BEG FOR IT

MEGAN HART

ISBN-10:1-940078-34-2
ISBN-13:978-1-940078-34-2

Cover by: Chaos
Cover art:
http://www.istockphoto.com/portfolio/grinvalds

Also by Megan Hart

Dedication

For Mine
ICYHWM

Chapter One

Her boy.

Her first and, as it had turned out, her only boy. Over the years, Corinne had thought of her boy in the middle of hot afternoons when she yearned for a glass of iced coffee, sweetened to perfection, and there was nobody to prepare it just the way she liked it. Nobody to bring it to her. She'd thought of him, too, when she itched and twitched for something that seemed to dance beyond her grasp, leaving her empty when she should've had everything she could want to fill her up. She thought of him now in the darkness, stretched out on the king-sized bed that she could still only bring herself to use half of.

Corinne thought of her boy when she wanted to remember that once upon a time, she had not been an overworked and overwhelmed single mother in a precariously situated job with an unexpectedly burdensome mortgage and an ex-husband disgustingly contented with his new wife and family. Once upon a time, Corinne had been cherished and worshipped and adored.

She'd been a fucking queen.

Well, that had been one long damned time ago, Corinne told herself as she rolled over to slap some sense into her alarm clock. It would've been way too tempting to snuggle back into her pillow's lumpy comfort, but it was already half an hour past the time she ought to have been up and in the shower. Also, the bed itself was a tangled mess, sheets kicked off in the night because she'd been way too hot in this late September heat wave for anything but her pajamas.

Once she'd slept naked in her boy's embrace, neither of them minding the stickiness and the sweat. The memory of it sent her rolling again, this time to bury her face in the pillow to stifle a long, low groan. Frustration, at first, mingled with a latent but stirring arousal.

She'd giving up dating over the past six months or so. Her last few dates had been all right. Guys who were nice enough. Guys with kids and mortgages of their own and jobs they weren't certain were going to last the month. She'd gone out with one guy five times before they slept together, and after that she'd found herself unable to rouse enough interest to return his calls. The sex had been bland, which was bad enough, but worse, in the morning he'd stared her down over scrambled eggs and made mouth noises about "the future." It should've been what she wanted. It was what her single girlfriends said they wanted while Corinne nodded along.

The truth was, she wanted something far less…conventional.

She'd looked for it, casually, in the first months after her divorce. The specialty dating site had seemed promising enough—you could check off your likes and dislikes the same as the vanilla sites, but this one included choices like "pony play" and "cuckolding." Identifying herself as a dominant woman had led to an influx of men fairly demanding she top them. Bewildered by the attention, Corinne had tried to start off with conversations that had usually turned quickly into something else. To her surprise and disgust, she'd found herself inadvertently domming a few guys who'd managed to piss her off enough to make her reply with more rudeness than she would have otherwise. That had been enough for her, and back to vanilla land it had been, without much more success.

That long, low moan turned into a strangled sob she tried to hide by biting her pillow, but though her jaw clenched, the pitiful sound still leaked out. She wept, hating herself at first before giving in to the emotions ripping through her, leaving her raw. She was forty-two years old, mother of two, divorced for almost two years, and she didn't weep for anything that had been her life with Douglas.

She wept, instead, for the loss of her boy.

Corinne forced the tears away quickly, refusing to indulge in a hurt that had happened fifteen years ago. She could've screamed if she wanted. There was nobody to hear her. Her younger sister, Caitlyn, had shown up a few weeks ago with a duffel bag and a story she still hadn't told, but she'd gone to Delaware to visit their parents for the weekend. The kids had been with their dad last night to attend a dance recital for their stepsister Allyson and would stay there through the weekend. Douglas's new wife—Karen—Allyson, and another stepsister Hannah, as well as a new puppy, were guaranteed to keep them occupied. In the beginning, Peyton had called home four or five times a day and texted quadruple that amount, while her younger brother Tyler had simply refused to talk about anything that went on at their dad's. It was a good thing, Corinne reminded herself, that the kids had adjusted to their new family. But now, in the big, silent house that had once been their family home and was now empty half the time, all she could think about was how fucking lonely it was without them.

Nothing good ever came of wallowing. Corinne got up and out of bed. She wasn't going to have time to stop at the diner this morning, though if she rushed a little she'd at least have the chance to brew a single cup of mediocre coffee to take with her.

In the shower, she got beneath the water before it had time to get hot. With a yelp, dancing and shivering, she turned so the spray could pound her back and shoulders, where she carried most of her tension. She put a hand flat on the wall as she reached for her washcloth with the other. She couldn't find it, though she was sure she'd hung a fresh one on the small hook just last night. Dammit. Teeth chattering, Corinne looked around but found no cloth, which meant she'd need to step out and get one.

These were the moments when being alone hit her so hard. When there was nobody to shout for, "Hey, can you grab me that washcloth?" Nobody to argue over what to watch on television. Nobody to remember to bring up the garbage pails, except her, and she always, always forgot.

Of course, one of the huge reasons why she and Douglas had ended up splitting was because he hadn't been the sort of man to do those things for her, at least not without a lot of reminding. It had always been so difficult with him. He wasn't a bad guy. Not a terrible husband. He was simply more interested in whatever it was he wanted than he'd ever been in taking care of anything else.

Her boy would've made sure the cloth was hanging on her hook before she even got in the shower, and if he hadn't, he'd have been there at once to bring it to her. Thinking of this as the water at last warmed to a reasonable temperature, Corinne let herself sink once more into memories.

He'd learned her. Known her. Sure, things had turned bad and it had ended, but that was always the way. If things weren't bad, they didn't end.

Corinne's hand slipped between her thighs at the memories of her boy on his knees, head bowed, rubbing her feet while she drank iced coffee and flipped through silly gossip magazines. All those hours spent on her feet waiting tables had left her with painful arches and cramping toes. Other men might feign a brief interest in massaging away the pain, but only so far as it meant them eventually getting in her pants. Her boy rubbed her feet until they no longer hurt, even if they both knew she didn't plan on fucking him.

That had been the difference between him and all the other men she'd ever dated. Other men had claimed they wanted to please her, and some of them had tried, but in the end it had always come down to them giving her what she wanted as long as it was also what they wanted to give her. Her boy had taken care of her needs before his own, no matter what.

"You don't want a boyfriend, you want a dog," one ex-lover had accused in the final fight that had ended that relationship.

He hadn't understood her at all.

With one hand still flat on the wall, she let the fingers of the other slide through her folds, finding slick heat between her thighs. When she brushed the tight knot of her clit with her thumb, everything inside her contracted. Tensing. Pulsing.

She thought of her boy in a slightly different position, still on his knees but his back and shoulders straight. Chin lifted. Hands crossed behind his back while he faced the corner for some small infraction she could no longer recall. Sometimes he'd sassed her just so she would be pushed to discipline him.

"Fuck," Corinne breathed and turned her face up to the water as she opened her mouth.

God, she missed kissing. Tangled tongues, sloppy wetness, the heat of breath on her face. A hand on the back of her head, keeping her close.

She tweaked her clit between her thumb and forefinger, slowly. Then faster. Her fingers curled and slipped on the wet tile. Her hips rocked, and she settled her feet a little wider apart. She wanted, needed, to be filled, but all she had was the thickness of her first two fingers. The heel of her hand pressed her clit as she fucked into herself.

She remembered taking him in the shower. Laughing, teasing, she'd told him he'd been a dirty boy and needed a good scrubbing. Compliant as always, obedient, her boy had allowed her to put him under the spray and had stood patiently while she soaped a cloth. It had quickly become too difficult to laugh around the sharp intake of her breath as she moved the cloth over his firm, taut muscles. He'd always been so, so lovely.

"Hands on the wall." Corinne's voice is low and a little harsh, the tone meant to trigger him. It triggers her, too, when she talks like this. Commanding but not cruel.

He turns immediately, those big strong hands going flat against the slick surface. Without being told, her boy places his feet shoulder-width apart, giving her room to reach through his legs to cup his already hard cock, if she wants. For now, Corinne only strokes the soapy cloth over his back. Shoulder blades jutting, shifting at her touch, he shudders.

Her boy leans to press his forehead to the shower wall, bending at the waist. Corinne nudges his feet with hers to get him to open wider, careful that neither of them slip. When his feet are far enough apart that he's leaning even farther, his ass easily accessible, she runs a finger down his spine. Counting the knobs there. Briefly circling the twin dimples at the base. Then lower, down the crack of his butt until she finds the tight pucker of his asshole, where she presses her fingertips and listens to him moan.

Her other hands slips between his thighs to cup his balls. She doesn't squeeze, though when he pushes back against her, she lets out a low warning tone and allows her grip to get a little tighter. Just enough to warn him.

"Please," her boy whispers. "Please, Ma'am."

Corinne let out a hushed cry as she withdrew her fingers from her yearning, hungry cunt and used them to rapidly stroke her clit. She'd fucked him in the shower, fingers, mouth, and tongue working him until he'd begged for the release she had not granted until he'd gone to his knees in front of her and given her two orgasms with his tongue. The water had turned cold by the time they'd finished, but neither of them had noticed.

She moaned his name, letting the thrum and beat of the water take it away so she could almost pretend she hadn't said it aloud.

Her breath sobbed out of her as she slid two fingers inside her pussy again, curling upward. She let herself go with the pleasure. No more holding back. Stroking her clit again in a steady, constant rhythm, Corinne urged her body toward the edge.

So close, so fucking close, and yet she couldn't manage to tip over. With a frustrated groan, she turned to press her back against the wall. Now the water spattered her breasts, teasing her nipples almost painfully. It washed over her belly and between her legs, and she tipped her hips upward to let it pound her clit. There, there it was, the stream from the showerhead nothing compared to a sweetly flicking tongue, but all she had at the moment. Corinne used both hands to open herself, exposing her pussy to the water's steady spray.

Her boy should be on his knees in front of her right now, she thought somewhat incoherently. His fingers gripping her hips. Digging deep. Holding her close to the expert, relentless stroking of his tongue against her.

Oh, yes. Oh, fuck yes. This was it, the point of no return, when everything up until now had been merely a tease. She was going to come, yes, right here, like this, and…

Corinne shook with it, aware of the sting of water in her eyes but not caring. Nothing mattered but the pleasure. Not her own harsh grunting or the stinging needles of water turning chilly or the fact she was definitely very late for work now. All that mattered was the ecstasy sweeping her away from everything that made her sad.

Panting, her inner muscles clenching, Corinne twisted the faucet to turn off the water. She stumbled with weak legs onto the bathmat and grabbed for her towel. Pressing it between her thighs, she let out another hitching sigh at the aftershocks the soft terrycloth gave her. She wanted to come again and again, spending the day in a never-ending chain of climaxes, stopping only to nap in the sweaty entanglement of her lover's limbs and to be fed cheese and grapes and to sip chilled wine.

The thought of this, finally, made her laugh. *As though that scenario would ever happen,* she thought as she bent to tuck her hair into the turban she made of her towel and went, otherwise naked, to the sink so she could finish getting ready. A day of nothing but pleasure? How long had it been since she'd been able to indulge in something like that?

A long, long damn time, Corinne thought as she stared at her reflection. The pink flush still spreading over her chest and up her throat gave her a small smile. At least she'd had a few minutes of gratification, anyway, and she should count herself lucky. A few of her friends had declared they no longer even cared about sex at all.

The day she no longer wanted to get off, Corinne thought, she hoped it was the one they put her in the ground.

Chapter Two

Before

Weekends at the diner are always crazy busy. It's one of the few places that is open twenty-four hours, where you can get breakfast all day, and so it's popular with the local college kids during the week and even more crowded on the weekends with people coming out after hitting Lancaster's downtown bar scene. Corinne works the late night shifts so she can take her business classes during the day at Millersville University. She's going to get an MBA if it kills her—and sometimes, it feels like it might.

She does envy those students who come rolling in around two a.m. with cash to spend on platters of pancakes they leave half-eaten and wasted. They leave her tips in stacks of pennies and nickels hidden beneath the lettuce they took off their cheeseburgers. Mostly, she envies them the ability to go to school and keep playing on their parents' dime while she toils away at this job that breaks her back and kills her feet, just so she can get her degree.

There's one group in particular that both amuses and annoys her. Three, four, five younger guys who seem to have known each other since elementary school, based on the nicknames they use for each other and how comfortable they are with casual, physical contact. Squeezing into a booth, hips and shoulders pressing, arms slung around each other's shoulders, feet on each other's laps. At first she'd assumed they were gay and crazily brave enough to flaunt in front of this rural city's judgment, but they've been coming into Triton's long enough now that she sees they're not gay. More like brothers, a pack of them, forged by friendship and not blood.

Reese is the quiet one. He always orders the same breakfast. Two eggs over medium, wheat toast, hash browns, coffee, and every few weeks, he adds a single pancake. He uses cream and sugar in his coffee but only a little syrup on the pancake, and he always, always leaves her a nice tip of folded dollar bills tucked beneath the edge of the plate.

Reese has a crush on her. Corinne knows this because she catches him watching her as she takes care of the other tables. When he thinks she can't notice him, he stares, but every so often she'll look up into the diner's mirrored interior and let her gaze move across the room, deliberately seeking out the sight of Reese's long-distance worship. On the nights when he doesn't come in, she finds herself still looking for his reflection.

Tonight, they're short-staffed and overcrowded. People wait for tables even though it's nearly two in the morning, and anyone with any sense would've gone home to bed by now, grouchy Corinne thinks as she weaves and bobs to get around Dino, the busboy, who's trying to clear off a table so she can seat someone else. Corinne's so busy she barely notices when Reese and his friends come in, at least until she finds herself at their table. They're jostling and joking, causing a ruckus as usual. Except for Reese, in the far corner.

At the sight of him, every bad feeling she's had this entire night, all the shitty tips and messed up orders and rude patrons…all of that melts away when she sees Reese's smile. He's a gust of clean, fresh air, and she breathes him in. For a moment it's like they're the only two in the diner, but only for a blink, because she shakes herself back into the real world. No time for goo-goo eyes. She sees him watching her in the mirrors as she walks away, and for the first time in all the months he's been coming in here, Corinne lets her gaze meet his in the reflection.

She smiles.

After a few seconds, Reese smiles too.

The next hour is a blur of coffee and late-night orders, but she keeps an eye on the clock for four a.m. Her salvation. Her shift will end, and she'll be able to finally get home, grab a steaming shower, and slip into bed. It'll be Sunday. She doesn't have class, and she won't have to go back to work until Monday night.

So caught up in the rest of the work, she doesn't notice when Reese's group heads out, leaving piles of cash on the table and Reese sitting alone, waiting for the check. She notices the look in his eyes though. Oh, yeah. She notices that, for sure.

"I'm about ready to go off shift," Corinne says as she scribbles the total on the bill and passes it to him. "If I leave before you're ready, you can take it to the register."

"I'm ready now."

The words leap from her lips, coasting on a smile. "Are you? You sure?"

Reese doesn't smile. He nods, his gaze never leaving hers. He's lined his icy eyes with dark liner that make them stand out even bluer. It's not a look she usually goes for, but something about this guy flips Corinne's switch.

"Yes. I'm sure," he says.

As far as come-ons go, it's subtler than she's used to, but that's what she likes about him. He's waiting for her outside when she comes out, and she somehow expected that. His shoulders are hunched, his hands thrust deep in his pockets, and he's blowing out a few frosty breaths into the late November chill.

"Are you coming home with me?" she asks.

"Yes, please." He smiles.

And *that*, that she fucking loves, the way he says it so politely, so hopeful and yet at the same time it's clear he has no doubt she's going to say yes. He's confident. Not cocky.

She lives close enough to the diner that the car doesn't even have time to get warm before she's pulling up in front of her apartment. Not that it has to—the heat between them is palpable. They haven't talked much on the ride over, but whenever she glances over at him, Reese is looking at her.

Inside, she hangs up her coat and turns to him, meaning to ask if he wants a drink, but she's in his arms before she has time to say a word. Reese pulls her close, his hands firm on her hips. She expects a kiss.

Instead, Reese goes to his knees in front of her.

Everything inside her shakes at this, his worship of her, his face pressed to her belly. Her hands go automatically to the top of his head, fingers threading through his hair. She cannot breathe.

She can feel the heat of him through the thin cotton of her uniform. He inches up the hem, sliding his hands up the backs of her thighs along the smoothness of her pantyhose. At the press of his mouth between her legs, Corinne mutters a cry.

Reese laughs and nuzzles her. Her fingers tighten in his hair until he looks up at her. His eyes blaze. His mouth is wet.

She finds her voice. "You want this pussy on your tongue?"

"Yes," he says. "Please."

Her grip tightens a bit more. His eyes go half-lidded, heavy with desire. She doesn't know why she says this, but something inside her has awakened. Something strong and powerful and incapable of being denied.

"Please…what?" She waits, breathless, uncertain what he will say, but when he speaks, his answer is perfection.

"Yes, please…Ma'am."

In that moment, everything Corinne has ever believed she wanted from a man falls away. She's been waiting, she thinks, dazed, as she stares down into Reese's face. Waiting her entire life for this.

Chapter Three

Stein and Sons had started off as the Stein Brothers back in the thirties, when Morty and Herb Stein had joined forces to provide a dairy delivery service to rural families who lived too far from town to make a regular trip but who didn't live on farms.

Morty had handled the actual deliveries. Herb had gone door-to-door not only to the farmers from whom they'd negotiated their supplies, but also to the families who'd needed convincing that the Stein Brothers could provide them with efficient, reliable, and, most importantly to Depression-ravaged central Pennsylvania, *thrifty* goods and services. They'd started with driving a single horse-drawn carriage and preparing invoices in the back room of their mother's house and ended up with a fleet of refrigerated tankers and a corporate headquarters. In the early to midseventies, renamed Stein and Sons, they'd been the largest local dairy delivery service in the entire state. Corinne could remember pouring Stein and Sons milk on her cereal while watching Sunday morning cartoons.

Of course all that had changed over time. No more home deliveries. Competition from other dairies. Issues with customers refusing to buy products that used bovine growth hormone. Slowly, the business had diversified and reorganized and downsized.

Stein and Sons morphed from a delivery service of bottled milk, cream, and cheese into a small dairy specializing in gourmet items such as goat's milk, artisanal cheeses, specialty yogurts, and hand-churned ice cream. With an on-site store and tours to capitalize on Lancaster County's thriving tourist business, Stein and Sons had a tidy little setup that would've confused its founders, but Corinne liked to think it would also have made them proud.

Chief financial officer. The title felt unwieldy when she said it aloud, though it looked just fine on all the stationery printed with her name. The company was so small that she did more than take care of the financials—she was also the head of human resources and director of operations…sort of. All the jobs had been bundled into one. They'd had to let go most of the other staff. Other than the off-site custodial staff that came in to clean three days a week, most of the time it was only Corinne and the secretary, Sandy, in the office. The fifty or so other employees who maintained the barns and livestock and worked in the production facility rarely, if ever, came in. It wasn't exactly what her early twenties self, waitressing at the local diner and busting her ass to complete her MBA, had pictured she would be doing, but Corinne guessed that could probably be said by a lot of people.

She'd started at Stein and Sons fifteen years ago in the accounting department and worked her way up, until here she sat in her own corner office with a big, shiny desk and a view of what had once been farm fields but was rapidly becoming obscured by neighborhoods populated with mini-mansions. She'd been through every downsize and shift in the company's focus. There'd been a few times she'd considered leaving for a position that paid more, but she'd never quite made the leap. She'd been too aware of how deceptively green the grass could be when fertilized with the manure of someone else's cows. Now she wondered if it was time to start seriously revamping her résumé.

There'd been rumors flying for months. Corporate takeover. A buyout. Mergers. Flat-out shutting down the entire production line and selling off all the assets. Dennis, Lynn, Patty, Jennifer, and Ryan—the Stein grandchildren who'd maintained their inherited positions within the company—had been reassuring the employees that nothing was going to change, no matter where Stein and Sons ended up heading.

Corinne doubted that was true. Everything changed, no matter if you wanted it to or not. Besides, she saw the numbers and the bottom line. She signed off on the paychecks and ran the quarterly reports. She'd been the one to let the rest of the office staff go when they needed to cut back on employee costs. Stein and Sons was in trouble, with no good way out in sight.

The board had turned down too many offers over the past couple of years, ones they probably should have taken back when the business had started off booming and they could've turned a hefty profit. It was now fizzling, without much to offer anyone. If they couldn't turn around sales in the next few months, they were going to go under.

"We're still not seeing enough growth," she explained to the men and women sitting at the conference table across from her. Someone had laid out some bagels with a carton of the dairy's garlic/rosemary cream cheese, and she'd already indulged herself in coffee with real fresh cream from the employee fridge. She was going to miss this if she had to leave.

"Patty was supposed to oversee the new marketing ventures," Jennifer said, turning to her cousin. "What's happening with getting the new products into local stores? Why aren't we increasing orders?"

"We're not only not increasing, we're losing them," Dennis put in.

Patty frowned and tucked a curl of graying brown hair behind her ear. "Look, it's not that easy. We're in direct competition with a lot of the local dairies we used to have business relationships with—"

"A million years ago," Ryan interrupted.

Patty nodded at him but kept talking. "And none of *them* are dealing with all this fancy stuff. It's straight up milk, cream, seasonal eggnog, ice cream, whatever. They're selling to the big conglomerates too, for more money than we can afford to spend on more product than we can possibly utilize. So even if they're not putting local products on the shelves, they're profiting by selling to the big kids' club."

"Exactly," said Dennis with a small thump of his fist on the table. "We need to serve a market with an expanded palate. That's what we're going for. We want to reach those folks who think nothing of driving into Philly for dinner because they're sick and tired of nothing but chain restaurants. The kind who pair cheese with wine. Hey, have we looked into maybe getting in with some of the local wineries? Maybe a themed cheese spread or something?"

Corinne had heard people like that existed in Lancaster County. Transplants from New York or Philadelphia or even D.C. who'd fled "to the country" and suffered a long commute so they could raise their kids to play endless seasons of soccer on fields that reeked of manure. She'd been born and raised here in south central Pennsylvania. She'd never driven to the "big" city just for the sake of having dinner.

"People around here don't want to eat herbed yogurt, Denny.

They want the kind with fruit on the bottom. They might go for some fancy cheeses, but trying to sell them anise and lavender ice cream is just going to end up making us look like fools." Patty said this last bit firmly, with a matching rap of her knuckles on the table. It was a habit most of the family had picked up from their parents, who'd learned it from their fathers, Morty and Herb.

"Look, we got into the Philly markets—" Ryan began.

"Only three, and only on a provisional basis. It's more expensive to ship there. If we had more customers it would make the cost of shipping maintainable, but we don't. We also have more competition from bigger dairies closer to Philly, and they've snagged the spots in the farmer's markets, places like that where we *might* have a shot. Yes, we can reach the sorts of customers who'd love a candied walnut and rosemary goat milk ice cream, but only if we find a place that will carry the products. All around, what Corinne's been saying is the simple truth." Patty turned to Corinne with a sigh. "Not enough growth. Guys, we have to face it. We're going to have to shut it all down."

Ryan sighed. He was in charge of product invention and testing. "We could go simpler. It doesn't have to be so fancy, I guess. Get back to basics, come at it from the nostalgia angle. Stein and Sons has been around forever."

"I don't want to sell. I never have." This came from Lynn, usually silent, which meant that when he did have something to say, everyone listened. Before anyone could chime in to agree or disagree, he held up a hand. Lynn had started off in the company working in the dairy barn. He knew more about the cows and goats than any of the others. His brother Dennis liked to tease that Lynn wore manure instead of cologne, and Corinne was privately inclined to agree, but no matter what he had caked on his boots, Lynn commanded respect. "But I think it's time we seriously considered the offer again."

The offer.

That's how all the owners referred to it, usually in a disdainful undertone or with a casually anxious sneer. For a company with a history of staying in the same family for generations without so much as a hint of a power struggle, the idea of passing the Stein Brothers legacy into the hands of a stranger had always been unthinkable. They'd received and passed up plenty of offers for other buyouts in the past, unanimously voting to keep Stein and Sons in the hands of its grandsons and granddaughters.

Now, *the offer.*

It had come in two weeks ago. An insultingly terrible offer, laden with restrictions and caveats that would've essentially crippled the company in the long-term. It would've gone straight into Corinne's trash file, but it hadn't come directly to her.

Lynn shook his head. "I don't know that we have any choice. Corinne's given us the numbers. We've tried everything we can think of. Nothing we do is working. It's time to let go."

"But if we sold, we wouldn't have the business anymore," Jennifer said. "It would be totally gone."

"It's going to be gone soon anyway, if we don't see some turnaround," Corinne said gently. "Something has to change. Or there won't be anything left to sell except the physical assets."

The cousins shared a look. Dennis cleared his throat. Patty sighed. Lynn looked stoic, and Jennifer's red eyes gave away her emotions. Only Ryan looked resigned.

"My dad always said to quit before you got fired," he said. "I'm sorry, guys. I wish I'd been able to come up with something that had really taken off."

Jennifer squeezed her cousin's shoulder. "Nobody's firing you. It's not your fault we can't convince anyone to expand their palates."

"I set up a meeting with the guy for you this afternoon," Lynn said to Corinne. "His name's Tony Randolph, and he represents the buyer. We need to discuss the terms. The buyer's intentions. I'll need you to get a real handle on what's going to be best for Stein and Sons."

"His intentions are to throw a couple of bucks our way and make us seem grateful to have it." Patty frowned. "That offer was almost worse than declaring bankruptcy."

"It's certainly nothing close to what we feel the business is worth, I know that." Lynn shook his head. "But this might be the best thing. It could be good."

"Not much about this can be good," Jennifer put in, then quickly pressed her lips closed.

"We have Corinne looking out for us," Lynn said.

Corinne slid a fingertip across her phone to bring up her calendar. "Thanks for the vote of confidence. Of course I'll go to the meeting. What time?"

"I said you'd meet him at the StockYard Inn at two." Lynn cracked his knuckles, then laid his hands flat on the table. "We trust you, Corinne. Hear what he has to say and bring it back to us. Help us figure it out."

She nodded, looking at each of them in turn. Softly, she rapped her knuckles on the table. "Okay."

Chapter Four

Reese Ebersole had bought and sold close to a hundred businesses. He'd acquired his first one twelve years ago using his meager savings, earned from his job bussing tables while he went to school, along with what had been left of the inheritance from his parents. The inheritance itself had not been substantial. He'd lost more money than his parents had ever earned in their entire lives. They'd meant it for him to finish school or pay for a wedding. Have a baby with a woman he loved. All the things they'd wished for him and would never see. Not because they'd both died far too early, but because Reese had never done any of those things.

He'd been too busy working. He'd had as many as thirty small companies in his portfolio, but currently owned only four that remained active. A string of kosher grocery stores. A tech company specializing in up-priced gadgetry appealing to people with too much money and not enough junk to spend it on. A media company with an emphasis on social media applications and development. The final company also specialized in something specific—catered holidays geared for überwealthy kinky people who wanted to travel in the lifestyle to which they'd grown accustomed. Bed and breakfasts with dungeons set up in actual dungeons, or buffet meals served on the bodies of naked, ornamentally beautiful men and women. The sorts of things they showed in the movies but normal people never did.

He had a penthouse flat in Philadelphia, a cottage in Ireland, a condo in Hawaii, and a pied-à-terre in Manhattan with a view of the Empire State Building. Mom would have tutted about the expenses of holding down so many households, especially without a woman to organize them. She'd have wanted to be sure each of them was fully stocked with toilet paper, milk, and eggs, and dishes that matched the silverware. Dad would not have been impressed with what he would have considered extravagance and indulgence. Dad would have counseled more caution. But beneath the criticisms, they both would've been proud, or at least Reese hoped. He guessed he would never know. He'd lost them both within six months of each other, long before he'd ever even made a bid on a business.

He'd stopped paying much attention to reports on his assets about two years ago when the numbers had reached a point where they'd become ridiculous, like playing with Monopoly money. Cash could buy and sell a lot of things, but Reese wasn't naïve enough to believe happiness was one of them. Other things—cars, houses, tailored suits, fine wines. Those could bring at least the briefest interludes of happiness. Very rarely, however, had anything brought him joy.

Well, fuck joy. He'd given up on that a long time ago. For now it was enough to have the money he wanted to do whatever he pleased. As far as Reese was concerned, Heaven looked a lot like a long, long string of numbers in front of a decimal point.

Once, Reese's Heaven had been something else to him, but that had also been a long, long time ago, before he'd become the man he was now. He'd learned to be ruthless. Uncompromising. How to cut a path for himself without caring much for who stood in the way. How to get what he wanted, no matter the cost. Reese had fled Lancaster County at twenty-three, but here he was again, and the gently wafting scent of manure that had drifted through the car windows as he drove had been enough to slam him back into the past and places he'd worked hard to forget.

Nothing he'd learned, it seemed, had taught him how not to look back.

"Still waiting? Can I bring you something to drink awhile?" The pretty brunette with the ponytail gestured at Reese's empty wineglass.

"Yes. Two glasses of the Rendezvous Orchard Cabernet."

"Do you want me to bring it when…she…gets here?" The lilt of the question made it clear she wasn't sure what to think about the fact Reese might very well be on his way to being stood up. Or maybe she was just surprised that anyone in this rinky-dink town had ordered from a fifty dollar bottle of wine in the middle of the afternoon.

"No. Now. She'll be here. She's just running late, I'm sure." He didn't check his watch again.

He'd been waiting for half an hour. It was unfathomably rude and far from professional, but he couldn't be surprised. Everything about Stein and Sons had smacked of small-town folksy standards, including handshake contracts and keeping what Reese thought of as country time. His parents had been that way. Languid and leisurely, getting there when they got there, wherever *there* was. And for his parents, it had never been very far.

She would be here. She had to be. He'd come all the way from Philadelphia. He'd had his personal assistant, Tony, confirm and reconfirm the meeting. She *was* going to show up.

Corinne Barton Levy, CFO of Stein and Sons.

Reese had been casually scrolling through one of the weekly emails he got from a service that collated information on companies ripe for buyout when he saw her name, and the past fifteen years had given him a roundhouse kick to the teeth. It would've be a lie to say he'd never thought of her in all that time; the truth was he'd never stopped thinking about the only woman to ever get him on his knees. Without a second thought, he'd forwarded the information to Tony with instructions on making an offer.

He'd known he was being a prick about it. The offer wasn't half of what Stein and Sons was worth, even if Reese acquired it only for the assets and never even tried to turn it around. He'd made the terms too harsh for the minimal buyout amount to be worth it, a virtual slap in the face, purposefully insulting. Yet they'd asked him for this meeting, which meant they were seriously considering his offer.

What would he do if they decided to take him up on it?

A small craft dairy company? Why the hell would he ever want to go back to where he started? He didn't even drink milk. He hated yogurt. And lavender ice cream…well, that just seemed like it would taste like shit.

He'd worry about that when it happened. He'd made worse deals without knowing it up front. Heading into something like this wouldn't give him more than a day's headache. He could pick it up and put it down in the span of a few weeks, especially if he simply liquidated everything, which, from a business standpoint, would make more sense than trying to make it successful.

The truth was, none of this was about the company at all. It was all about *her*. Unless she didn't show, Reese thought, and wouldn't that end up being an ironic boot to the ass?

Another five minutes ticked by before the girl brought back the glasses of wine, and Reese still sat alone at the table. He checked his phone for messages, but there were no texts, voicemails, or emails. Damn it, were they sending their cancellation by Pony Express? He stood, ready to ask for the check and walk out without waiting another minute. Screw Stein and Sons and Lancaster County. He was out of here.

"Sorry, so sorry," a feminine voice said, her words a rush, her tone sincere. The woman in front of him shook her head and put a hand on the back of the chair on the other side of the table. "I got stuck behind a buggy and there were a lot of looky-loos out today. I'm so sorry I'm late…"

Her voice trailed off as she looked up at him with those big, blue eyes rimmed with thick, dark lashes. She blinked rapidly, before her gaze went as sharp and focused as a finely honed knife. She straightened, all vestiges of apology disappearing and replaced by a familiar haughtiness that in the past would've tempted him to turn the tables and beg her pardon, but Reese stifled that urge neatly, like closing a book. He'd had years of practice, after all.

"Hello, Corinne," he said. "It's been a long time."

For a moment he was sure she was going to tell him to get bent, then stalk off. Maybe, he thought suddenly, terribly, unwillingly, maybe she'd slap his face first. He didn't take a step back, though he wanted to.

Corinne didn't leave, and she didn't slap him. To his surprise, she moved to embrace him, a second or so only, the press of her cheek on his. He breathed her in, blinking at the brief caress of her hair on his face before there was space and distance between them again. His cock was already almost fully hard.

"Reese, my God," she said. "How are you? What a wonderful surprise."

A second later she was in his arms again, like she couldn't stop herself from hugging him, and all he wanted to do was pull her closer and never let her go. Instead, Reese took her by the upper arms and pushed her carefully but firmly a step or two away from him. It was impossible to miss the way her mouth turned down, though she smoothed her expression immediately. They stared at each other in an endless silence.

"They told me I was meeting with a guy named Tony

Randolph," Corinne said finally.

"He's my assistant," Reese told her. "But I decided to show up, myself."

Corinne took a seat at the table. She looked at the two glasses of wine, then him. She took her napkin from her plate and settled it on her lap.

"I hear you have an offer for us," she said. "I suppose we should discuss it."

Chapter Five

Before

"Sit down."

The woman in the dark blue uniform is no-nonsense, a little frazzled. More than a little annoyed, Reese thinks, by their boisterous group. His friends chuckle and shuffle, edging into the diner booth, but at her command, Reese immediately complies. His ass finds the chair settled at the edge of the table. His heart pounds.

His dick leaps.

She doesn't even pay attention to him as she puts a handful of napkin-wrapped utensils in the center of the table, along with an equal number of menus. He's glad for that, because that means he can look at her surreptitiously without having to pretend he's not fascinated by her. This woman, the waitress, her name is Corinne, and she's almost always here in the late night hours when he and his friends leave the club and end up craving breakfast. She knows them all, by sight at least, which is why it's okay with everyone that she bosses them around like this.

It's especially okay with Reese, who would never admit aloud to any of the other guys that when he jacks off, it's to the sound of this woman's voice commanding him to stroke harder. Faster. Telling him to beg her to let him come.

"Coffee?" She nudges his shoulder with the edge of her order tablet. Brows raised. "You okay?"

Reese coughs. "Yeah, yes. Coffee. Sure, thanks."

Corinne's eyes narrow for a second as she studies him. "You'll never get to sleep if you drink coffee now."

He won't sleep anyway—it's already past three and he needs to be up at five thirty to help his dad with the cows. "That's okay."

"No." She taps her pen against her lower lip for a second. Her gaze is intense. Burning. "I don't think so. You get tomato juice."

"But I don't—"

"Juice." She bends to whisper in his ear, but quickly and subtly.

His friends are all so busy making noise that nobody hears her but him. Again, his dick leaps in his jeans. Reese shifts at the pressure, and Corinne looks into his lap with a knowing, secret smile that only sets him on fire even more.

He doesn't like tomato juice, but he drinks it anyway. The reward is another of those smiles she gives him when she comes to take away the dirty plates. And then, even better...

"Good boy," Corinne mouths at him as everyone else gets up, tossing crumpled and sweaty dollar bills onto the table as her tip.

He lets everyone leave without him. Uses the bathroom, where he washes his hands and splashes cold water on his face, running wet fingers through his hair until it stands on end. His face in the mirror is pale, considering how hot his cheeks and throat still feel. His eyes are wide and have gone dark. The eyeliner is smudgy. He wipes some of it away, but not all of it. His father hates that he wears makeup to go out, but Reese thinks Corinne likes it.

She's waiting for him in the parking lot when he comes out, hitching his collar up around his neck.

"You need a ride," she says. Not a question.

Reese nods. "Yeah, my friends, they ditched me."

"They didn't ditch you. You told them to go on ahead. You wanted me to offer you a ride home again."

It's his turn to smile. "You caught me."

Corinne laughs. Shakes her head. "Get in, then."

They don't talk much on the ride. She plays the radio, low. The glow from the dash highlights the shadows under her eyes. Every so often she glances at him, and he can feel the weight of her gaze. She's assessing him.

Reese's cock is so hard it actually hurts.

Corinne doesn't take him to her apartment, which is a disappointment. She pulls into the first few feet of the long farm lane. In the distance, he can see a light on in the farmhouse kitchen. His father. Reese's eyes are gritty with lack of sleep, he's coming down off the high of clubbing and he wishes desperately he'd had the coffee he'd ordered.

She puts the car in Park.

"You should get inside, I guess." For a moment, Corinne peers out through the windshield, down the dark lane to the house and barn beyond. She twists a little to look at him. The fringes of her hair flutter now over her eyes. "Time to milk the cows."

She doesn't sound like she's mocking him. More like she gets it. Most people around here do. Here in the heart of Amish country, Lancaster is a city surrounded by rolling hills and lots of farms. Milton Hershey got his start here because of all the dairy farms he needed to make his chocolate, before he'd gone on to build his own town.

"Yeah."

"You look tired, puppy."

At the endearment, a soft, low, and helpless groan trips its way past his lips. When she puts her hand on his crotch, kneading the bulge there, Reese cannot stop himself from rolling his hips into her touch. He aches. Physically aches.

"Shhh," Corinne whispers, though he hasn't said anything. She leans across the center console to put her mouth next to his ear. Hot breath. The flick of her tongue on tender flesh.

He can't stop himself from moaning. Her hand tightens, squeezing. Almost pain. She laughs softly; the sound thrills him.

"You wanted me to touch you," she says against his neck.

Reese draws in a breath. "Yes."

"I've thought about this pretty cock." Her voice gets rough and rasping. She unzips him. Unbuttons. His cock is so rigid it springs free into her hand without effort, and at the touch of her fingers, flesh on flesh, Reese is afraid he's going to spill all over them both. "Touching you. Tasting you."

"Please…" he manages to breathe.

"Tell me how you've thought about it. About me." Her fingertips stroke along the wetness leaking from his cockhead. "About what we did."

Reese's entire body is clenching and tense, but he focuses on her voice. Then on her face. He doesn't dare look down at her hand squeezing him just beneath the head of his prick. He'll come for sure.

"I think about it all the time. You riding my face. How you tasted and smelled. How much I loved your pussy on my mouth."

Corinne's breath hitches. "Oh. Fuck. That, yes. That was good."

"I want to make you come again, that way. Let me." It's not quite a plea, not really begging, but he sees by the flash in her gaze that she likes the way he asked.

"You're already late," she tells him. "You don't want your dad to get angry."

His father will probably already be angry. There isn't much Reese can do about it. They've been clashing for years, and it seems like nothing Reese does anymore will make the old man happy. He's given up trying.

When Corinne withdraws, Reese lets out a gasping plea, snagging her wrist to keep her hand on him. Immediately, her expression turns cold and dark, a fire extinguished. She says nothing, merely looks at the circling grip of his fingers, but he releases her at once.

"Sorry. I just wanted—"

"You want what you want," she answers sharply.

Reese frowns. His balls ache, but so does his head. There is a weight behind his eyes that will only get worse the longer he goes without sleep or the nudge of caffeine.

"Everyone does," he snaps.

Quicker than a blink, his jaw is in her fist.

"You," Corinne says, squeezing and releasing him, "don't talk to me that way. Behave yourself."

And though he is horny and annoyed and exhausted, all Reese can think of is pleasing her. Not just so she'll get him off, though he can't stop himself from wanting that release. No, he wants to please her for reasons he can't fully understand, has never tried to decipher, and generally tries to pretend he doesn't feel.

"I'm sorry," he says and adds, softer, "Ma'am."

Her smile tips up a bit on one side. "I like way that sounds on your tongue."

"I like the way it tastes," Reese whispers.

Heat flares again in her gaze. She gestures for him to move toward her. To kiss her. Her hands thread through his hair. Her mouth is open. Sighing, moaning, shivering. She nips his lower lip and pushes him away, turning her face when he tries again to get at her mouth.

"Go, now," she tells him. "I'm not going to fuck you in a car on the side of the road."

Disappointed, he sits back. The sky is getting pink. There are lights on in the barn. He's really late.

"No," Corinne continues thoughtfully, drawing his attention back to her. "Next time, I'm going to fuck you in a nice, soft bed."

With a strangled groan, Reese lets his head fall back against the seat. "You're killing me."

"Yes," she says, "but softly."

He turns only his head to look at her. "Will you let me take you out?"

"On a real date?" She looks faintly surprised.

"Yes. Of course, on a real date." He's annoyed again, not sure why.

Corinne lets her tongue dent her lower lip for a moment before she answers. "Yes. Dinner. A movie. The works."

"The works," Reese agrees. A yawn fights its way out of him. He rubs his eyes. His cock is not much softer, but he's trying to will away his erection at least enough so that he can get out of the car. "I really needed that coffee."

For a second he thinks she's going to turn stern again. Part of him hopes she does. He can't get enough of it.

But Corinne smiles and shakes her head. "No, puppy. What do you do after you help your dad in the morning?"

"Go back to sleep until it's time for the afternoon milking."

"Right. And so you're sleepy now, but you'll be back in bed in what. An hour?"

"Less than that," he admitted with a glance at the sky. "He'll have done a lot of it already."

"And if you'd had coffee, you wouldn't be able to sleep. You'd be up all day, running on empty."

It's the truth, and he knows it.

"I don't like tomato juice," he says. "Tastes like pennies."

Corinne smiles. "Fair enough. I'll remember that."

He leans across the center console to kiss her once more, taking a chance that she won't chastise him again. The kiss is sweet and lingering. When he tries to draw away, she holds him by the collar for a moment, staring deep into his eyes.

"Good boy," she says.

And Reese is lost to her.

Chapter Six

He'd ordered her a glass of Cabernet Sauvignon. Her favorite. After all these years, and he still remembered. It shouldn't have meant anything, but try as she might to pretend it didn't, all she had to do was sip from her glass to be reminded of how once upon a time, Reese Ebersole had been hers, completely and utterly.

He'd ordered the meal for her as well, and she ought to have been annoyed but found herself amused, instead. Charmed, a little. He got it mostly right. She'd have preferred grilled chicken instead of shrimp, though he couldn't have known she'd started keeping modified kosher after she got married. He had chosen the right dressing for her salad and exactly the appetizer she'd have picked for herself, though.

"Most men don't order for their dates these days," she murmured, taking off the shrimp and setting it aside without comment. "It's considered a little overbearing."

"You're not allergic," he said with a glance at the cast-off shellfish.

"No," she said, and offered him no more explanation than that, because she didn't owe him a damned thing, especially not about the changes she'd made to her life as part of her now-defunct marriage.

Reese stroked a thumb along the sweating edge of his water glass, drawing her attention to his hands. God, how she'd always loved his hands. Strong enough to break her, although he never had…at least never physically.

"Anyway," he said, "this isn't a date."

Corinne arched an eyebrow. "Of course it's not. I was joking."

"I guess my sense of humor's changed since the last time we saw each other," Reese replied.

At least he was acknowledging there'd been a last time. He'd greeted her the way a stranger would and had seemed surprised when she hugged him. Corinne sipped her wine, relishing the earthy flavor.

"I never thought I'd see you here. I knew the offer was coming from Ebersole Enterprises," she said after a moment. "I did have a minute where I thought… But then, no. How could it be? What kind of coincidence would that have been?"

He sat back in his chair. "I find that hard to believe."

"Hard to believe what?" She studied him. "In coincidence?"

"That you'd have even for a second imagined it might have been me."

The tone of his voice was hard to read. Corinne paused before answering, then said carefully, "Why wouldn't I?"

"I find it hard to believe you've spared a passing thought for me in the past fifteen years, that's all." He shrugged and gestured to the passing waitress, who turned at once, all big eyes and bouncy, swinging hair. "Another glass of Cabernet for Mrs. Levy."

Corinne shook her head. "Actually, no, I'll take an iced coffee, please. Cream and sugar."

She waited until the girl had left before she added crisply, "One glass is enough. I have to drive, not to mention I have to head back to the office after this."

Reese said nothing.

"And it's Ms. Barton. Not Mrs. Levy. I never took my husband's name." She paused again, watching him. When they'd been together, she'd prided herself on being able to know his emotions just by looking at his face. Now she had no idea what he was thinking or feeling. "Should I ask how you even know that?"

"I saw it in the paper when you got married."

It wasn't an implausible explanation, but something in the way he cut his gaze from hers told her it wasn't quite the truth. Corinne frowned, not at his words but at the way her stupid heart had lifted at this casual admission that he'd somehow paid attention to her life. "Anyway, we're divorced."

"I'm sorry to hear that."

He didn't sound sorry. He sounded vindicated. Corinne felt her frown threatening to become a scowl, and she deliberately smoothed her features.

"Don't be sorry. It's for the best. He's very happy with his new wife and I—"

"And you're very happy with your *career*, I'm sure," Reese said in a low, angry voice.

It was her turn to sit back and look him over. "Yes. I am, as a matter of fact. Why do you make that sound like some kind of sin?"

Interrupted by the arrival of the waitress with the appetizer of Thai sweet chili spring rolls and Corinne's iced coffee, they were quiet until the girl left. Then Reese leaned forward to speak across the table.

"You told me once you didn't believe in the idea of sin."

"It's a turn of phrase," Corinne told him. "And by the looks of things, you're not exactly an unsuccessful slug yourself, so why are you being so judgmental about my career? Or about anything in my life, for that matter?"

His mouth thinned. "Right. Of course, what you do isn't any of my business."

Something occurred to her. She narrowed her eyes. "You knew. Didn't you? That I worked for Stein and Sons. You knew I'm the CFO, and that you'd be meeting with me."

"I did," he told her without so much as a blink or the faintest blush of shame.

A vivid memory of the red imprint of her hand on his cheek reared up inside her head, so fierce and gut-punching that she recoiled. He noticed too. She knew he did. Again, she wanted to slap him, right there across the table in front of everyone, for that single tilting quirk of a smug fucking grin.

Of course she didn't slap him. Normal people didn't go around slapping people in public. Or in private, she reminded herself, shoving away the memories again, harder this time. *Put those motherfuckers in a box*, she thought. *And close that goddamned lid.*

"This meeting is over." Corinne stood and shouldered her bag. She tossed her napkin on the table. "Thanks for the wine. I trust you'll take care of the check."

Head high, back straight, she headed for the parking lot without looking from side to side. She couldn't. If any tiny thing distracted her, she was going to burst into huge, ugly sobs.

This was not how she'd imagined seeing him again. In her dreams they ran into each other at a party, both of them dressed in their best. He was with another woman, she another man, but that didn't matter. The second they caught eyes across the room, he'd move through the crowd toward her. He'd take her hand. Kiss the knuckles. Ask her to dance. He'd pull her close and whisper in her ear that he'd been a fool to ever leave her.

God, she was so stupid.

At her car, Corinne dug for her keys in her overstuffed purse, but they eluded her beneath the drifting tide of receipts and permission slips and used tissues with pieces of gum inside. It was a mom purse, like her shoes and her hair and her entire freaking life, and then shit, she was crying. Silent, painful sobs tore at her throat. She closed her eyes and gripped the roof of her car, hating how something so ridiculous and simple could make her so fucking sad.

He was surprised she'd ever spent a minute thinking about him in all these years? Of course he couldn't know how sometimes all she felt like she did was pine away for the past, and her boy, and how it had felt to be young and kinky and in love.

Love.

She could admit it now, looking back, though for years after it ended she'd told herself it hadn't been anything close to that. Corinne had learned the hard way that love could never be assumed or even really understood. You could say the words a million times without making them true; you could deny them for eternity and never make them false.

"Here."

She looked up through the blur of her tears to see Reese. Corinne swiped at her eyes. He took her bag from her with a gentle tug. Dug through it. Pulled out her keys. He clicked the remote to open the driver's door, then carefully snapped the carabiner around the strap of her purse exactly as it was meant to be done so that she wouldn't lose her keys in the first place.

He handed her back her purse along with a paper sack emblazoned with the StockYard Inn logo. "I had them box up your salad. You should take it along."

"I don't want it."

"You'll be hungry later," he said. "Then you'll want it."

Corinne dabbed at her eyes and gave him a long, hard stare. She did not take the bag from him. "The question is, Reese, what the hell do *you* want?"

"We have terms to discuss," Reese told her. "A business meeting. Remember? This isn't personal, it's not about you and me."

Corinne opened her car door and tossed her purse onto the

passenger seat. She straightened to look him in the eye. "Oh, no?"

Reese shook his head.

"You're a liar," she told him. "And you're not any better at it than you used to be."

Then she got in her car and drove away.

Chapter Seven

Before

They are lying in her bed when Corinne says to him, "I could own you forever."

He has already spent hours between her thighs, worshipping her with his tongue and fingers; she has so far denied him access to her pussy with his cock, and he's throbbing. His balls are tight and hard and full, and a minute or so ago, Reese would've said that burying himself inside her heat was what he wanted more than anything else.

At her words, though, the spinning world seems to slow and stop.

"You want to…own me?" He pushes up on his hands to look at her. His mouth is full of her flavor, sweet and tangy. His cock, pressing the softness of the bed, twitches. He has to hold himself back from pumping his hips. It won't take much to make him spill, and she hasn't given him permission.

Corinne looks faintly surprised, as though she hadn't been expecting him to question her. Or maybe it was her own admission that so shocked her, because now she sits up, withdrawing from him. She pulls her knees to her chest.

Reese sits up too, though he is on his knees with his heels pressing into his ass. His cock bobs, tapping his belly, and he watches her look at it. Her smile leaves him light-headed. He wants to take his hardness in his fist and stroke, stroke until he explodes, but that's *his* weakness. He needs to be stronger for her. To prove himself. He crosses his hands at the wrists just behind his lower back.

A sigh shudders out of her when he does that. "Fuck, you are so beautiful."

Her praise sends a rush of crackling, electric heat all through him. He can't help letting his back arch a little. The motion thrusts his hips forward. It's not enough to make him come, but it's enough to tighten his balls and his asshole too.

Corinne reaches to swipe the string of precome off the head of his dick with one fingertip. Keeping eye contact with him, she tucks the finger in her mouth and sucks it clean with a soft moan. Reese's entire body jerks at the sound. When she slides another finger into her mouth and sucks them both, he swears he can feel that sucking wetness on his cock, which is exactly what she obviously wants him to feel.

"So fucking beautiful." Corinne trails a fingertip along the underside of his shaft, toying for a second in the small divot beneath his cockhead. "Such a pretty purpley red. Leaking. For me?"

"Yes," Reese says. "All for you."

She's toyed with him plenty. Teasing. Edging him until he's sure he won't be able to hold out for one more second, only to ease off and leave his cock twitching with no release. He hates the denial, the persistent fullness in his balls. He hates his frenzy, how everything focuses on his cock, his balls, his ass, how his entire world shrinks until all he can think about is coming.

But he loves it too, because Reese loves her. The games they play turn him on more than anything ever has. More than that. They fulfill him. It's like Corinne is the key that unlocks a door to rooms he didn't know existed.

She grips his shaft with a fierceness that makes him gasp. She pulls him toward her, and Reese moves, eager to keep her grasp from hurting him. When she offers her mouth, he kisses her. She strokes him, balls to head. His cry is muffled inside her mouth. Her tongue swipes his. She takes his lower lip in her teeth and bites, not hard enough to draw blood, but still painful.

He's so hard he's sure he's going to break.

"Do you know what it feels like, for me?" She licks the spot she bit and locks her gaze to his. Her stroking hand slows, fingers squeezing just behind the head.

He couldn't come now if he tried, but Reese knows better than to even make the attempt. No matter how much he yearns to spatter her belly, no matter how much it hurts to hold off, it's a point of pride. He's given her the right to command his orgasm, and damn it, he's going to do his best to please her.

"To look at you, that lovely erect cock so thick and hard and dripping for me. To know how much you want to come. But you won't, will you? Until I say?" Her other hand cups his throbbing balls. Her thumb strokes the seam behind them.

At the press of her fingers on his asshole, Reese mutters a plea.

Corinne looks at him. There's nothing teasing in her gaze now, only a fierce and focused intensity. Her grip on his cock loosens. She strokes. She presses her fingertip just inside the tight ring of muscle.

"This hungry little asshole," she whispers. "Begging for me to fuck it."

"Yes…" More words spill out of him, a few of them coherent but most an entreating mumble. And then, "Yes, please, Ma'am, please. Fuck me. Own me. I am yours."

"You *are* mine." Corinne yanks him forward again by his cock so she can get at his mouth.

Reese's hands grip the headboard behind her. She nudges his thighs apart with hers. Her finger slides in deeper. Her other hand strokes, stopping short of palming his cockhead, and oh, thank God, because if she did that he wouldn't be able to hold back…he can barely hold back now…the finger inside him curls a little, pressing that magic spot that keeps him begging.

"Please, Ma'am, I'm going to come, please…" He shakes, helplessly thrusting into her grip. Grinding onto her finger. "Please. More."

Another finger pushes inside him. There's no lube. The stretching hurts, but not enough to stop him from moaning. She's being gentle enough not to cause any damage, but if anything, she's holding back too much. He's too far gone, needs more. All he can think about is the pressure in his balls. She makes circles on his prostate, pressing and releasing. Her stroking hand grips him behind the cockhead again, effectively blocking his orgasm one more time.

It doesn't stop more precome from leaking out of his slit. Thicker now, turning white. "Oh God, Ma'am, please, please, let me taste you."

"You've already made me come three times," Corinne whispers against his mouth.

"I want to make you come again, I want to please you—"

She lets go of his cock and slaps his face. For an exhilarating, horrifying second, Reese is sure he's going to fucking lose it, just jet all over her luscious tits and maybe even her face, oh, shit, oh, no… She slaps his face lightly again, then grips his jaw to bring his face to hers.

"It's not about what *you* want to do to please me," she says, "it's about what *I* want you to do to please me. And what pleases me is when you obey."

If ever Reese had not understood humility before, the fingers in his ass and the sting of her slap have certainly taught it to him now. If he moves, fucking onto her fingers, he's going to come. If she touches his cock, he's *sure* he's going to come. And if she slaps him again, oh, fuck. If she slaps him, he might just fucking die.

Her next touch is a caress, soothing. Then she drags her palm over the wetness now steadily dripping from his cockhead. Lubed, her hand glides over his shaft. Up. Down.

Looking him in the eyes, Corinne starts up that steady, circular pressure on his prostate again. She strokes him faster. Stops. Then again, all the while slowly and firmly fucking his ass with her fingers.

"I'm going to come," Reese manages to say, or at least almost say. Some of the words are garbled.

"Oh, yes, baby. Come for me."

She's no longer moving either of her hands. He's taken over all the moving. Thrusting into her curled hand, rocking his hips to grind himself onto the fingers inside him.

His orgasm rushes like a freight train, battering him. He comes so hard that he sees stars. His grip on the headboard hurts his hands, a pain of which he's aware but can't be bothered to ease, not while every single nerve is firing with pleasure.

Thick white fluid spurts out of him, too many gushes to count, and even when he stops jetting, the pressure on his prostate sends a few more spasms surging through him. He wants to collapse, but even in the aftermath of that epic climax, Reese manages to keep himself upright. Still shuddering, he opens his eyes. He expects her to be smiling or maybe even laughing the way she sometimes does when she allows him to climax, though he likes to believe it's with joy and not because she's mocking him.

Corinne is looking at him, but to his shock and concern, tears glitter in her blue eyes. As he watches, one single droplet escapes her lashes and glides over her cheek. It takes a bit of work to unkink his fingers from the headboard, and they're stiff and sore when he does.

He takes her in his arms, turning them both so he can cradle her on his lap. They're both sticky, and this position sends a reminding twinge in his ass, but he stretches out his legs and tucks her against him. Corinne presses her face to his chest.

"What's wrong, baby?" Reese asks with a kiss to her hair.

"I meant what I said."

Her voice is muffled against him, and he has to shift a little to get her to look at him so he can ask her to repeat herself.

"I meant what I said," Corinne says again. "I could own you forever."

Reese brushes his lips to hers, tasting salt. It kills him that anything could ever make her cry, especially something he's done. "Don't you know, Corinne? You already do."

Chapter Eight

He shouldn't have let her get to him, damn it.

"Anyway, that's all there is to this stuff." Tony closed his laptop lid and then the folder next to it. "You're really going ahead with pursuing this? I thought you said their CFO walked out of the lunch without even talking about the terms."

He'd let Tony believe Corinne's sudden departure was because of the insulting offer, not Reese's history with her. As far as Tony knew, there was no history with Corinne. "She did. But when you told me about the call from their president asking to reschedule for Monday, I figured they were still interested enough to make this happen."

Tony shrugged. "Okay. Sure. I needed to get out of the city for a few nights anyway. Breathe the fresh country air. Mmm, smell that air."

"Wow, nice sarcasm," Reese told him.

"What can I say, it's a gift." Tony grinned, then looked at the desk between them. "So that's all the paperwork, and I have my notary stuff with me, so if they do decide to sell, we're all set."

"That's enough for tonight. You can go, take a break."

"You want me to order you some dinner?" Tony tucked away his phone and stood, all six feet five inches of him. He pushed the folder across the desk toward Reese. "I'm going to order in and veg out, catch up on some TV."

Reese twisted to look up at him. "You're not going out? It's Friday."

"I'm sure Lancaster is a hotbed of excitement if you know where to go," Tony said, deadpan, "but tell you the truth, I'm beat. If you tell me what you want to eat, though, I'll be glad to get something for you. There have to be some places that deliver, right?"

"Don't forget, this is hick city." Reese laughed.

Tony tilted his head. "It's not that bad. There's a certain charm to it. All the fields. The cows and stuff. I saw three buggies on the way here; that was pretty cool. I'm going to check out some like, quilt shops and stuff tomorrow. Buy me some of that…what's it called? Red pepper jelly. You grew up here, have any recommendations?"

"Not really." Reese stretched, cracking his neck with a wince. His back and neck were killing him, and he desperately needed a run. Or a massage. Something to help him shed some of this fucking tension.

Tony stood and, without a word, went behind Reese to work his fingers into the knots at the base of Reese's neck. "No love for the old hometown?"

"No." Reese groaned, letting the other man work away at the painful spots. "Shit, that's good."

Tony worked a minute or so longer, then patted Reese's shoulders. "Want me to see if the hotel has a spa service or anything?"

"Remember, hick town." Reese rolled his shoulders as Tony gathered his things.

"I bet things have changed since you were here last. Give it a chance. You might be surprised." Tony excused himself, leaving Reese alone in the oversized hotel room.

The business suite would never win any awards for its decor, but the design was functional and practical, two qualities Reese appreciated. The king-sized bed seemed comfortable enough. He wasn't going to sleep much tonight, he was sure of that.

His phone beeped and he snapped it up, sure it would be Corinne calling to apologize. Her boss hadn't been too pleased about her abandoning the meeting, that had been clear. He'd been apologetic to the point of awkwardness about it.

Reese should've told the guy right then the entire offer had been something of a scam. How he'd never intended them to take it, that Reese been caught up in a personal issue with their haughty CFO, and the only business he'd meant to finish was the unfinished business between him and Corinne. Of course he'd said nothing like that, and of course the message was not from Corinne with her hat in her hands. She wasn't going to apologize to him, and he ought to have known better.

The message was from Tony, double-checking that Reese didn't want any food. He was ordering pizza and wings. Reese's stomach grumbled. He shot back a text.

Beer?

They won't deliver it, Tony replied. *But we can nip down to the place around the corner if you really want to.*

Around the corner was some divey looking corner bar with neon in the window. An idea struck him, and Reese tapped a query into his phone, then shot back a text to Tony.

I have a better idea. It's a little longer to walk, but you'll love it.

Ten minutes later they were sweating in the late September heat and walking away from the hotel. Reese shouldn't have been surprised the old place was still in business—diners rarely seemed to go under. They might change ownership a couple dozen times, but they usually managed to survive.

He paused on the sidewalk to look up at the long silver building lit with blue lighting. The sign was different. A new logo. Same name though. Triton's Diner had been around forever.

Tony gave him a curious look. "You don't want to go in?"

"My dad used to take me here when I was a kid. Saturday mornings. We'd get up early. He'd make sure all my chores were done. Then we'd 'sneak' off to town to have eggs over medium and pancakes. Mom always knew, but she pretended she didn't. They made the best hash browns here I've ever had in my life." Reese laughed ruefully and shook his head. "It looks the same. But not."

Tony put his hands in his pockets and rocked back and forth on his heels. He didn't say anything. He waited. It was one of the qualities in him that Reese appreciated most. That ability to know when silence was better than speech.

"Let's go in," Reese said.

Inside, the young waitress who seated them sported multiple piercings in her ears and lip and nose. Her artificially black hair was carefully arranged in a fifties pinup style, including a headscarf. A pattern of stars outlined her temple and snaked toward the back of her neck.

"Coffee, hon?" She even had the diner waitress patter down.

"Two coffees. You still serve breakfast now?"

"All day," she said with a grin.

When she'd taken their orders and filled their mugs, Tony watched her head behind the bar and into the kitchen. He put a hand over his heart. "I'm in love."

Reese chuckled. "With a girl?"

"I could be in love with a girl who looks like that." Tony gave Reese a dreamy eyed grin.

The food was up in minutes. Steaming hot, eggs prepared to perfection. Hash browns glistening with grease and still the best Reese had ever tasted. He and Tony ate in companionable silence punctuated only by requests to pass the ketchup or more sugar for the coffee.

It was the most satisfying meal Reese had eaten in a long time. He wiped his mouth with a napkin, then sat back in the booth and rubbed his stomach with a sigh. Tony laughed.

"Better than pizza and beer," Tony said. "Good idea."

"Dessert? We've got a killer lemon meringue. It will blow your mind." The waitress made goo-goo eyes at Tony, who returned the look with an equally soppy one of his own.

"Sold," Reese told her.

Tony sipped some coffee, not making a secret of how he was admiring the view of the waitress walking away. "So what's it like, coming home?"

"This hasn't been home for a long time." Reese hardly ever talked about growing up on a dairy farm here in Lancaster County. He tried to hardly ever think about it.

"Got it. And growing up here has nothing to do with buying this dairy. Right." Tony gave Reese an assessing look. "Nostalgia?"

Tony didn't know the half of it.

"I'm trying to buy that dairy because I think I can make some money off it. The same way I've done with every other business I bought. It has nothing to do with where or how I grew up. It's totally a business decision." Reese scraped up the last crispy bits of yolk-soaked hash browns and licked the fork clean. He caught Tony's look but very carefully gave nothing away with his own expression. Tony didn't need to know the truth. "You have another opinion?"

Tony shifted in his seat. "I know that you've never dealt with any place that makes food or beverages before. Not even a restaurant. There were plenty of opportunities to get into that sort of thing, but you've always steered away, even though restaurants can be some of the fastest things to turn over."

"Who says I couldn't own a restaurant, if I wanted to?"

"You looking to buy a place?" The waitress had reappeared with two plates of pie and another round of coffee. "Eddie's trying to sell, if you're really interested."

Tony grinned at her, eyeing the name tag pinned to the front of her blouse. "Hi there…Gretchen. Awesome coffee, by the way."

"Why's he selling?" Reese ignored Tony's batting eyelashes, though they seemed to have caught the waitress's attention.

"He wants to retire to Florida." Gretchen shrugged and topped off their mugs, then stood back to give Tony a contemplative look that turned into a small, interested smile after a moment. "Says it's too cold here in the winter. He's had this place for about thirty years."

"Eddie Malone." Reese nodded. "My dad knew him."

The waitress shifted her flirtation from Tony to give Reese a curious look. "Yeah? Who's your dad?"

"Uh…well, he passed away," Reese told her, which wasn't the answer to the question she'd asked but one she accepted with a nod.

"Well, Eddie's trying to get rid of this place. If you're really looking."

"I'm not," Reese said. "But thanks."

With another shrug, she left them. Tony gave him a long look as Reese forked a bite of orgasmically tasty lemon meringue into his mouth and pretended he had no idea Tony was trying to dig out more information from him.

"I've worked for you for eight years," Tony said finally. "You can't tell me there isn't more to this dairy acquisition than just making a profit. I've run the numbers for you. I've done the due diligence. Sure, it's possible that with your magic touch you could make it work, but you made them a shit offer. It's almost like you didn't want them to take it in the first place."

Reese chewed pie. Swallowed. He gave Tony a bland grin.

Tony frowned. "Fine, don't tell me. Drag my ass out here to the middle of nowhere to pursue some weirdly sudden artisanal cheese fetish. It's my job, I get it."

"It's your job," Reese agreed mildly.

"I live to serve, master."

Reese frowned. "Don't call me that."

"Fine. My liege?"

Tony was joking and had no idea why it made Reese a little

uncomfortable. Like he'd never spoken to Tony about where he'd grown up, Reese had never told him about the sorts of games he used to play. "Cut it out."

Tony stabbed the air between them with his fork. "You can't hide it from me forever."

"I'm not trying to hide anything," Reese began, and his words cut off at the sight of Corinne coming through the diner's double front doors.

She wore a pair of faded jeans and a stretched out T-shirt sheer enough to hint at the outline of her bra beneath. Her long, dark hair had been pulled into a messy bun, though a few tendrils had escaped to curl and stick to her neck. She looked tired.

She was beautiful enough to stop his heart.

She saw him in the next second, and the pleased, anticipatory look she'd had when she came through the doors became immediately shuttered. She'd put on her guard.

It fucking broke him that he was the cause of that. In the times before, all she'd ever had to do was look disappointed in him, and he'd gone to his knees for her. Literally. Once, making Corinne happy had been the only goal Reese ever had.

Tony twisted in his seat to look where Reese was staring. "You know her?"

"It's the CFO of Stein and Sons."

Tony's eyebrows lifted. "She's—"

"She's the CFO," Reese repeated harshly, "of Stein and Sons."

"Ah. Look, how about I head on back to the hotel and turn in. I'll see you tomorrow morning?"

"Yeah, I'll go with—"

Too late. Corinne had crossed the tiny dining room to stand in front of their booth, hands on her hips. Mouth a thin, grim line. "What the hell are you doing, Reese? Stalking me?"

"I'm finishing my dinner," he told her. "Actually, it was breakfast. Just at dinner time. Breakfast all day."

Tony looked startled at the blather spouting from Reese's mouth. Corinne noticed Reese wasn't sitting alone. She shook her head and frowned, probably against the start of a tirade. She nodded at Tony.

"Hi," Tony said. "You must be Corinne. Tony Randolph."

Now she looked embarrassed and held out her hand. "Oh.

Tony. You work with Reese. Hi, nice to meet you. I thought *we* were supposed to meet."

"I changed it, I told you," Reese said.

"I'm just on my way out. I'll see you Monday at the meeting…?" Tony stood.

Reese watched Corinne's gaze go up, up, up. At the small curve of her smile, no different than the looks Tony eternally garnered from men and women alike, Reese winced from the stab of jealousy. He was an idiot. She could look at whomever she wanted to. Hell, she could drag Tony off into a corner and fuck him into next week, if they were both into it, and although before tonight Reese hadn't thought Tony might even have considered it… Fuck.

He was getting out of control.

Both Tony and Corinne were staring at him. Keeping his expression bland, Reese leaned back against the diner booth as though he didn't have a goddamned care in the world. He didn't seem to have fooled his assistant, who was still smart enough not to say anything about it, but he gave Reese a look that said he'd be asking about it later.

When Tony had gone, Corinne turned as though she meant to leave too. Reese snagged the soft fabric of her jeans at the knee, letting go at once when she looked down at his hand, then at his face. He'd seen that look before. He'd overstepped.

"Sit," he said. Then, more gently, "Please?"

Corinne slid into the booth across the table from him. "What kind of game is this?"

"*This* is called coincidence. I had no idea you'd be there tonight. How could I?"

"You want me to believe you come back into town after about a million years, trying to buy the company I work for, and you show up at the diner where we first met, and that's a coincidence?"

He would always remember the first sight of her behind a coffee pot with a plate of eggs and potatoes in her hand. This might have been the place his father brought him on Saturday mornings, but it was also the place with strong memories of her. Reese frowned.

"I wanted something to eat." He sounded defensive and cursed himself for giving her any hint that she was affecting him.

Her gaze softened, though her mouth did not. "So you came for breakfast."

"It always was the best I ever had."

"I bet it still is." Her eyes met his, held his gaze. Challenging him the way she'd used to, and it wasn't about the breakfast.

Reese shrugged, giving Corinne the look his last lover had called "the smug bastard expression." Amber had hated it. He was sure Corinne wouldn't like it any better.

Corinne, however, smiled. She tilted her head and looked him up and down, and though it had been a long, long time since she'd studied him that way, he'd never quite forgotten how it had felt to be the center of her attention. Object of her affection. Nobody else had ever come close to making him feel for even one second what Corinne had done with such casual cruelty.

"Maybe you should tell me what's going on," she said when he didn't speak.

"I buy and sell businesses that are faltering, and I grow them and sell them for a profit," he told her. "I saw Stein and Sons listed in a report I get about small businesses that are considered to be in need of acquisition."

Impulsive. Mom had said he was impulsive, in response to Dad's somewhat harsher assessment of "flighty." Reese had grown to think of it as following his gut.

Corinne's smile twisted on one side. "And you...what? You saw I worked there and decided to buy it? So you could somehow fuck with my life, Reese? What the hell?"

"Is that what you think of me? I guess I shouldn't be surprised. You never did give me the benefit of the doubt."

Corinne's smile disappeared entirely. "I guess that must be what *you* think about *me*."

More words wanted to shoot from his mouth like bullets, finding the best places to hurt her. Over the years he'd often imagined it, some grand speech that would put her in her place and leave her reeling, maybe even begging him to forgive her. Now faced with the chance, all Reese could think about was how he needed to tell her the truth. Things had ended between them because of broken trust that had never been repaired. It had changed and ruined everything between them, and it had changed and sort of ruined him too.

"I wanted to see you again," he said finally.

"Coffee, hon?" The waitress caught a glance of Corinne's face and frowned. She looked at Reese. "Oh. Sorry. I can come back?"

Corinne shook her head. "Coffee's good, along with a cup of ice, please. And I'll have some of that Stein and Sons full cream Eddie keeps. Thanks."

When the waitress left, Corinne looked at him. "You wanted to see me again."

He nodded.

Then, shit, she was going to cry. Tears glittered. Her lips quivered. How could he have ever thought that was what he wanted, to hurt her?

He wanted to take her in his arms and kiss away the tears, but didn't move so much as an inch. Too much time had passed. He didn't know her anymore.

"You could've just called me or something," she said when she won the struggle to get herself under control. "Found me on Connex, for God's sake."

Connex had paid for his house in County Galway, Ireland, but he wasn't going to tell her that. "I don't have a Connex account."

The waitress brought the drinks and the cream. Corinne took her coffee the way she always had. He remembered. Three sugars. Enough cream to turn it white, but she would refill her cup several times without adding more. She added the coffee to the cup of ice and stirred.

"It's a terrible offer, and you know it," she told him after she'd sipped.

He wasn't going to admit that. "It's a fair offer, considering the losses the company has taken over the past few years and the changes in the marketplace."

"You really want to run a small town specialty dairy? This isn't some tech company that you can oversee from afar," Corinne said, then raised an eyebrow at his look. "Yeah, I did my own research on Ebersole Enterprises. You're a hands-off kind of corporate mogul, aren't you? You like to buy up businesses, tear them apart, and sell off the pieces."

"Not always," he replied.

Her chin lifted. "You do it often enough."

They stared at each other over the table, but Reese refused to allow himself to get lost in her gaze. Fathomless, blue, he'd more than once dived into those eyes and let himself drown.

"From everything I was able to find out about Stein and Sons, you're looking at the total dissolution of the business before the end of the year, unless things change," he said.

"Which is why you think you can sneak in with that horrible offer, right? I read the terms. You're not obligated to keep any of the existing board, staff, or employees. So what does that mean? You're going to come in and fire us all?"

He'd done it in the past, when it made sense for the business, but he'd only put those terms in there this time to make it less likely the board would approve the sale. "I'd do what was best for the acquisition."

"You'd do what was best for yourself," she said in a low voice. "Whatever you needed to do for you."

He scowled. "You're not being fair."

"Something tells me this isn't about being fair."

"Corinne..."

"I cannot in good conscience suggest to my board that they take your offer, Reese. But they're desperate. So they'll probably take it anyway. You're going to come in and rip it to shreds, put them out of business. Put people out of their jobs, and what do you expect them to do? There aren't a lot of positions for goat cheese artisans around. And what about me? I've been with Stein and Sons for my entire career. Did you think about that? How I might need my job to support myself? My kids?" She took a slow, shuddery breath. "I have two children. They're my life."

"You can find another job. You don't make goat cheese."

"Sure, because finding a new position that pays me what I'm paid, with my benefits, my flexible hours, yes, that's so easy at my age. Starting over." Her lip curled slightly. "Says the man with the yacht."

"I don't have a yacht," Reese told her quietly.

"No, because you get seasick," she shot back at him.

It was true. She remembered. The words hung between them, somehow accusatory.

He wanted to kiss her.

He wanted to hate her.

He wanted to save her.

"I'll see you at the meeting on Monday," he told her, and left her sitting alone in the diner booth.

Chapter Nine

Before

It's been a long, lazy day of nothing but bed and tea and kissing. They'd gone to bed with the dawn and slept for some hours before Reese woke her with the stroking of his fingers between her legs, finding her clit with that same unerring precision he always did. He'd given her an orgasm, and they'd fallen back to sleep.

Now he's on his back, one arm above his head, his face turned from her. Corinne had woken a few minutes before and gone to the bathroom to pee and brush her teeth, to generally freshen up a little. She creeps back into the bedroom to stand next to him, looking down at his peaceful, sleeping face. His lips are parted, a soft puff of breath escaping every so often. His brow furrows, eyes moving behind his closed lids.

Dreaming.

Of her? she wonders. Certainly she dreams of him sometimes, mostly when they aren't together but sometimes even as he sleeps beside her. They've been doing that more and more over the past few weeks. He hasn't quite moved in with her, not yet, but he might as well have. He's had another falling out with his father that she hasn't wanted to ask too much about, waiting for him to tell her on his own, but she knows it has to do with Reese quitting the farm.

She can imagine how disappointing it must be for his dad to find out his only son doesn't want to continue with the family business, and how hard it will be on the farm's operating budget to replace Reese with higher paid labor. She knows it's been hard on her boy, who has been looking for a job to replace the farm work, without much success. They've spoken of college—he wants to continue past the two-year business degree he already has. He needs money for a place to live, a car, food. School is not the priority.

She could ask him to move in with her, she thinks. Two could live as cheap as one, as the saying goes. She's already covering the rent on this apartment and all her expenses with the waitressing. She's eight months away from finishing her degree and already has a couple of job offers lined up for her. Accounting is far from what she'd dreamed about spending her life doing, but it will be better than the late night shift at the diner, long-term.

Besides, she thinks fondly, her boy will make her life easier, even if he can't contribute financially right off. When he isn't job hunting, he can mop the floors and clean the toilets and cook for her, she thinks with a small shiver of delight, imagining him at those domestic chores wearing only a pair of lace panties and a blush—he hates when she orders him to wear panties, but he loves that he hates it. Oh, Corinne thinks with another slow, rolling shiver, he will do her laundry. All of it, washing and drying and folding.

Reese shifts in his sleep, the sheet slipping down to reveal the firm muscles of his bare belly and the fine line of dark hair disappearing below the edge of the fabric. With a small, careful tug, Corinne pulls the sheet farther down to reveal the sweetly sleeping head of his cock, half-hard. He takes a slow sip of breath, but doesn't wake.

He is so fucking beautiful.

Slate-blue eyes he likes to line with black, thick dark hair to match. His body is lean and tight from working on the farm. Before Reese, there'd been more than a few guys. High school, college, then after. She has five years on him, after all. It bothers him, she thinks sometimes, that she's had men before him, and he's had only a girl here or there. Nothing like what he and Corinne share. She could tell him forever that it's different with him, but she's not sure how to convince him. Reese knows he's attractive because he's been pretty his whole life, but Corinne still reminds him. It's important to her. Making him believe it.

Once, years ago, her parents had given her a five-thousand-piece puzzle that had been nothing but black with a single crimson cherry in one corner. It took her the entire Christmas break to finish the puzzle, hours spent searching through the identical pieces to create the picture—until at last, at the end, she'd been able to fit that red cherry into the final, empty space.

In her life, Reese is the cherry.

They found their way to each other and managed to discover the rarity of two people whose darkest desires aligned. They don't talk much about the things they do that set them apart from other couples. For Corinne, Reese's innate desire to serve and please her came not as a surprise, but as a relief. He doesn't call her a bossy bitch or promise to give her whatever she wants, so long as whatever she wants is what he feels like giving her. She asks. He provides. It makes the sex smoking hot and kinky as fuck.

It's work too. If he's going to trust her to make the best decisions for him, she has to be willing and able to do that. It's a big responsibility that has nothing to do with fucking. Some days, Corinne is overwhelmed with the honor of her boy's belief in her; that she will always know best. It has made her realize how selfish she's been in the past. How much being with him has changed her.

When she pulls the sheet entirely off him, he stirs. His cock thickens, growing against his thigh so the head nudges his belly. Sometimes she wakes him by sliding up his body to straddle his face, letting her pussy tickle his lips until he moves, hungry and feasting on her. Today, though, seeing his cock rising awakens a different desire inside her.

Corinne moves onto the bed between Reese's legs, letting her hands run up the insides of his thighs to push them apart. His muffled gasp of surprise make her giggle against his skin as she runs her tongue along his secret inner flesh. He writhes, hips thrusting automatically, but her murmured command stills him.

She loses herself in his scent and warmth and the way his muscles tense and release beneath the tracing tip of her tongue. When she adds a light scratch of her fingernails, he writhes again. This time, she sits up.

Her nails dig deep, pinching tender flesh. This only makes him arch harder, into the pain. Not away from it. This is where Corinne finds her pleasure. Not solely in the causing of agony, but in knowing that she's turning him on.

"I told you to stay still."

"Sorry…"

She decreases the pressure of her fingernails in his skin, then runs the tips of her fingers over the marks she left. Reese shudders. Kneeling between his legs, Corinne pushes his thighs apart, wider and back so his knees bend. Reese makes a noise of protest, shifting to look at her with pleading eyes but an open mouth, lips glistening from his tongue.

"No?" she asks calmly, though her voice dips lower, rasping. "I was thinking of getting ready for work. I could just go do that—"

"No!" His gaze catches hers for a second before his head falls back against the pillows. His hands fist on the bottom sheet.

He opens himself to her.

Fuck, that's it. Right there. His obedience, especially with that tiniest hint of reluctance, totally flips her switch. She shakes inside with it, that power over him.

Her fingertips tickle him. She watches the muscles in his belly leap. Watches him swallow, hard, as his head tips back, exposing the line of his throat to her. His chest hitches with a half-strangled breath. When she pushes his knees back farther, exposing more of him to her, Reese lets out another small, muttered noise, this time not of protest but of utter, complete acquiescence.

Corinne bends back to loving him with her mouth and tongue and the press of her teeth on the marks she already left. She nuzzles him, her hair brushing his balls. She can feel the heat of him on her cheek. Eyes closed, she presses harder, teeth nipping. Her hands slip beneath his butt cheeks, her thumbs pressing the twin trigger points in the hollows framing his asshole.

The first time she'd ventured into touching him there, Reese had jerked himself away from her touch, closing himself off so fast she'd barely had time to taste him. He'd laughed nervously, twisting to roll her beneath him. Putting her in the "right" place, she'd thought at the time, and had let him do it, because they'd been brand new and still learning each other. Even now months later, he hasn't fully embraced how much he loves it.

Now, waiting for him to go still again, Corinne simply breathes on him. She lets the hot tickle of air tease him. His thigh muscles have gone rock hard, and so has his cock. Neither of them moves for an eternity, until at last she lets just the tiny, pointed tip of her tongue flick him.

She doesn't laugh when he cries out, though his reaction fills her with an overwhelming delight. She doesn't moan, either, though she wants to. Instead, she gives herself up to loving him with her mouth again. Soft kisses, tender swipes of her tongue. No teeth this time, though her nails dig lightly into the meat of his butt. She doesn't scold him when his hips move. Knowing he can't keep himself from moving pushes her own hips down, grinding her clit against the bed.

Reese has spent hours worshipping her pussy, and Corinne gives him the same attention and adoration now. She runs her tongue up along the seam of his balls to the base of his shaft, adding the pressure of her fingertip on his asshole without dipping inside. Her hair falls across her face, brushing his skin. She's on her knees, one hand on his thigh, the other between his legs, so turned on she doesn't even need to touch her clit to start the delirious, building pressure of orgasm.

Clear fluid drips from the slit of his cock, stretching from the head in a thin strand to puddle on his belly. Her head spins at the sight of it, that clear and evident proof of his arousal. His helpless reaction to everything she's doing. It's a flame set to the gasoline pool of her desire, igniting her.

"I fucking love it when you leak for me," she whispers.

Reese laughs softly and looks up at her. "I can't help it."

"That's why I love it so much," Corinne tells him.

Looking into his eyes, she swipes through the slickness on his skin, then presses those fingers a little deeper inside him. He's already wet from her tongue, but lubed this way she slips in easier, a little faster even than she'd intended. Reese mutters a cry and grips her wrist.

"Hush," she whispers, not moving, giving him time to adjust.

He's not holding on to her to keep her from pushing inside, though. He's urging her to go deeper. Still kneeling between his legs, one hand on his shaft and stroking, Corinne eases her fingers inside his heat. Twisting her wrist, she curls slightly upward, pressing.

His cock leaps in her grip. His fingers bunch the sheet, tugging it free at the corners. A series of small, desperate moans slip out of him, along with a single word.

"Please."

"Please what, puppy?"

"Please…fuck me."

Who could ever understand this? she thinks. How much she loves when he begs her that way, how tender it makes her feel toward him. How much pleasure she gets from making him feel so good.

Her fingers curl again, a come-here gesture inside him. She strokes his cock, making sure to palm the head and coat him in slickness. Then she grips him firmly just under the head, jacking him without moving up and down along his length, avoiding the sensitive tip. He's so stiff she can feel the rush of his heartbeat beneath his shaft's thin skin.

"I'm so wet for you right now, it's dripping down my thighs," Corinne says.

Reese moans, hips thrusting a couple times before he stops, obviously remembering she's told him not to move. "I want to taste you…"

"I thought you wanted me to fuck you."

He laughs, breathless. "Yes, that too."

"Like this?" Her fingers curl, pressing, and she moves them in and out. His reply is a garbled mutter she has to take as affirmation. She laughs too, and the sound stutters out of her throat, also a little choked with emotion. "You are so fucking beautiful, Reese."

He'd argued with her the first few times she'd told him that, but he knows better, now. "Thank you, Ma'am."

Corinne lets her hand stroke up and over the head of his cock. "My good boy."

At the words, his cock throbs, and more precome oozes out of him. Her clit pulses, her hips rocking forward as she clenches internally. She's so turned on that time seems to slow, everything surrounded in a glow.

There is something she's been thinking about for some time now but had not yet brought up to him. They'd fallen into this relationship without really talking about the things they both liked, finding their way together with one small reveal at a time. No whips, no chains, nothing that draws blood. Nothing like the things she's read about in the few books she bought online, the ones that say you need contracts and safe words and aftercare. Their negotiations have been informal, a mutual give and take. They're doing it wrong, according to anything she's ever read, although everything they've ever done has only felt right.

Withdrawing her touch, she moves up his body to straddle him. She lets her hands stroke down his arms to circle his wrists, bring them up next to his shoulders, an act he gives in to without resistance. She kisses his mouth.

"Reese…"

"Yeah?"

"I want to fuck you," Corinne whispers into his ear.

He turns his head slightly so his lips brush her cheek. "Yes, please."

"I want to *really* fuck you."

He says nothing for a second. Neither of them move. His erection, trapped between her ass and his belly, pulses. She can slide down an inch or so and take him inside her. She's so wet he will slip in without friction. But that isn't what she wants, and she thinks he knows it.

"…How?" he asks, finally.

She presses her face to the side of his neck. She rocks a little on his dick, moving so her pussy enfolds him, though he is still not inside her. "I have something."

Corinne had bought her first vibrator at age twenty-one from the back room in the cheesy adult video store that featured LIVE GIRLS DANCING (which, she presumed, was way better than dead ones). She'd worn her share of sexy lingerie. She'd even gone to a couple of those home "toy" parties hosted by her giggling friends who'd shrieked and covered their faces at the sight of anything remotely off-center. Even so, nothing had prepared her for the wealth of choices. She'd gone online to look for what she wanted, and finally found it after wading through pages of reviews and descriptions that had by turns thrilled and confused her. Her purchase had arrived in a discreet brown package, bigger than she'd thought it would be. She'd tried it on a few times, feeling ridiculous. *Will I feel silly in front of him*, she thinks suddenly, knowing this desperate desire inside her is going to urge her toward taking the chance of looking foolish.

This thing she wants, this thing she's been dreaming about for a long time even before she knew it was actually possible…if she can't ask it of Reese, she can't imagine who she'll ever be able to ask it of.

His hand strokes down the back of her hair. "What kind of something?"

She pushes upward to look at his face. "I can show you."

Most of the time she can read Reese's face as easily as though he has a ticker tape describing his thoughts scrolling over his forehead. Not right now. His gaze has gone shuttered, expression beyond neutral. Blank.

Then his brow furrows. His lips press together. He gives a single, sharp nod.

"Show me."

She isn't certain her legs will hold her when she gets up from the bed and goes to the closet, where she'd put the box on the top shelf so it could stare at her and mock every time she pushed it to the side to get at her stack of winter sweaters. Everything about her feels numb, so that she might stumble on unfeeling toes. She can feel him watching her as she walks the few short steps. Watching the way her body moves as she pushes up on her tiptoes to pull down the box. She knows he loves the way her hair hangs down just above the dimples at the small of her back, and normally she'd have swung her hips to give him a little extra show, but now all she can manage is to keep herself steady as she turns, box in hand.

Reese has pushed up, sitting. His cock hasn't softened. If anything, the anticipation has seemed to make him impossibly harder, thicker. It's started to flush that telltale dark red she's learned to recognize and crave.

Confidence, Corinne thinks. She owns this. She will ask him, and he might say yes or he might say no, but at least she can *ask* him. This is Reese, her good boy—no matter what he answers her, she doesn't need to worry about him thinking she's some kind of freak or sexual deviant.

Does she?

For the most part, Corinne has never worried about her preferences. She knows what she likes and what she wants, and if previous lovers helped her hone those interests, Reese has been the one to expand them. To help her explore. Hesitating now, she understands more than ever why Reese has often seemed more reluctant. When you open yourself up to someone about your deepest desires, it becomes so much easier to be afraid they will reject you.

She opens the box and takes a deep breath, holding it out as she waits for his reaction.

"Oh," is all he says.

She closes the box, preparing to back away and return it to the shelf. No, to put it straight into the trash. Already the heat of embarrassment is creeping up her throat into her cheeks; there have been few times with him when she hasn't felt in control, but all the times when he must've felt this way are circling around now to bite her.

"No, don't do that." Reese reaches for her. "Come here."

She does, pressing one knee to the bed to hold the box out to him. He opens it and sets aside the lid. He lets his fingers trail over the smooth rubber dildo and matching harness, then the bottle of lube nestled beside the toys.

"You want to fuck me. With this."

She nods. "Very much."

He closes his eyes for a second or so, head bowing slightly. When he speaks, it is in a voice so quiet she can't hear him. His uncomfortable cough seems enough of an answer, though. When she starts to withdraw, he catches her wrist.

Again, as before, not to stop her but to urge her on.

"Yes," he says. "Please."

That simple answer, the "please," the way his eyes meet hers without cutting away—she is completely lost to him in that moment. *And forever will be*, Corinne thinks as she leans to take his mouth with hers. He has agreed to give himself to her, and she is going to take him.

"I don't know...I'm not sure..." Reese adds when the kiss breaks and their foreheads press together. "You've done this before?"

"No, honey. Never."

He grins and looks relieved. "No?"

"No. You're the first. I'll be careful." She slides her hand between them to grip his cock, still hard as iron. She passes her thumb over the head to feel the wetness and revels in how he shudders at the caress. "We'll go as slow as you want."

His rough kiss takes her by surprise, and more so when he pushes her back onto the bed to roll on top of her. His belly presses her clit, urging a gasp from her. He kisses her so hard she'll be bruised, later. The tip of his prick slips inside her, not from any effort but because his body fits so naturally with hers that in this position, that is where his cock wants to be. It goes no further than that. Reese keeps himself from sinking all the way into her by pushing on the bed with his hands.

Corinne waits to see if he's going to move. She can tilt her hips. He'll be balls-deep inside her in a second. Then there will be no stopping it—they will move together until they both come. She can let him have this, if he's going to take it. She can let them both slide away from what she's asked from him and what he moments ago declared he would give.

Reese doesn't fuck into her. He kisses her again. He shifts to let the tip of his cock slide over her clit in a few steady, even strokes that have her craving to be filled. His tongue strokes hers. Then he moves from her mouth to her throat, pausing to sample each of her nipples until she cries out and tangles her hand in the back of his hair.

He moves back to her throat, nipping and sucking. Then her ear. His breath, hot, caresses her, and his tongue flicks at the tender earlobe until she writhes beneath him. She tilts her body, but he shifts so he slides along her cunt without pushing inside.

"I want you to fuck me," he whispers in her ear. "I want it so much, I thought about it, I never thought you would...I didn't know. I want it so much it hurts."

He quiets, breathing hard against her neck, still supporting himself on his arms. Corinne turns her face to kiss his cheek. She embraces him, urging him to cover her with his full weight.

"Get on your back," she says after a second or so, feeling his heart pounding so hard against her she is surprised it doesn't leap right out of his chest.

They roll. She gets off him to slip into the harness, which requires only a few adjustments of the buckles at each hip to fit her just right. She strips away the protective film at the bottle's opening and uncaps it, then coats the shaft with a thick layer of lube.

Kneeling between his legs, she puts her hands beneath his knees to support them. She settles the tip of her cock against him, not pushing. Not rushing. After a second or so, she uses a hand at the base of it to guide it, pressing slowly. It's different than when she uses her fingers. Harder to judge his comfort level, because she has no sensation in the rubber phallus.

"More," he says. "I'm okay."

Inch by inch, she enters him, until she's seated to the base. The dildo has been designed to press her clit, though the sensation surprises her. His eyes lock on hers. Their fingers link, gripping the outsides of his thighs.

Corinne moves, withdrawing as slowly as she'd pushed forward. Then in again. Out. His body accepts her, and better than that, his cock has gone as dark a purple-red as she's ever seen it. Every sound he makes urges her on, a little faster. A little harder. The pressure on her clit builds and she tries to hold off, tries not to go mindless with it, because she doesn't want to hurt him, but oh, fuck, oh yes, it feels so good, she's so close, she's going to come from this and can't believe it.

She's not even stroking his cock, but Reese is making those noises she knows mean he's going to come soon. Corinne slows the pace, teasing herself and him. Fascinated by the sight of his face. She's never seen him look quite like this. His eyes are open but glazed. If he sees her, she thinks it must be through the same fuzzy glow that surrounds him.

"I'm gonna come!" His cry echoes, tipping her over the edge.

Orgasm tears through her. Her pace stutters from the pleasure. She can't concentrate on anything but riding this, wave after wave of ecstasy. She fucks into him with short, jagged motions and he shouts hoarsely, coming in thick, white spurts.

"I love fucking you, Reese," she says. "I love you, oh, fuck...I love you."

The words are out of her before she can stop them, but if he hears them he doesn't say anything. They're both caught in the tsunami of orgasm, tumbling and rolling with it, incapable of doing anything but letting the waves take them. With the aftershocks still coursing through her, she slows the thrusting. Her nails have dug marks into his thighs. His cock is spent but not yet soft.

Carefully, Corinne eases free of his body, noticing how he winces. She goes to the bathroom and stands for a moment, weak-kneed and semidelirious with what has just happened. The rubber cock juts from between her thighs, and she no longer feels ridiculous. She feels powerful and grateful and, in the aftermath of her outburst, a little bit anxious.

She shouldn't. Still naked but without the accessories, she slides into bed so he can spoon her, and the press of his kiss to the back of her neck beneath her hair is familiar and cherished.

"I love you too," Reese tells her.

Chapter Ten

"It seems like a lot of cash to throw at a failing business, and I'm far from one to look a cash cow in the mouth, so to speak, but it seems too good to be true." Lynn said this in his careful, measured voice. "Can I ask, Mr. Ebersole, what prompted you to change the terms of the offer?"

Corinne sat in stunned silence. She'd arrived early to this morning's meeting to find Tony and Reese already in the conference room. New paperwork. New terms.

A brand new offer.

"After discussing some things with Ms. Barton, I came to the realization that I'd vastly undervalued Stein and Sons." Reese steadfastly did not look in her direction. "With some more research, I've determined that there's a lot more potential here than I'd previously thought, and with my contacts in the greater metropolitan areas, I'm thinking I could really turn this business around."

"Instead of just selling off the pieces of it?" Patty asked with a look at Lynn.

Ryan shifted in his chair. "You think you can get us in the hands of customers who like what we're selling?"

"And the mouths," Reese said. "Which is where you really want to be, right?"

Everyone laughed except Corinne, who managed a smile that strained the corners of her mouth. She'd tossed and turned every night since Friday, caught up in the memories. Only this time instead of sweet and sexy melancholia, she'd been fighting a slowly rising fury. With Reese for showing up this way, for this fuckery, but also with herself for the way, even now, she still wanted him.

At least she wanted what he had been.

Within half an hour, the deal was done. Signed, sealed. Delivered. Hands were shaken. The sense of relief in the room was palpable.

Corinne stayed back after everyone had filed out to take Reese and Tony on the factory tour. She should've been relieved, the way everyone else was. The board would be paid enough to make giving up their family business worthwhile. They could all retire. She would be getting a raise big enough to make her suspicious. Big enough to make sure it was going to be really, really hard for her to find another position to match it.

In her office, she tidied her desk and called the kids, who'd just gotten home from school. Last year she'd been paying an after-school sitter, but now that Peyton was nearly twelve, Corinne allowed them to say home alone until she could get there, usually no later than five. It helped that Auntie Caitlyn could be there for them in case of an emergency. Still, Corinne liked to text or call them around this time to make sure they were okay.

"Hey, buddy," she said when Tyler answered the phone. "How was school? Anything exciting happen?"

"Not really."

"Anything bad happen?" It was the same series of questions she asked both of them every day. Sometimes there was an answer. Sometimes not. Today Tyler told her a long story about how a kid in his class was getting in trouble for posting an unflattering picture of their teacher on one of his social media accounts.

She spoke with her son for a few more minutes, then with Peyton. By the time she got off the line, she felt much better. At least until she looked up to see Reese standing in her doorway. Seeing her disconnect the call, he stepped through.

"I thought you were going on the plant tour," she said.

Reese closed the door behind him. "I've seen a barn and milking stations plenty of times. I didn't need to go."

"You didn't need to do that," she told him with a lift of her chin toward the door.

"Yes, I did. I need to have a private talk with you, Corinne."

She gave him an arched brow. "Hmm, let me guess. New management says no personal phone calls allowed on company time? Sorry, bossman, I'll be better about it next time."

"Don't." He stood in front of her desk, his gaze dark. Stormy.

Corinne had seen Reese angry a number of times. Their relationship, despite the power and control issues at the core of it, had still been one of the most emotionally open ones she'd ever had. Probably exactly because of that dominance and submission component. She could see that now, although at the time she'd just thought it was the way things should go with all relationships. It had taken her a lot of failures to see how rare it was to have that level of connection.

"Don't what?" she murmured.

"Don't act like I'm the bad guy."

She laughed without much humor. "I could hardly say that, could I? I mean, you're practically a white knight, am I right? Riding in here on your charging steed to rescue us all? Save us?"

"I haven't saved this company yet," he said. "But I can. I will."

"So, you think you just saved *me*?" The question slipped out of her, unbidden but brutally honest. She wanted…no, needed, to know.

His hands went flat on the desk as he leaned forward to look at her. His fingers curled on the smooth wooden surface. He took a breath, then another.

"You don't have to worry about taking care of your kids now, do you?"

She swallowed a rush of emotion. "Is that what this is all about? Me and you?"

She watched the pulse throb in his throat. She got up and went around the desk to stand in front of him as he turned to face her. This close, she could smell his cologne.

"What are you wearing?" Corinne asked in a low voice.

His tongue swept along his lower lip, leaving it glistening. "Something by Armani. It's called Code."

"I like it," she said.

Something glittered in his gaze. She should walk toward him, she thought. Or he should take those two steps to her.

Neither of them moved.

"I don't like that cologne, whatever it is." Corinne takes a long, deep breath of the skin of his throat, then bites. She holds his flesh between her teeth, teasing him with the idea she might actually take out a chunk, leave him bleeding. She knows she never would. She's not sure Reese does, though.

He groans. That noise, guttural and helpless, makes her lose her fucking mind. It makes her want to hurt him and heal him all at the same time.

She releases his skin but can still taste him. "Don't wear it again."

"Yes, Ma'am."

She puts a hand on his shoulder, pushing him down to his knees. Inches her skirt up to reveal the edges of her panties. Her boy moans again. When she buries her fingers in his hair, tangling them tight, pulling hard, he looks up at her with a dreamy, blurred gaze.

"Tell me what you want," Corinne murmurs. Her voice sounds thick and sweet as syrup, dripping off her tongue.

Her boy smiles. "To make you happy."

Her finger traces the line of his jaw. Her fingers curl lightly around his throat. She could choke him, but she doesn't. Even so, he closes his eyes, still smiling, and leans almost imperceptibly into her embrace.

"Hurt me," Reese whispers.

"Why did you buy this company, Reese?"

He didn't look away from her. "Because it's what I do."

"It wasn't to…" Her breath hitched. It was hard to swallow, her throat tight. Too much emotion. She took a step toward him. "To protect me? To take care of me?"

She was wrong; she saw that immediately in the twist of his lips and the way his gaze shuttered. He took two steps back from her, far enough to be certain there was no way she could reach and touch him. His look of utter disdain hit her like a stone through a glass window.

Shattered.

What had she really thought? That after all this time and all that had passed between them that any decision he ever made had anything to do with her at all? How could it?

Hadn't she learned already that she wasn't worth the effort of being cherished?

Hadn't Reese been the one to teach her that very painful lesson?

She'd seen it at once written all over his face and could have gone the rest of her life without hearing him seal it with his words, but of course he said them anyway.

"I think you've got the wrong idea," Reese told her. "I'm not your boy anymore."

Chapter Eleven

Before

"He's going out again, Mother." This is what Reese's father says while looking directly at his son. "Look at him. What are you wearing? Girls' clothes?"

The hot pink skinny tie had been a gift from Corinne, true, but it's still from the men's section of the store. The soft cotton panties he's wearing under his dark jeans, though—those are girls' clothes for sure. His dad would have a heart attack if he knew his son was wearing panties. Reese is pretty sure that's a big reason Corinne has asked him to. She's never met his father, but she knows exactly how to push every single button Reese has.

When you're wearing my panties, it reminds you constantly that you're mine," she had told him two days ago as he knelt between her thighs to press his cheek to her skin. Her hands had stroked, stroked through his hair. He could smell her pussy, so close and yet denied him for the sole purpose of making him crazy with desire.

"I could never forget that I'm yours, Ma'am.

She'd never asked him to call her that. It had slipped out of him the first time they were together, an automatic expression of polite address, and her reaction had been electric. He didn't call her Ma'am all the time. Just when he wanted to watch her eyes grow dark with arousal and see her nipples grow tight. It was his version of her asking him to wear panties.

"Answer me," his father says with a thump of big fists on the table, drawing Reese's attention back to the present.

Reese shrugs. "I'm not wearing girls' clothes, Dad."

"You're wearing makeup."

"It's just…a thing." Reese shrugs.

"You look like a fairy."

"I'm not wearing wings." Reese grins, but his father doesn't. There'd been plenty of times when Dad had been able to take a joke, but it seems more and more like he's set on turning into a grumpy old man who never laughs at anything. "Dad, c'mon. It's a pink tie and a little eyeliner. Not a big deal."

"You'll be out all night in that pink tie, doing what? Wasting your money and your time."

"It's fun, Dad. That's all." Reese tugs at the knot of the tie. "Here, I'll take it off, if it offends you so much."

When he shifts, he can feel the softness of the cotton riding up his ass crack. The panties are meant to fit Corinne, too small on him. She's right about how they keep him constantly reminded of her.

"Never mind," his father says. He shakes his head in disgust and waves a hand in Reese's direction. Dismissing him. "Go out. Go waste your time and your money, come home with a sick belly. You already have the sick head."

Reese had been backing out of the kitchen to avoid the tirade, but this stopped him, dead still. "What's that supposed to mean?"

His father won't look at him. He keeps his attention on the paper spread out on the table in front of him. The after-dinner cigarette smokes in the ashtray. Stinking. Reese's father looks at what's in front of him so he doesn't have to see his only child.

"Dad."

His father gives another of those dismissive waves, but Reese isn't going to let him get away with it this time. He steps closer to the table, forcing himself into his father's line of view until the old man looks up with a long sigh rooted so deep in his guts it seems to take forever to slip from his lips. Reese puts his hands on the table and leans forward, trying to catch his father's eyes.

"What did you mean? Sick in the head?"

Finally, looking pained, his father raises his head. "Go. Just go. And if you're going to stumble in with the stink of alcohol on your breath tomorrow morning instead of being ready to help with the milking, you might as well just stay out and not come home."

"Are you kicking me out?"

"I'm sure," his father says with a slightly curled lip, "that one of your *boyfriends* can give you a place to stay, if you need one."

Reese doesn't know what to say to this. A dozen responses rise to his tongue and are swallowed, making no sense. He can't wrap his head around this accusation that feels like it must've been building inside his father for a long time.

"I have a *girlfriend*."

"Sure, you do. That's why you bring her around so much."

Reese hasn't brought Corinne around because she works nights, because his parents are old-fashioned and might not understand about her being a few years older, they would ask her embarrassing questions about if she goes to church and if she plans to marry him and push out babies. Even if Reese can't imagine his life without Corinne as part of it, they aren't anywhere close to that sort of relationship commitment yet. It's occurred to him that she might not want to actually marry or raise a family with him. She's never talked about it, never even hinted. In another couple of weeks, they'll have been together for an entire year.

"I don't bring her around because I'm afraid you'll be rude to her."

At this, his father looks up. His glasses have slipped down his nose. Tufts of hair burst from his ears, his nostrils. His eyebrows have grown immensely thick and gray. All of his dad's hair has turned gray, and Reese discovers he can't remember when that happened.

When's the last time they went to the diner together for breakfast? Reese can't remember. When's the last time they did anything but snipe at each other? Reese can't remember that, either.

He's sure his dad's going to say something so Reese can combat it. They can have a fight. It'll be a little ugly, but Reese might be able to get some of the things off his chest that have been bothering him for a long time. His dad will yell and scold and accuse.

Instead, his father simply shrugs. His face holds no expression. Disappointment would've been easier to face than that utter lack of emotion.

All of Reese's arguments dry up. He actually has nothing to say to the old man; that's what he realizes as he straightens the knot on his tie. He can't do much about the slide of cotton into his ass crack, but there, again, he is thinking of Corinne and what she does to him. And for him. How she makes him feel, as though he's all full up and needs nothing more than to be with her, making her happy.

His dad wouldn't understand, Reese thinks, watching his father ignore him. If Dad had ever wanted to make someone other than himself happy it had been a long, long time ago, and hell, it seems as though he's even stopped trying to please himself.

Without another word, Reese stalks out of the kitchen and down the long country lane to the main road, where he finds Billy and Jonathan waiting for him. They're going clubbing, and at the end of the night, they'll drop him off at Triton's Diner. Corinne will serve them all coffee and eggs and pancakes, but Reese is the only one she will take home.

Chapter Twelve

"There isn't anything I can do about it, except maybe quit. And I'm not going to do that, not only so he doesn't get the satisfaction, but of course because I'm not stupid enough to let what happened in the past ruin what I have going on now. I don't want another job. I like the one I have." Corinne mixed cake batter as she spoke to her sister, who was sitting at the breakfast bar allegedly looking up job prospects on her laptop. From the way Caitlyn occasionally giggled, Corinne suspected she was surfing Connex, instead.

Peyton had volunteered to bring in a dozen cupcakes for the bake sale. Typically, since the girl had spent the weekend with her dad and the new family, she'd been too busy with lots of other projects to remember that someone, somehow, needed to provide the treats. That left it up to Corinne, who hated baking, especially the last minute emergency aspect to it..

"Sprinkles," Peyton said. "All different colors of sprinkles. But no coconut shavings, because coconut is the devil's—"

Corinne watched in amusement as her daughter's cheeks turned pink. "Uh-huh?"

"Dental floss!" Peyton burst into giggles.

"That's not how that goes," Caitlyn murmured.

The phrase was "coconut is the devil's pubic hair," uttered by Corinne any time she had to deal with the foul stuff, but now she laughed as hard as her kid was. "Dental floss. Right. Good one. Dental floss isn't that gross, though."

"Tyler must think it is. He never flosses his teeth." Peyton made a face, wrinkling her nose and glancing into the living room where her brother was busy with some video game. "Or brushes them, either. And he pees on the seat, and he doesn't flush… I wish I had my own bathroom here like I do at Dad's."

When she and Douglas had bought this house, it had been with the idea of settling for what they could afford without financially strapping themselves. Since at the time both kids were toddlers, neither she nor her ex-husband had looked ahead to the day when the sharing of their bathroom would lead to power struggles or other complications and cause so much domestic strife. Well, there were other things she'd need to change about this house before she could consider adding another bathroom. The kitchen, for one, with its outdated appliances and linoleum.

"Well," Corinne said lightly, "I'm sorry that our house isn't as big and nice as Dad's new one, but I can talk to Tyler about being more considerate in the bathroom."

Before Peyton could answer, the house phone jangled, catching them all off guard. The landline rarely rang, especially this late in the evening. It was almost bedtime.

"Yeah?" Corinne kept her voice hard, ready to put the smackdown on a telesolicitor. "Are you aware that you're calling past nine p.m.?"

"I forgot about your phone rule," said a familiar male voice. "I apologize, I should've called earlier."

"Reese. Hi." Turning, the phone's long cord twisting as she did, Corinne kept her face away from Peyton's curious look. The kid had eagle eyes, and Corinne didn't want to give anything away with her expression. She also avoided Caitlyn's scrutiny. Hell, she wasn't sure what she was going to say or do.

"I have some questions on a few things about the accounts, and—"

"And you couldn't wait until tomorrow morning?"

"You've taken tomorrow morning off," he reminded her. "You won't be in until the afternoon, and I'm heading back to Philadelphia in the morning to tie up a few things."

He paused. She wondered if that was meant to be an innuendo. If it was, there was no way she was going to react to it.

"I won't be back in Lancaster until next week," Reese added. "I didn't want to wait."

"What kinds of questions?"

Reese hesitated before answering, though when he did speak his voice was strong and confident. A bit overbearing, actually. Arrogant. Another of those slow, rolling shivers that had so often run through her when they were together made its twisting, curving journey into her nervous system. He was putting on a show for her. Pushing her buttons, trying to get a rise out of her.

"I want to go over some of the numbers with you, make sure everything is properly squared up. There are some discrepancies."

"In *my* work?" She'd closed her eyes, one arm crossed over her belly to tuck her elbow into her palm while she held the phone to her ear. She opened them to see both her daughter and sister staring, and she waved them out of the kitchen with a fierce look.

"I have questions. That's all."

She pictured him in the business suit he'd been wearing in that restaurant, the first time she'd seen him in fifteen years. Now she pictured him in that same suit but on his knees in front of her, head bowed. Hands behind his back, crossed at the wrists, the position he'd so willingly gone to for her, so many times.

I think you've got the wrong idea. I'm not your boy anymore.

He could not have been more clear. She could not have been more stung. Lifting her chin now, cheeks heating, Corinne opened her eyes. From upstairs she could hear the faint noise of Caitlyn urging the kids to get ready for bed.

"It's getting late, Reese. I need to get my kids settled for the night."

"This can't wait," he said. "I'll need to talk to you about it tonight. Put your kids to bed and call me back."

Corinne had never been a switch. It was true that after Reese, she'd never had another boy the way she'd had him, and that she'd settled into a pattern of traditional, vanilla relationships that had rarely even hinted at her proclivities. But she had definitely not gone in the other direction, ever, not in her personal or working life. At his arrogant assumption that she would rearrange everything to give him what she wanted, she smiled without humor. The rusted-shut tumblers of a long-abandoned lock began to click open, one by one, inside her.

"Tell you what," she said. "Why don't you come over here. They'll be in bed and I'll be able to address your issues without distraction then. Forty-seven minutes."

Not forty-five. Not an hour. Forty-seven, a specifically odd number, meant to remind him of who was in charge. Meant to make him think hard about making sure he got it right.

"Fine," Reese replied in a steely voice, giving her no hint as to whether or not he'd remembered all the other times she'd set him such a specific task. "I'll be there."

Chapter Thirteen

Reese pulled into her driveway exactly forty-five minutes after they'd hung up from the call. It would take two minutes to get from the car to the house. Arrival time, precisely forty-seven minutes.

He didn't get out of the car.

He turned off the ignition and slipped the key into his pocket. He gathered the handful of folders he'd brought along. Patted his pocket to make sure his Parker fountain pen was in its place. He waited, hating the fact his heart had started to pound faster with every passing minute that he was late.

When I tell you to be ready at a certain time, puppy, I expect you to be ready. I despise being made to wait. It's disrespectful.

Corinne's words from the past echoed in his mind. Yet here he was, dallying in the front seat of his car on purpose just to fuck with her because she'd had the audacity to pull that forty-seven minute business with him, like even after all this time he was going to jump at her command.

Inside the house, the upstairs lights went out. A minute or so after that, the front porch light also went dark. Then the ones in the front room. She wasn't going to wait up for him.

He'd pissed her off. Good, Reese thought as he got out of the car. She needed to remember that things were different now. So did he.

Standing on her porch in the dark though, at least ten minutes after she'd told him to be there, he wondered if he'd pissed her off so much that she wasn't going to answer the door. He didn't want to ring the bell, mindful that her kids were supposed to be sleeping— kids. The thought of it made him reel just enough to take a step back so his heel hung off the porch. Corinne had children. She'd had an entire life after him.

What the hell was he doing? Badgering her on a Sunday night, insisting they go over these stupid numbers that ultimately weren't going to matter, not once he fully took over and the new budgets and strategies for growth were implemented. Why the hell was he on her porch when he could've phoned the office or even had a video meeting next week to talk about stuff?

Before he had the chance to turn and go, however, the door opened. Silhouetted in the glow from the hallway behind her, Corinne leaned in the doorway. She wore a pair of soft, clinging yoga pants and a tight T-shirt with a deep V that hinted at cleavage. She'd pulled her hair on top of her head with a few tendrils escaping to draw attention to the line of her neck. She held a glass of red wine.

"So. Are you coming in, or are we going to talk on the porch? I warn you, the mosquitos will devour you."

Reese squared his shoulders. "Yeah, I'm coming in."

She stepped aside to let him pass, closing the door behind him. "Shoes off, please."

He'd already been toeing them off, remembering her house rule that had been in place back in that drafty old apartment on Queen Street. When he glanced over his shoulder, she was watching him with a small, faint smile as she sipped her wine. She caught him looking, and her expression changed. Got a little colder. She pointed her chin toward the rug at the side of the door.

He had to bend to pick up the shoes so he could put them on the rug, and he'd never been more aware in his life of another person's gaze upon him as he did. She was watching his ass. He knew it. Watching him do as she'd ordered him to do. He would've acquiesced to anyone's house rule about shoes because his mother had raised him to be polite as a guest in someone's house, but this time, instead of neatly settling his leather oxfords on the rug, he tossed them in a jumble.

Behind him, he heard a soft, low sigh.

When he turned to look, Corinne was staring at the messy way he'd left the shoes, one arm crossed over her belly so she could rest her elbow in her hand. Her wine was still sloshing in the glass, her lips wet with it. Her tongue slipped out as he watched. Tasting.

She looked him right in the eyes then, and said nothing. She didn't have to. She knew exactly what he'd done and why he had done it, or at least she thought she did. For fuck's sakes, *Reese* wasn't exactly sure why he'd done it, other than if he'd ever believed he could keep his shit together in the presence of this woman, he'd been fooling himself all along.

"Kitchen." Corinne lifted her glass toward the end of the corridor. "We'll sit in there."

He followed her, of course. Her kitchen was big and bright and cheery, decorated in a red and black color scheme that didn't surprise him. The kitchen on Queen Street had been smaller, but similar in decor, minus the report cards, school photos, and crayon drawings mostly covering the outdated fridge. A platter heaped high with cupcakes sat in the middle of the island counter. Glass sliders led to a stone patio out the back, and he caught a glimpse of a fire pit and a vast, sloping yard. Everything about this room spoke of a nice, suburban life and family. The complete opposite of his life.

"Wine?" She held up the bottle.

"What kind?"

With a raise of her eyebrow she turned the bottle to show him the label, which featured a colored line sketch of a zombie. "It's called Malicious. It's a Malbec."

She pulled a wineglass with a big bowl from the others hanging beneath the cabinet, and set it on the counter. She filled it. Put the bottle down. Held out the glass to him without coming closer.

He would have to step forward to take it. Of course he did. "You still buy wine based on if the label's pretty."

"How else are you supposed to do it?" she teased and lifted her glass, watching him over the rim of it as she sipped. "I suppose you rely on the advice of your personal sommelier."

"I research," Reese told her. "It's not that hard."

"Neither is picking out a bottle with a fun label," Corinne said lightly. "Are you going to drink it, or are you going to waste it?"

"It's already in my hand."

"Good—" Her voice had dipped, but she cut herself off with a small cough and cut her gaze from his.

He wanted to take pleasure in the sight of her discomfort but couldn't. He took a long sip of the wine and lifted the glass with a nod. "It's good. Yeah."

"So," Corinne said crisply, "what is it, exactly, that you wanted to talk about?"

He took a seat at the breakfast nook, which had been styled to look like a retro diner booth. "This looks familiar."

"It's from the diner. About four years ago, Eddie did some renovations and auctioned off a bunch of the stuff he was replacing. I grabbed this and some other things that are still in storage until I can get around to fixing up my kitchen the way I'd like it to be. My ex didn't like the diner look."

"So as soon as you split up you put this in?"

She nodded. "Yep."

"A good way to stick it to him, I guess."

Her eyes narrowed. "It was a good way to start working toward turning this kitchen, which he now no longer uses, into a space that would please me."

It had been a dickish thing to say, and he knew it. "You always did know exactly what you wanted and how to get it."

That should not have been a dickish statement, but he came out sounding like a total asshole anyway.

"It's my house. Why shouldn't I have it the way I like it?" Corinne asked in a clipped, controlled voice.

"You should always have everything the way *you* like it. Right?" *Three strikes*, Reese thought. *You're out.*

He'd have deserved it, too, if she'd lost her shit with him, but all Corinne did was press her lips together and look at the glass of wine in her hand. It seemed that time had given her better control over her temper. Reese wasn't sure that was the reaction he'd wanted.

"It's getting late. Please show me what it is you have questions about so we can go over it."

He spread the folders open in front of her to show the printouts he'd culled from the stacks of material Tony had prepared. "There are a couple of accounts that don't match up. Some past end-of-year things."

She tilted her head to look over the papers he was pulling out. With a frown, she tugged one set closer to her. "Yeah…these are from right around the time we switched to the new software. I took care of all that in the new system."

"There's no record of any of that."

"Of what?" she asked sharply.

"Of the updated files."

Corinne took a sip of wine before answering. "Where'd you pull this from?"

"Tony gave it to me."

"Where did he get it?"

Reese sat back in his chair. "It was all part of the original information that Lynn sent us when we were collecting data before we decided to make the offer."

"It didn't come from the updated package I put together."

"I—"

"It didn't," Corinne said. "It couldn't have. The stuff Lynn put together was culled from older files he'd tried to access after a computer backup failed. He's a great guy, but he's not the most tech savvy. And, if you've done any research into this company at all, you know that they're all great people, but it's still a small, family run business and occasionally the way it's been handled reflects that. If you'd asked me, though, I could've made sure you were working from the most current information."

"I am asking you!"

"No," she told him with a slow, deliberate shake of her head. "You're trying to show me up. Aren't you? Because you had to dig pretty deep to find something remotely problematic with the way I've handled the financials for Stein and Sons. And wow, did you dig. So here's my question for you, Reese. Did you pull out all that crap because you wanted something to rattle me with, or did you just want an excuse to see me alone?"

Reese pulled the folders out of her hands and piled them. "That's a completely unprofessional accusation."

"It would be unprofessional of *you*, if that's what you did."

He'd spotted a spin-lid garbage can in the corner and stood now to toss the files into it. Her accusations, professional or not, had hit too close to home. He turned to lean his back against the counter, facing her.

"You know, I've bought and sold more businesses in the past twelve years than you could possibly guess."

"A hundred or so, right?" she said easily enough. "I told you, I looked you up."

"Then you should know I'm—"

"A powerful businessman. I know." She got up from the table and moved toward him, stopping just out of reach. She took a long, slow slip of her wine. "Expensive suits. Houses all over the world. You're very important, and very, very rich. You're one of Philadelphia's top ten eligible bachelors."

She must've read one of the many gossipy type reports that had gone around the internet once or twice when he'd been foolish enough to get involved with that sort of thing.

"You should know that I'm good at what I do," Reese said. "I don't waste time or resources on things that don't matter."

She smiled thinly. "And you should know that I'm also good at what I do, and I don't need my time *wasted* on things that don't matter."

Somehow, he suspected that neither of them were really talking about the business.

"Good to know. When I get back to the office next week, I'll expect to have all the updated information showing me these the discrepancies and how they were resolved, with authentication."

Corinne put her half-full wineglass in the sink. It took her a few seconds longer to turn than necessary, but when she did, her expression was neutral. "If you're planning to accuse me of some kind of impropriety or...I don't know what. Embezzling?"

"No!" Shocked, he took a step toward her before stopping himself. "What?"

She crossed her arms. "Because that's what it sounds like, Reese. So if that's where this is leading, you should tell me right now, because then I can have my resignation letter on your desk tomorrow morning."

"That's it," he said. "That's what you do. You get challenged the least little bit, and you want to quit."

"Me? That's a good one. I'm not the one—"

"Mom?"

Both of them turned toward the lanky blonde girl standing in the doorway with a curious look on her face. She had Corinne's eyes. Shit. The daughter.

"What's up, Peyton?" Corinne's tone had changed. Lighter, sweeter. Concerned. She didn't look at Reese.

"Are the cupcakes ready?"

"Yeah, honey. I'll put them in the container for you and make sure they're in the car for when I drop you off at school after the dentist."

"Okay, good. I wanted to be sure you didn't forget." Peyton looked at Reese, then her mother.

"This is Mr. Ebersole. He bought the company I work for. He's here to go over some paperwork."

Peyton nodded, assessing him frankly in a way that reminded him so much of Corinne that he wanted to laugh, but didn't. With a backward glance, she left the kitchen. Corinne looked at him.

"My oldest. She volunteered me for the bake sale."

"You hate to bake," he said.

Corinne's brow furrowed. "You remember."

"I remember a lot of things."

"Yeah," she said, looking into his eyes. "Me too."

Chapter Fourteen

"You really think he came all the way to your house on a Sunday night just to talk to you about discrepancies in the files? C'mon, Corinne. There's no way." Caitlyn spread a thick layer of port wine cheese on a cracker and crunched it messily. Mouth full, she went on. "The guy buys and sells companies like trading cards. You think he can't really tell when something is funky or not? Also, isn't that what his assistant is supposed to do?"

Corinne stretched out her toes, wiggling them as she admired the polish. It had been a long, stressful week. Reese had not fired any of the current barn or production plant staff, but he'd had her start interviewing potentials for the positions she'd let go over the past year, as well as some others that had been formerly been filled by the board members. All of *them* had taken the payout she was beginning to wish she'd been offered.

"Maybe he's trying to make you his new *assistant*," Caitlyn said in a half-horrified voice.

Though it was Corinne's weekend with the kids, Douglas had taken them to his nephew's bar mitzvah. Corinne and her sister had planned to spend the entire Saturday giving themselves manicures and pedicures, drinking wine, and eating snacks while watching as many hours of their favorite TV show, *Runner*, as possible.

"Let's watch season eight," Corinne said, ignoring her sister.

"Eight? No. Eight's the season we pretend didn't happen." Caitlyn shook her head. "That's the season when the writers went on strike and they came up with that alternate timeline! How can you want to watch Eight?"

Corinne laughed. "Okay, Five."

"Five's good. Get that queued up; I'll fill our glasses."

Back in minutes with full wineglasses and some more snacks, Caitlyn settled into the couch next to Corinne. Both of them sang along to the opening theme song, which had no words, so they made up the lyrics randomly. They'd both seen most of these episodes at least three times already, so there was plenty of time to talk.

Caitlyn, Corinne knew, was going to keep circling back around to the subject of Reese unless she did the big sister thing and cut off baby sis at the pass. "So. What's up with the new job? Any luck?"

"Ugh. Did Mom tell you to ask me that?"

"No. I just wondered how it was that you were able to make it out here for such an extended visit, that's all. What happened with the last one, anyway?" Corinne sipped the wine, a Cabernet she'd picked up because the label had featured a mermaid with a sugar skull face. The empty bottle would join the others in a row along the top of her kitchen cabinets.

Caitlyn's mouth twisted. "I got fired."

"Ah."

"Yeah. Go ahead, you can say it. 'Again?'"

"Again?" Corinne imitated her sister's snide tone, then softened her voice. "Kid, what happened?"

"I got caught three times without covering up my piercing." Caitlyn pointed to the delicate jewel in her nostril. "It was against corporate policy. I didn't want to take it out, so they had me wearing these little round adhesive bandages that were always falling off. That's all."

"Sucks." Corinne shrugged. "So, you're looking for something else?"

Caitlyn took a long, slow sip of wine and then bent forward to riffle through the plastic bin of nail polishes. She plucked out a bottle of sparkly crimson and held it up. "Yeah. Of course. Sure. Eventually."

"Eventually." Corinne laughed and shook her head. "How is it that you manage to drift from thing to thing and always end up somehow on top?"

"I'm a kitty cat," her sister said with a grin that seemed a little forced. "Landing on my feet, even when you toss me out the window."

"I take it that means that what's-his-name is history too?" Corinne had never met her sister's last boyfriend, though she'd seen plenty of pictures of the two of them on Caitlyn's Connex account. Her sister hadn't mentioned him since arriving at Corinne's doorstep a month ago and, used to her sister's come-and-go boyfriends, Corinne hadn't pressed for information.

"Oh, yeah. Ancient. Speaking of what's-his-name," Caitlyn said. "Let's get this turned back to Reese."

Shit. Her plan at distraction had failed. Corinne sighed and also bent to dig around in the mess of bottles. She found a dark, iridescent blue that Peyton had brought home in a goody bag after a sleepover party. Busying herself with opening it, Corinne didn't look at her sister.

"There's nothing to talk about."

"You don't think it's the universe trying to tell you something?" Caitlyn asked.

Corinne snorted. "Like what?"

"I don't know. He was your one, and here he is, back again."

"My *one*?" Corinne snorted again, this time with laughter. "Please. My fucking *one*? You're crazy."

Caitlyn looked serious. "Hey. I remember how it was with you two."

"You were like, twelve. You had no idea how it was with the two of us, I promise you that." Corinne shifted to get her toes up on the coffee table, but gave her sister a look. "Reese Ebersole was not my *one*."

"He's back in your life after fifteen years, Corinne, because why? He just happened to buy the company you work for? That doesn't seem a little extreme to you?"

"It's what he does," Corinne said flatly, remembering what he'd said in her office. "If he just wanted to get back in touch with me, he'd hardly have to buy a company to do it. It's coincidence, that's all."

"It's serendipity."

Corinne spread a light coat of blue polish on her toes. It was too thin. The color barely showed through. She was going to need a lot more coats to get it anywhere close to the color it was in the bottle.

"He used to paint my toes for me," she whispered around a sudden lump in her throat. "However long it took, no matter how much work it was to get them perfect."

Damn it, she didn't want to ruin sister-time with tears over a relationship that had ended years ago. She didn't want to cry over Reese at all. But there they were, the heated wet sting sliding over her cheeks and into the corner of her mouth, tasting bitter.

Caitlyn put her arm around Corinne's shoulders. They didn't say much after that. Corinne cried for another minute or so before grabbing a handful of tissues from the box on the end table and swiping at her face. She blew her nose and gave her sister a watery smile.

"Enough of that. I am so not going to even give him another second of my time. Not like that, anyway. We're going to have to work together, and that's it. Whatever happened between us was a long time ago. It doesn't matter now."

"Who are you trying to convince? Me? Or yourself?"

"Both," Corinne admitted. She studied her toes, thinking she would leave them as they were, too pale a shade or not. "But I can tell you without a doubt, Reese Ebersole was not, and never will be, my one."

Chapter Fifteen

"You don't have to go back there, you know." Tony said this from the doorway to Reese's office, where he'd been leaning. "Cow country, I mean. I can handle everything for you. Or we can set up a regular weekly video meeting. It's not like you've never bought a company and handled it from here before."

Reese gave Tony a long, steady look. The other man grinned. Reese did not. Tony shrugged and held up his hands.

"It's a new acquisition. I want to make sure things are going the way I want them to," Reese told him.

Tony snorted, then quickly settled his expression into something that was meant to be bland but didn't quite make it. "Sure. Yep. That's it. It has nothing to do with—"

"Don't." Reese glared.

Tony shrugged again. "Hey, listen, far be it for me to judge your motivations. I'm just angling for a trip back there so I can maybe grab a bite at that diner. And that waitress's number."

Reese leaned back in his chair and put his feet on the desk. He wasn't fooling himself, or Tony, with pretending to get any actual work done at the moment, anyway. "What's up with that?"

"Can't stop thinking about her." Tony shook his head. "She's...something else."

As long as Reese had known him, Tony had never mentioned liking women sexually, not even once. "I thought..."

Tony laughed. "Yeah. Me too. I mean, I knew better. There've been a few ladies in my past. Just not lately. Hell, there hasn't been anyone lately that I'd consider something special."

It had been the same for Reese, not that he was going to say that out loud. He and Amber had parted ways more than six months ago, and if it hadn't been acrimonious, it hadn't been particularly amicable, either. He hadn't thought it would matter so much to him that a woman wanted him mostly for his money, not until the fact of it had been staring him in the wallet.

"What about that one guy you were seeing?" Reese asked.

Tony gave Reese a look. "We didn't click."

Reese laughed. "Fair enough."

"You sure you don't need me to be in the office for you?" Tony fluttered his lashes. "I could use a change of scenery. Get out of the city, you know? Cast my net on fresher waters? I could try out being straight for a bit."

"I need you in Philadelphia," Reese said firmly. "I need to check in on my parents' old house anyway. I'm thinking about selling it."

It had been vacant since they'd passed away. He'd sold off the farmland to a developer who'd surrounded replaced the barn and fields with brand-new construction. A property management company had been taking care of the old farmhouse, making sure nobody vandalized it, that the house itself was kept in proper repair, that sort of thing. It had been rented a few times over the years, but was empty now.

"I can work from there as well as I can work from here," Reese added when Tony didn't reply. At the sight of his assistant's raised eyebrows, Reese frowned. "You don't think so?"

"I know you can work from wherever you want to, man. I've watched you do business on the beach and in the back of a cab. And fine, I'll stay here in the office to keep things up to date if you need something. I just think…"

Reese waited, but Tony didn't finish. "What?"

Tony moved out of the doorway to sit in the chair on the opposite side of Reese's desk. He leaned forward to put his elbows on his knees, and gave Reese a long, serious look. "Are you okay?"

"I'm fine." Reese put his feet on the ground with a thump and frowned. "Look, why don't you just handle the arrangements the way I pay you to do and leave my emotional well-being out of it."

Tony's eyes narrowed, but if Reese had offended him, he didn't say so. Instead he gave Reese a half smile and stood. "You got it. I called the management company about getting someone in there to clean it up. It'll be done by the end of tomorrow. I arranged for your personal mail to be forwarded to the office here, and I can take care of whatever looks important to get sent on in a weekly package, or I'll bring it with me when I come out."

"Who says you're coming out?"

Tony grinned. "Hey, look, you can work remotely, and of course I'll stick around here to keep the cogs greased, but Lancaster *is* only an hour away from here and I sure think I can be way more efficient if I come out there to meet with you at least once a week. Maybe a breakfast meeting. Nah, too early. Lunch. We'll just order breakfast."

"At the diner," Reese replied with a smirk. "Got it."

When Tony had gone, Reese turned back to his laptop, though he wasn't getting much work done. His assistant was right. Reese didn't need to go back to Lancaster at all to handle business there, much less for an extended stay in his childhood home. It was all about Corinne.

Since showing up back in her life he'd been an asshole to her, and though there was a part of him that wanted to convince himself she deserved it, he knew that wasn't true. It hadn't been true back then, either, but somewhere along the way being an asshole had become such second nature to him that he wasn't sure how to stop.

Amber had accused him of it. So had more than one of the women who'd come before her. None of them had lasted very long. He'd been cruel, Reese could admit, if only in his lack of attention, his sometimes deliberate refusal to give his lovers what he knew they wanted.

Throughout the years, Reese had placed a lot of blame for the past on other people. His father for being unbending and close-minded. His mother for not defending him. Corinne for not giving him a second chance, though even at the time he'd known he didn't deserve one, not after the way he'd behaved. He'd blamed lovers for walking away when he'd been the one who forced them to go. And in all this time, he'd never stopped thinking about her and the mess he'd made because he'd been too focused on himself. He had let her down, and every success he'd had since then had been somehow hollow. The question was, Reese thought, was he going to have a chance to make things right with her? Was that what he wanted?

Or maybe the real question was, how could he have ever wanted anything else?

Chapter Sixteen

Before

Reese has never been so content as when he's on his knees for her. Waiting. Ready to do whatever it is his queen desires.

Right now, on his knees with his hands crossed at the wrist behind his back, all he can think about is tasting her. She's been teasing him for an hour with the promise of her beautiful pussy. His cock is so hard it's dripping, slick with precome that Corinne has cooed over, swiping her finger along it to lick right in front of him while he throbs.

They're due to be at his parents' house for Thanksgiving dinner in three hours.

Corinne, wearing only a pair of tiny black lace panties, is fixing her hair in front of the mirror on the dresser. She glances at him in the reflection and gives him that slow, somehow secret smile that is just for him. She smoothes a curl and tucks it into place, then turns to lean against the dresser.

When she parts her legs and slips a fingertip over the front of her panties, Reese groans. "Please…"

Corinne laughs and leans to take his face in her hands. She kisses his mouth, but when he uncrosses his arms from behind his back to grip her hips, her fingers tighten on his jaw. Hard.

"Behave," she whispers. "I told you not to move."

Standing, she can easily press her pussy to his eager, waiting mouth. He breathes her in through the lace, but he does not move again. With a murmur of approval, Corinne at last pulls her panties to the side and lets him lap at her heat. The taste of her has his hips bucking forward, and this time, she slaps his face lightly as she pulls her body away from his questing tongue.

"Bad boy," she says. The slap wasn't hard enough even to sting, but her disapproval does.

Again, she takes his face into her hands, this time to look deeply into his eyes. Her kiss feathers over his lips. Reese shakes with the effort of not moving to take her in his arms, to pull her against his face. To push her onto her back right there on the bare bedroom floor and fuck her hard enough to wipe that smile off her face.

"You hate it when I slap you," she whispers. Her tongue flicks against his lips before she takes the lower one between his teeth and bites, stretching the tender flesh just hard enough to hurt before she lets go and soothes his skin with another kiss. "But you love it too. You want to get me on my hands and knees right now, don't you? Put me in my place with that thick, pretty cock in my cunt. Don't you?"

"Yes…"

Another slap, this one harder, turning his face.

"Yes, what?"

"Yes, Ma'am." The words come out with a bit of a snarl that makes her laugh, and she's right. He does hate it when she slaps him, even though he fucking loves it at the same time because he likes the pain. He likes that when she hits him, her nipples get hard and her eyes glaze.

"I like to hurt you," Corinne breathes into his ear as her hand slides into his hair and pulls. Her shin goes between his legs, pressing his erection against his belly. "I love it. I love the sounds you make, Reese. I love how hard your cock gets, I love how you leak for me, I love it when you can't hold yourself back any longer, but I love how hard you try because you know I want you to last."

She pulls his hair harder, tipping his head so she can get at his mouth. His knees hurt. His hands sting from how hard he's making fists to keep himself from grabbing her. His cock aches, his balls heavy and tender.

"I love you," Corinne says into his mouth.

He sighs. "I love you too."

To his surprise, Corinne gets on her knees in front of him. Once more, she takes his face in her hands. "I'm nervous about meeting your parents."

She has not told him that he can move, but he takes the chance of disappointing her to take her in his arms anyway, because she needs his comfort more than he needs to avoid disobedience. Because this is part of how they work; he needs to know when it's all right to break out of the game to give her what she needs.

"Why?" He nuzzles her throat, pulling her close as she buries her face against him.

"Well…it's a big deal, right? Big family dinner. I know you and your dad haven't been getting along—"

"That's not because of you."

"It's partially because of me," she says. "Because you've moved in with me, left the farm. I know he blames me a little bit for turning your head."

"My dad doesn't know anything about me. I wanted to leave the farm long before I met you, Corinne."

She snuggles against him and they shift so he can sit instead of kneeling. His knees cry hallelujah. His cock, on the other hand, is still tortured when she cuddles herself into his lap.

"I want them to like me, I guess. That's all."

"They'll like you." He's not actually certain of that, but it's a small lie.

She looks at him, not convinced. "Uh-huh."

"I love you. If they don't…well." He shrugs.

She kisses him lightly on the mouth. "I want to fill your ass with that new toy I bought you, so that when I look at you across the dinner table, I'll know you might be talking and eating and laughing, but you're totally going to be thinking about me fucking you when we get home."

He'll be thinking about that anyway, and she knows it. The thought of that—the heavy rubber toy stretching and filling him while he has to face his family…it's too much. His cock leaps, another trickle of clear fluid sliding from the tip, but his expression must show his concern because Corinne frowns.

"No?"

"Please, no." He won't be able to deal with it. Not in front of his father.

"Puppy, if I want you to wear that toy for me, you will. If I want to put a collar and a leash on you and parade you through the living room on your knees, you'll do that too." Her voice has gone stern and cold for a second, her gaze assessing him before she softens. Another kiss, this one lingering. She caresses his hair, petting. Her ass rocks against his cock, teasing. "But I won't ask you to."

Reese presses his face to the warmth of her throat, his eyes closed. "I can't. I want to be able to, but I just can't."

She puts her arms around him, holding him even though she's still sitting on his lap. They rock a little bit. She hums some soothing noises into his ear.

"I might ask you to do things you think you can't do, or things you think you don't want to do," she says against his skin. "But I won't ask you to do what you absolutely can't do."

He's relieved, but also disappointed. "I'm sorry."

"Hush." She pulls away to look into his face. "Don't be sorry. All of this, everything we do…it's no good for me if it's not good for you, too. If you don't want it and love it—"

"I do. I do love it and want it."

"I know." She smiles, though her brow's still a little furrowed.

He shifts to move her weight a little on his lap. "I'll be thinking about you fucking me no matter what I'm wearing."

"I know that too." In a smooth motion, she turns and straddles him, taking his cock deep inside her so fast he cries out. Her hand goes over his mouth. The other goes behind his neck to cup him.

Corinne begins to ride him. Her pussy, hot and slick, grips his cock until he can't stand it, or he doesn't think he can, and then she slows. Stops. Squeezes him with internal muscles without moving. Her hand over his mouth to keep him quiet.

Then somehow, they've rolled and he's on top of her, fucking hard and deep and fast. Her knees come up to grip his sides. Her nails rake his back, then down to score his ass with stripes of pain that only urge him on. They kiss, bruising each other and then pulling back. Softer. Slower. He doesn't want to come until she does, and she needs more than this slamming.

Reese pushes himself up on one arm to use the other hand between them. Corinne arches into the touch with a low, urgent cry. Again, her body tightens on his, and he's close, so close, but he keeps himself from going over by concentrating on her. He pinches her clit lightly between his thumb and forefinger, thrusting so slowly now he's almost not moving at all.

Corinne is always beautiful to him, but when she orgasms, she is transformed. Sweat glistens on her upper lip as her body tenses. She is lost in the pleasure, and Reese loses himself in watching her. She cries out his name. Her pussy pulses, milking him, and he can't hold back any longer. They finish together. When he can focus his vision again, he looks down at her.

She's smiling, but she puts on a stern tone. "Now I'm going to have to shower all over again. We're going to be late to dinner."

"It was worth it."

Corinne laughs and pulls him down to kiss her mouth. "Always. With you, it's always worth it."

Chapter Seventeen

Corinne would be damned if she let Reese Ebersole see for even one second how much his presence in the office rattled her. She wasn't used to answering to anyone higher up when it came to daily office dealings—Lynn and the others had rarely been present in the office except for the board meetings, and Corinne had been left to do her job as she saw fit. Reese had made it overtly clear that the only reason he was settled into the formerly vacant office next to hers was because he needed to keep a close and personal eye on how things were going with the changes he'd put into place. He was checking up on her, and it rankled. Well, she wasn't going to give him the pleasure of knowing how much she despised his hourly pings to her instant message requesting random information. She would never let on that every time he called her into his office, she wanted to tell him to go fuck himself.

She would never show that each time she met his gaze, all she could think about was telling him to get on his knees in front of her and eat her pussy like it was her birthday.

That's what she'd told herself this morning as she'd dressed carefully in a charcoal pencil skirt paired with a stark white blouse that tied with a bow at the throat. Her hair in a tight French twist. Pearl earrings. Shit, the only thing that saved this outfit from being a parody was that she refused to wear tottering stilettos and had instead slipped into a pair of cute, hot pink kitten heels with a pointed toe. She looked fucking amazing, though, she thought as she poured herself a mug of coffee in the break room, and if looking good was like putting on armor, Corinne had been battle ready for the entire week.

"Corinne. I need to see you in my office."

Her back straightened, but she didn't turn to even offer him a glance. She continued stirring sugar and cream into her coffee.

"Sure."

"Oh, and bring me a cup while you're at it, would you? Black."

Oh.

No.

He.

Did.

Not.

But he had, yes he had, and it actually made her want to laugh. Not with humor, exactly, but a thickly bubbling near-hysteria that would've totally wrecked her calm demeanor if she let loose so much as a single chuckle. She hadn't turned. He hadn't left the break room. She could feel him watching her.

Waiting.

Well, Reese could wait until an angel and the devil did the do-si-do, she wasn't going to give him the satisfaction of getting a rise out of her.

"No problem," she answered smoothly, still without turning more than her head, ever so slightly. "Be right there."

She waited until she heard him leave because she couldn't trust herself to keep her hands from shaking as she poured the coffee. Some of it still sloshed over the rim. She wiped it carefully with a napkin and carried both mugs into his office. Even more carefully, she set his in front of him so that not a drop splashed.

She didn't sit.

"The financials from last quarter," Reese began, then paused.

Corinne said nothing.

"They're in good shape."

"Well," she said, "I'd expect them to be. You did have me redo them in the new program you prefer."

Never mind that Stein and Sons had been using the same software for the past five years, a program she'd personally picked out because it was easy to use and had all the functions she needed. The program Reese was insisting they switch to was glitchy and far less user-friendly. If he was making busywork for her, he was going to be disappointed to discover that she wasn't going to complain, at least not to him.

When he didn't say anything else, didn't even sip the coffee he'd asked her to serve him, Corinne tilted her head. "Is there something else?"

"No," Reese answered in a tone that sounded more like yes.

She didn't wait for him to add anything. She left his office and went into her own, firmly shutting and locking the door so he couldn't burst in on her. Not that he would, she reminded herself. He would simply message her and expect her to drop everything and run in to service him.

She would do it too, Corinne thought with a curl of her lip. In that moment she couldn't tell whom she hated more. Reese for putting her through this rigamarole, or herself for letting him.

Chapter Eighteen

Before

Thanksgiving at his parents' house is always a good time. Food, music, laughter. Games of cards spread out on the dining room table with plates of pie and mugs of coffee. Reese's family is enormous and they all gather in the old farmhouse every year.

He's never brought a girl home before, and everyone notices but nobody gives him a hard time. Well, not too much. They all like Corinne, of course they do. There's nothing about her that isn't easy to like.

Corinne's camped out on the sofa with one of Reese's cousins, looking at the photo album from her recent wedding. Reese has brought Corinne a mug of coffee and a piece of pie.

"No," she says, offhandedly, "not pumpkin."

It's not a chastisement or anything. Not even a command. He's so used to her gentle corrections that it doesn't even seem strange to him that he takes the plate of pumpkin pie back to the kitchen and returns with a slice of apple that she takes from him, her face tipped up so he can kiss her before she goes back to looking at the pictures.

It feels natural to take a place on the floor at her feet, especially since with all the guests in the overfull living room, seating is at a premium. And Reese is content to lean with his back against her legs, her fingers every so often brushing the back of his neck. When she hands him her empty mug, he takes it without question to the kitchen for a refill.

His father has been watching him, apparently. At the counter as Reese fills Corinne's mug, his father takes a seat at the kitchen table. He gestures to Reese's mother for her to cut him a piece of pie, even though the tins are directly in front of him, and she has to come around the table with a plate to do it.

"Sit," his father says. His mother flees the kitchen.

"I have to take—"

"She'll wait," his father says. "Sit down."

Reese sits, wary. He and Dad haven't been getting along for a long time, but he'd thought that at Thanksgiving there'd be peace, at least for the night. "Yeah?"

"How's it going? Living with her."

"Good. It's all good." Reese turns the mug in his hands.

"You find a job yet?" Dad digs into the pie with his fork, chewing steadily without looking away from Reese's face.

"Not yet. I'm looking into some bank loans for school, though. And I have a lead on some part-time work."

"You're living off her? She supports you?"

Reese frowns. "Well…yeah, I mean…I'm going to get work, Dad."

"But until then, you're the housewife?" His father's disgust is clear in his tone.

Reese goes cold inside. Then hot. His throat and cheeks burn, but he keeps his voice steady when he answers, "I take care of things around the house, yeah. Corinne goes to school and works."

"Pussy." Pie flecks his father's lips and clusters in the corners of his mouth.

Reese looks away. "Don't."

"She has you trotting to and fro, bringing her coffee and pie? What else does she have you doing? Folding her panties?"

"Sometimes wearing them," Reese replies, voice cold and hard and sounding somehow distant, even to himself.

He means to be shocking. To stun and hurt his father. It appears to have worked, because Dad's mouth works, but nothing comes out.

"I thought you'd just be happy I'm not gay." Reese wants to get up from the table. He wants to take Corinne's coffee to her and sit there while his family laughs and talks; he wants to play a killer game of Spoons and then have another piece of pie. He wants to go home with the woman he loves and sleep beside her and wake up in the morning, and if she asks him to do a load of laundry, he'll do it. He'll do whatever she asks. "I don't expect you to understand. But, Dad, it's not your business."

"It's disgusting."

Reese flinches, though the words are no surprise. "I love her. I want to make her happy. That's all."

"I love your mother, and I want to make her happy, but you don't see me prancing around in her underwear!"

"Reese?" Corinne is paused in the doorway, looking concerned. "Hey, is everything okay?"

"You ready to go?" Reese stands, leaving the coffee on the table.

Corinne's look of concern changes to surprise. "Sure. If you want to."

"Yeah. I'm ready. Let's go." Without a look at his father, Reese ushers her out through the family horde, weathering the hugs, kisses, and goodbyes. In the driveway, he holds out his hand for her keys and slides into the driver's seat, although it is Corinne's car and she usually drives.

"What happened?" she asks as he steers them down the long, winding country lane toward the main street. "Did you and your dad have a fight?"

"Something like that. Nothing new. It's fine." Tight-lipped, Reese switches on the radio so they don't have to talk.

At home, she tells him to go take a shower. He doesn't want to. They showered just before leaving for his parents' house. He's not dirty. He and Corinne face off in the bedroom; Reese feels alternately hot and cold. Itchy in his skin. He wants to pace.

"I told you to do something," Corinne says sharply. "But feel free to keep arguing with me, and see what happens."

He can't stop himself from arguing. He keeps thinking of his father's words and the look of disgust and disappointment on his face. "I don't want to take a fucking shower, Corinne! I just want to go to bed."

She gives him a cool shrug. "Fine. But you're not getting into bed with me without taking a shower first. Go sleep on the couch. No. The floor."

He pauses. She means it, he's sure of that. She teases him sometimes, sure, but right now there is nothing but calm steadiness in her expression as she stares him down.

He does not have to obey her. He could, in fact, force his way into the bed, and there'd be very little she could do to make him get out of it. They both know, though, that he won't do that. Breathing hard, angry, his nails biting into his palms, Reese sneers.

"Fine. I'll take a fucking shower."

"Go."

In the bathroom, he strips out of his clothes and throws them defiantly on the floor, then gets under the spray before it's even hot. Cold water needles him into a gasp. It warms quickly, but even so, that first onslaught is enough to take his breath away and leave stinging patches all over. Minutes in, the steam wreathes him, and in the fog and the heat, Reese lets his forehead fall against his arm as he leans against the shower wall. The water washes away most of his anger, leaving him with a hollow feeling in his stomach.

He dries off and hangs up the towel, then puts all his clothes in the basket. Naked, he goes to the bedroom. Corinne is propped up in bed, reading, and when she sees him she pulls back the covers and pats the bed in invitation.

Wordlessly, Reese slides in beside her. She puts an arm around him, letting him press his face against her breasts. Her hand strokes down his back in patterns of three, then one then three again. She's soothing him.

"I'm sorry," he says finally. "I needed the shower."

"I know, puppy. It's okay." She kisses his wet hair and makes a noise, prompting him to move so he can look up at her. She caresses his face. "I'm sorry you and your dad can't seem to get along."

He talks to her for a long time about his father.

When he goes quiet, Corinne says, "I think you should go talk to him. Be the first to reach out. Didn't you tell me that you guys used to go to Triton's a lot? Invite him to lunch or something."

Surprised and angry that she's not taking his side, Reese sits up. "What? Why? He's not going to listen to anything I have to say. He's made his judgments, and that's it as far as he's concerned. I'm not going back to work on the farm. Is that what you want me to do?"

She hesitates. "It's a job—"

"No! Shit, Corinne. I hated working on the farm. If you don't want me to live here anymore, just fucking say so."

She'll be pissed off now. She'll discipline him for the language, the tone, the attitude. She'll hurt him, maybe, and then maybe she'll fuck him. Suddenly, Reese wants that more than anything.

"I love having you here. Don't be rude. And if you don't want to work on the farm, you don't have to. But I think you do need to go talk to your dad and try to mend things with him."

"Are you ordering me to?"

She frowns. "Of course not."

He quiets and sits with his back to the headboard, their shoulders touching. He doesn't look at her. The calm he'd gained from the shower is gone; his stomach is tense and tight again. When finally he slides beneath the covers and turns on his side, facing away from her, Corinne says nothing. She turns out the light. She spoons behind him, her hand flat on his naked belly. She kisses him between the shoulder blades.

"I don't want you to hold onto a grudge that you might regret, that's all." Her soft words float through the darkness over him. "I'm looking out for you."

"I know."

He doesn't listen to her, though, and Thanksgiving Day is the last time he speaks to his father until his mother dies of a stroke two months later.

Chapter Nineteen

"He's trying to get under your skin, that's all." Caitlyn had listened to Corinne's tirade over dinner.

Overcooked pasta and limp salad, Caitlyn's work, still appreciated even if it hadn't been top-notch cuisine. The kids had scarfed down everything on their plates and begged to disappear into the TV room to play video games, and although she usually tried to keep Friday night family night to honor the Sabbath, Corinne had allowed it tonight. She'd been too agitated to really eat, though she appreciated baby sister's attempt at repaying her for the use of the guest room for what was becoming an indeterminate amount of time. Now she pushed her plate away.

"That is not how we work," Corinne said.

Caitlyn swiped a piece of garlic bread through the sauce and crunched it, talking around the food. "That's not how you *used* to work, maybe. It's obviously how he wants it to work now."

Corinne had never talked much to her sister about the way things had been. At the time she and Reese were a couple, Caitlyn had been way too young. By the time her younger sister had been old enough for them to share sexy stories, Corinne had been married to Douglas and fully entrenched in the vanilla life of a suburban wife and mother. She'd never spoken much to anyone about her relationship with Reese, actually, too aware of how not…normal…the other mothers in the playgroup would have thought it was to bend your man over and fuck him in the ass.

"Yikes," Caitlyn said at the look on Corinne's face. "Don't freak out!"

"I'm not freaking out, but you don't really know…I mean…" Corinne shrugged and twirled more pasta onto her plate.

Caitlyn made a face. "I know you think it's weird."

"Actually, I never thought it was weird. It was the only time I ever felt like everything made sense." Corinne cleared her throat, hating the way her voice rasped. "I think it's rare, though. To find a connection like that..."

"When your kinks align," Caitlyn said.

Corinne laughed a little self-consciously. "Yeah. That."

"Hey, we all have them. Some of us have kinkier kinks, that's all. And don't you think he feels the same way? He remembers. Why else do you think he's being such an asshole? I mean, he's acting in the exact opposite way he did when you were together, right? He's being all bossy and stuff."

"He's beyond bossy," Corinne said with a scowl.

"Would it bother you so much if it wasn't him? If some random dude had come in to buy the company and was throwing all this bullshit your way?"

Corinne shrugged. "I wouldn't like it no matter who was doing it."

"'Corinne does not take direction well.'" Her sister cackled, pointing a finger. "That was on your report card in the fifth grade, remember?"

"Yes. Yours was 'Caitlyn has difficulty coloring inside the lines.'"

Both sisters laughed. Corinne finally gave up on eating the soggy pasta. Caitlyn snagged another piece of garlic bread from the basket and used it to point at her sister.

"Point is, we are who we are, and we've probably always been that way. So no, you wouldn't be happy if anyone had come in and started ordering you around, but it's particularly egregious that it's Reese."

"Ooh. Good word."

Caitlyn fluttered her lashes. "Thank you."

"He used to be my boy," Corinne said, suddenly angrier than she'd allowed herself to be. "My fucking boy, Caitlyn. He...he was mine."

Her voice trailed into sadness.

"Now he's just fucking with me, and I hate it. Not because he's trying to prove to me he's the boss or whatever. But that he would take what we had and try to erase it that way." Corinne swallowed against the lump in her throat. "I mean, the whole reason we broke up was because he wasn't able to commit. We'd been together for two years, I was just about to start working for Stein and Sons;

everything could've been great. But he was dead set on running away from everything. Even me. When I asked him to meet me one last time so we could try to work on it, he never showed up. And he knew the consequences of that, Caitlyn, because I'd warned him if he didn't show that we were through. That was it, he walked out on me, and he never came back. It was ugly and harsh and horrible, but it was also fifteen years ago. What's the point of coming back around now to rub my face in how much he is not ever going to bend to me? What's the fucking point, if it's not to hurt me?"

"Maybe you should ask him that."

"Ugh. Gross. That's almost as bad as asking him why he can't just love me. I'll make sure to be drunk with my makeup smeared all over the place too, because that's classy." Her phone buzzed from where she'd put it on the counter to charge. When she didn't get up to answer it, Corinne shrugged at her sister's look. "What? The kids are with me. You're here. Who else would be calling me?"

She got up anyway to look at it, her mouth twisting into a sneer when she saw the caller ID. Caitlyn's brows rose as Corinne put the phone to her ear with a muttered greeting. Then her sister put her hands over her mouth to cover up the laughter.

"Reese," Corinne said. "What do you want?"

Chapter Twenty

She should not have agreed to this.

The long farm lane of her memory was still there, though it had been paved into a much wider street lined with big houses on small lots. The house at the end was the same though. Two stories, white painted siding, green shingles on the roof and matching shutters. The barn and outbuildings were gone. She parked by the side porch, noticing that it looked a little newer than the rest of the house, as though it had been recently repaired.

She sat in her car longer than she needed to. Fussing with her lipstick and hair. Her clothes, her armor, were more casual than what she'd been wearing to work the past week, but only because showing up at his house late on a Friday night wearing a pencil skirt and kitten heels would've been weird. She'd settled for the pair of leggings that made her ass look fantastic, along with a flattering striped top and ballet flats. Now she was second guessing the choices though. She didn't want to look like this was a…well, a date.

The truth was, Corinne wasn't sure what, exactly, this was meant to be.

Reese opened the door almost before she'd knocked. "Hi. Come in."

She waited until he'd moved aside before she entered into the small but cheery kitchen, decorated in colors that had been trendy so long ago they'd gone from outdated to vintage to trendy again. She hung her purse and coat on the back of a kitchen chair without waiting to be asked. Then she turned to face him.

"So," she said.

"So, I guess we should…do you want something to drink?"

"I have to drive home." Of course she had to drive home. She wasn't going to sleep over. Fuck, why had she even said such a thing?

Reese had already been pouring a glass of red, but paused. "You sure?"

"What exactly do you want, Reese?"

He put the glass on the counter. By the look of the bottle, he'd already gone through a couple already. "I think we need to talk."

Corinne crossed her arms. "About?"

Reese leaned against the counter, one leg crossed at the ankle. He wore a pair of low-hanging jeans and a concert T-shirt from a band she didn't know. It clung far too tightly to his chest and arms. His feet were bare.

She hated him.

"Look, can we go into the living room? If you won't have a glass of wine, at least we can sit on the couch. Be more comfortable."

Eyes narrowed, she nodded and followed him down the short hallway and into the living room. It didn't look much different from the last time she'd been in it, though at the time she hadn't been paying much attention to the decor. "Same furniture."

"Yeah, I never really did anything to it." Reese drained his glass and set it on the end table as he took a seat. "Sit?"

He'd asked, not commanded, so she did, perched on the edge of the cushions, plenty of space between them. She wished she'd asked for a glass of water, at least. Her throat scratched.

"We didn't get off on the right foot," he said.

Both her brows rose. "You think?"

"Look...I just wanted you to know that I really did buy Stein and Sons because I thought I could turn it around. And I intend to do that. I'm good at it. Maybe you find that hard to believe..."

"Why would I find that hard to believe?" she broke in.

Reese fixed her with a look, one she remembered. He'd been drinking long before she got there. For courage? Heat kindled in her belly at the thought.

"I mean to make it a success. And I wanted you to know."

She stared at him for a long, long moment before the question rose inside her, slipping over her dry tongue. "Why is it so important to you that I know, Reese?"

"I want..." he began and stopped.

His brow furrowed. Hands clenched, he got to his feet and paced in small, tight lines back and forth in front of her. The hems of his jeans whispered along the carpet. At last he stopped, head bowed, fingers still curled into fists at his sides.

"Because I want you to know," he said. "I just…do."

She could have stood, then, and left him to suffer whatever damage he'd caused. She should have. The past had happened and could not be lived over; nor could it do anything to change what was happening now. She ought to have walked away from him in that moment and kept moving forward with her life, away from everything they'd been and what they no longer were.

She didn't.

"Shhh, puppy," she whispered and opened her arms to him. "Come here."

He wouldn't, that's what she had time to think before Reese pivoted on his heel and came to kneel in front of her. His face pressed into her lap so that her hands found the soft brush of his dark hair. She petted him, both of them silent. He heaved a sigh so heavy that his shoulders lifted and fell, and the heat of his breath caressed her through the thin material of her shirt.

They stayed that way for a while. She didn't count the minutes, not by the ticking of the clock or the beating of her heart. They could sit like this for an eternity, she thought, and it wouldn't seem too long.

His fingers slipped beneath her thighs, and he looked up at her with glazed eyes. Parted lips, slick from the swipe of his tongue. Corinne ran her hand over his face, then a thumb over his lower lip. Reese closed his eyes and pressed his mouth against the palm of her hand.

"I want you to be proud of me," he whispered so low she almost couldn't hear him.

The words were a fist, punching her in the gut. "Why?"

"Because everything I've ever done," Reese murmured, words slurring, "has been about forgetting you or impressing you or making you proud. I've lived my whole fucking life for you without having you in it."

"You're drunk," Corinne said.

Reese nuzzled into her lap. "Not much."

She let her fingers tangle in his hair to tug his head up so he had to look her in the face. She whispered his name. He pushed up on his knees, so they were eye to eye.

"We haven't been together for a long time," she said.

"Yeah. I know."

"You could have called me. Written me a letter, even. You could have done anything but ignore me, but that's what you did. We had that fight, and I never heard from you again," she said.

Reese flinched, eyes closing for a minute. Shame-faced. "I know. You told me if I didn't show, that was it. We were over. I was angry."

"But you never even tried." When he didn't answer, she added, "So, why now? All these years later?"

"Because…I could," he answered simply, like that was supposed to make sense.

It did, somehow. Years had passed in which it might not have mattered if he'd called or written or hell, even friended her on Connex, because even if he'd come to her with an apology or a declaration of undying love, there'd been no room in her life for him. So here they both were, older and in different places in their lives.

"Look at me," she told him. When he did, she took his face in both her hands to stare into his eyes the way she'd done so many times when they were young and had never thought what they'd had would disappear. "The problem is, Reese, that all those years ago, I fell in love with you. And I've never managed to find a way to fall back out."

He kissed her then. Soft and slow and sweet and somehow yearning, his arms going around her. He tasted like good red wine. He broke the kiss, their foreheads pressed together, but before she could speak he was kissing her again. Harder this time, breathing a small sigh that turned into a moan when she gently sucked his tongue.

How many times has she dreamed about him, and this? For ages Corinne had imagined what it would be like to taste him again, only to discover now how fickle memory could be. He was even better than she remembered—or maybe she was. Both of them older, with more finesse, or maybe it was the years of longing that flavored this kiss. She didn't care. He was kissing her, then pulling her into his arms and onto the floor so she straddled him. His cock was hard under her, and his hands went up automatically with her fingers curling around his wrists to settle on the floor beside his head.

Corinne paused, breathing hard. When she rocked the tiniest bit against him, Reese bumped his hips upward and rolled them until he was on top of her. In seconds he'd pinned her wrists to the floor by her ears. She didn't struggle.

"What do you need, honey?" she whispered.

"You. I need you."

She arched to press her body to his. "I'm here."

His kiss moved over her mouth, down her throat to the scooped neck of her shirt. His hands slid up over the soft, loose fabric, pushing it up and over. Her nipples were already hard, poking the lace of her bra, and Reese mouthed each one as his hands cupped her. He moved back to her neck, pressing his open mouth to her sensitive skin. One hand went between her legs. Corinne cried out at the stroking slide of his fingertips against her, the soft material of her leggings no barrier to his questing touch.

Another moment after that, Reese slid his hand beneath the waistband and into her panties. His fingers pushed inside her before she was ready for him, and shocked, she cried out again. This was moving so fast, but there was no way to slow it down. Not with his mouth on hers and his fingers fucking into her, his thumb pressing her clit. It had been too long for her without anyone's touch, but most especially his.

Reese moved down her body again, fingers slipping out of her so he could wrestle her leggings over her hips. Her panties came down too, leaving her bare to his lips and tongue. At the first lick, Corinne arched, helpless to keep herself still.

It had always been so good when he did this. Reese worshipped her with his mouth, both hands moving beneath her ass to lift and hold her in place. He eased off right before she came—he'd always been able to tell exactly how close she was. Her low, frustrated cry urged a chuckle out of him, and the soft puff of his laughter against her was a fresh torture that had her writhing.

Settling her back onto the rug, he knelt between her legs and opened the button of his fly with one hand while the other continued to stroke her clit. He paused long enough to shove his jeans down—nothing but bare skin beneath. His cock sprang free. He worked the denim down, using one foot to push his leg free. Then the other. Kneeling again, he tugged his shirt off over his head and tossed it to the side.

Time had sculpted him. He'd always been lean and muscled and still was, though he'd grown bigger. Broader shoulders, bigger arms, his chest and thighs both harder and more rounded. His cock, too, seemed impossibly longer and thicker than she'd remembered even in her fondest recollections.

He stroked it as she watched. "You always liked to watch me do this."

"I still do." She pushed up on her elbow to get a better look.

"I want to be inside you," Reese said. "But I don't have anything."

Corinne hesitated. Everything had been force and fire a few minutes ago. They hadn't used condoms when they'd been together before—she'd been younger and stupid and trusting and on the pill. She couldn't get pregnant now because she'd had her tubes tied after complications with Tyler, but there were other reasons to be careful. Mesmerized by the slow stroking of his hand, though, she didn't make a protest at first.

"I've been with a lot of women," he told her.

"Are you trying to make me jealous?"

He shook his head. "No. Just...I didn't want you to take a risk with me that you weren't ready for."

She lay back, thighs parted to give him a good, long look at her treasure. "Touch me, Reese. And touch yourself at the same time."

"Like this?" His hand moved between her legs. Fingers tweaking her clit. She was so wet he slid two knuckles deep inside her without effort, then out to circle the slickness over the tight knot of nerves.

"Fuck, yes. That. Oh...fuck."

She wanted to watch him, but pleasure kept forcing her eyes to close. Her hips lifted, rocking. He fucked deeper into her, then out, taking the time to concentrate on her clit long enough to bring her to the edge before easing off. His other hand took care of himself, faster and faster, jacking just below the head. Sometimes he thrust into his fist instead of stroking, and the sight of that drove her wild because it matched up perfectly with the timing of his fingers pushing in and out of her.

"How many women?" Corinne asked with an edge in her voice.

"A lot."

"You made them come?"

"All of them." Reese groaned. He moved faster. His touch stuttered a moment, but that only sent her higher and higher, closer to the edge.

Her muscles tensed, pleasure building. She had to remind herself to breathe. She was going to come any second. She wanted him with her.

"You fucked them," she muttered, not a question, but he answered her as though she'd made it one.

"Yes. Shit, yes, I fucked them."

Her gaze locked on his. Her body bore down on him. Her fingers dug into the rug at her sides as she moved with him, perfectly in sync despite the fact he wasn't fucking her with his cock.

"How many of them," Corinne asked, "fucked you?"

His body jerked at her words. Reese shouted, hoarse, something that might've been her name or a prayer or a curse or a plea, or possibly a combination of all of those. Thick, hot fluid covered her belly. The smell of it, of his desire, this proof of how much he wanted her, finally tipped her over and she rode the waves of orgasm as she shook and lost herself inside it.

Some minutes after that, he'd spooned behind her, a hand flat on her belly in the stickiness he'd left behind. His face pressed to the back of her neck, pushing aside the fall of her hair. They breathed together, one breath. Two. Perfectly matched in this the way they'd been with everything else. She was drifting into sleep when he spoke, waking her.

"None of them ever did," Reese said. "That was only ever you."

Chapter Twenty-One

Reese had never particularly despised Monday mornings, but today he was looking forward to going into the office about as much as he would have enjoyed a kick to the crotch. Since waking up alone on his living room floor Saturday morning, he'd already been feeling like he'd taken a knee between the legs. The sight of Corinne's closed office door didn't help make anything easier.

He should have called her.

No, fuck that. *She* was the one who'd snuck out without a word, not even a note. If anyone should've picked up the phone, it ought to have been Corinne…except Reese knew that wasn't the way things worked. Not with most women, and certainly not with her.

He wanted to blame the booze for Friday night, but the truth was that two and a half glasses of Merlot were nowhere near enough to have made him out of control. He'd known exactly what he was doing when he'd called her to come over. When he'd kissed her. He remembered every second of it and couldn't forget it.

What if *she* wanted to?

She'd crept away before the dawn and he hadn't heard from her since. What if she were regretting everything that had happened? What if he'd done nothing but make a colossal fool of himself over her?

Grouchy, Reese logged in to his email to take care of a few things. He shot off a few replies, then forwarded the rest to Tony, who was due here in Lancaster tomorrow. After that, he pushed back in his chair, fingers laced behind his head, and closed his eyes to replay Friday night.

The taste of her. The scent. The sound of her moans. The clutch of her body on his…

With a discontented mutter, Reese let his feet hit the floor. He looked at his desktop's instant message window. There she was, the small bright green circle next to her name showing her online. He typed quickly, before he could change his mind.

I NEED A MEETING AT 11. MY OFFICE. BRING REPORTS.

Her answer came a moment later. *OK*

Okay? That was it? Frowning, Reese typed again.

MAKE SURE THEY'RE THE MOST RECENT, THE CORRECT ONES

This time, she didn't answer.

He was being an idiot, and he knew it. It was only ten in the morning now, and he didn't want to spend the next hour thinking about her. He didn't even give a damn about the reports—Stein and Sons had been in a financial mess, but it hadn't been because of anything Corinne had done wrong. All he was doing was looking for an excuse to call her into his office, when what he really needed to do was just go in, take her in his arms, and kiss her until she couldn't breathe.

Instead, he changed into a pair of shorts and a T-shirt from his gym bag and went for a run. Reese didn't love running, but that was part of why he did it. He had to concentrate on putting one foot in front of the other and not on what he was going to say to Corinne about what had happened. By the time he got back, sweating and sore, it was closer to noon than eleven.

She was waiting for him in his office. Today she wore a sleek black skirt that hit just below the knee, with a little pleat in the rear that showed off the backs of her knees when she shifted. Her blouse, a pale green dotted with tiny black dots, had him remembering the times when he'd fed her spoonfuls of her favorite ice cream flavor, mint chocolate chip. She'd pinned her hair up in a soft twist that made him want to tug it free of the pins and sink his face into it.

"I went for a run," he said unnecessarily, because the way she looked him over made it clear she could see exactly what he'd been doing.

"Would you like to take a shower or something? You've already kept me waiting. I can handle another twenty minutes."

Reese took a long, slow pull from the bottle of water he'd stopped to grab from the break room fridge. He watched her eye his throat as he swallowed. Then his mouth when he licked his lips.

"Used to be that you liked me sweaty."

"You will want to stop pushing my buttons, Reese," Corinne said in a soft, dangerous voice. She took a step or two closer. "You called this meeting with a demand for me to bring you 'correct' reports like I've never provided you anything you needed before, which is not true and extremely insulting. You showed up late, which was also disrespectful. And if you want to talk about being unprofessional, that last comment borders on sexual harassment."

He blinked.

"You've made it very clear that our past relationship is of no consequence to our business dealings," she continued in that same low, stern voice that had once been enough to get him to his knees in front of her.

It was making his cock twitch, no way to hide an erection in his thin running shorts. God help him, he'd brought this on himself. He didn't move when she took another step toward him, which put him within grabbing distance...if she chose to touch him.

"Therefore, Reese, I expect that you will treat me with the respect I am due. Is that understood?"

Fuck, that look. That voice. He'd been playing with matches and had started a fire.

"Yes," he answered.

Corinne's gaze flashed. Her lips parted. He could see the flash of her tongue as she slid it along her teeth.

"Yes, what?"

Ma'am. Yes Ma'am. Please, Ma'am.

"Yes, I understand," Reese replied, knowing what she wanted but refusing to give it to her.

Her gaze fell to the bulge in the front of his shorts, then met his eyes. "I've already told you once not to push my buttons, Reese."

He laughed. "Or what? You'll spank me? You really think that's going to work on me, anymore?"

Without blinking or turning away from him, Corinne reached to the cup on his desk. With unerring precision she slid the wooden ruler from amongst the pens and pencils. She drew it between her hands, gripping it lightly in front of her. Reese was so immediately and inexorably aroused that he actually thought he might need to sit down. Sit, or fall from knees gone weak.

Corinne tapped the ruler lightly on the underside of her palm. "Since you acquired Stein and Sons, do you feel your behavior toward me has been respectful and professional?"

He didn't answer her.

The ruler tap, tap, tapped on the underside of her palm. If his cock had ever been this hard, Reese couldn't remember it. The look she gave the front of his shorts only made it worse, because he could square his shoulders and lift his chin and refuse to give her what she wanted, but there was no way he could hide how much she affected him.

"Do you think it was appropriate of you to come to my house?"

Silence.

The ruler tapped.

"Do you think it was appropriate for you to request that I come to your house, for you to be drunk—"

"I wasn't," he gritted out. "I'd been drinking, but I wasn't drunk."

Corinne let a small slow hiss slip between her teeth. "That's one."

"My list is getting longer," Corinne says. "Keep testing me, Reese. See what happens."

He knows what is going to happen. She will refuse him the sweetness of her pussy on his tongue, or she will tease his cock for an hour before she'll let him enter her. She will have him kneel, naked, hands behind his back and forbidden to touch her or himself while she makes herself come and all he can do is watch. Corinne has dozens of ways to discipline him. Hundreds.

"Keep testing me," she says again, the words an offer, a command, a promise, and a threat all wrapped up in a wicked smile. "See what happens."

"I had two and a half glasses of wine. It wasn't enough to impair me."

"So you ordered me to come to your house after work and you put your hands and mouth on me, all without the influence of alcohol?" This time, she smacked the ruler hard enough beneath her hand to make a cracking sound.

"I don't need to be drunk to want to fuck you."

Her eyes narrowed; he hated himself for the way the words had come out, but something inside him pushed him to it. Years had passed in which he'd dreamed of saying all the things he'd wanted to tell her. Of closing the door that had stayed open through every other broken relationship.

"Oh, yes. I know." Another crack of the ruler on her skin had him swallowing hard. Her gaze never left his. "That was not my question, Reese. I asked you if you thought it was appropriate. Considering that you are technically my boss. Do you think it was professional of you to invite me to your house after you'd been drinking?"

"No."

"To touch me?" This time, she slid the wooden ruler through the half circle of her fingers; it made a whispering sound.

His fists clenched at his sides. "No."

"No...what?"

"No, it wasn't professional or appropriate."

Corinne straightened. "No, it wasn't professional or appropriate...what?"

"I love it when you call me Ma'am." Corinne's whisper tickles his ear as she nuzzles him. Her fingers are sliding over his chest and belly to cup his cock, still half-hard though only moments before he'd been exploding inside her.

He puts his hand over hers, reminding her without words that in the aftermath of their lovemaking, he's sensitive. "You do? How come?"

"I don't know. It's kind of silly."

He turns his face to find her mouth with his. She tastes of salt. Their kisses are lightweight and floating.

"I just know that I love it," she tells him.

"Then I'll always say it," Reese replies. "As long as you want me to."

"You didn't have to come over," he said in a low voice. "You didn't have to let me touch you. Or kiss you."

Corinne tilted her head, just so, and Reese held back a groan. She looked at him the way she'd used to. Assessing. Considering. Narrowed eyes and that small, smug smile. He couldn't see them, but he knew her nipples were hard.

"Your pussy's getting wet for me," he managed to say, though every word snagged and ripped on his clenched teeth.

She drew in a breath, her eyes going heavy lidded for a second. "Oh, yes. Yes, Reese, I'm so wet for you right now, all I can think about, actually, is sliding up the hem of my skirt and having you lap it all up."

He'd taken a step toward her before he could stop himself, but with one look she stopped him in his tracks. Another look would've sent him to his knees in front of her, right there with his cock busting out of his shorts, but Corinne held up a finger. The other hand let the ruler dangle.

"No," she breathed. "No, you don't deserve a single lick of this pussy. Not a single drop of my honey. Do you?"

"I'm not going to beg for it. I don't do that anymore."

A lift of her brow sent a surge of arousal burning through him. "I imagine you don't have to. But you *want* to beg me. Don't you?"

"This is not professional, Corinne. If you want to be judgmental about it, at least I asked you to come to my house. I didn't…I didn't corner you in the office…" It was hard to keep his voice from shuddering at the way she gave him another small head tilt. Her gaze swept him up and down.

"There's a wet spot on the front of your shorts. Your poor cock. It must ache, it's so hard." She kept her voice low, but glanced behind him, over his shoulder, before latching eyes with him again. "You didn't lock the door."

"No."

"Anyone could walk in. And what would they see? That thick, hard cock tenting the front of your shorts. So desperate to get inside my cunt that you're already almost coming right there." She curled her fingers upward and let the ruler fall against her palm.

His cock leaped at the sound of that soft thwack. More liquid oozed from the tip, wetting the fabric. "So tell me to lock it, and I'll put you on the desk, I'll be inside you in half a minute."

Her expression went hard. "Absolutely not. You come back into my life after all this time thinking you can be disrespectful? Insulting? That you can use this job as an excuse to somewhat punish me for what happened between us? You will not lock that door. You will not get to taste me, or fuck me again until I decide you deserve it, and you will stand there knowing that at any second someone could come in and see you this way."

"I will not beg," he warned her again.

Corinne's eyes narrowed further. "Hold out your hands. Palms down. Fingers straight."

He wasn't going to do it, Reese thought, even as he felt himself obeying. At the first crack of the ruler against his skin, he bit back a grunt—it hurt more than he'd anticipated, but not enough to garner that sort of reaction. It wasn't the pain. It was the look on her face.

She had never been more beautiful to him than when she was making him hurt.

Again, the ruler cracked down on his knuckles. A schoolboy punishment, fetishistic the way a cane might've been, and all the worse for that because of the way his entire body tensed when she raised the ruler again. His balls throbbed. He could see nothing but Corinne. Feel nothing. Hear nothing but her voice.

At the final crack of wood on his skin, the ruler split and broke. One piece fell to the carpet where it bounced. Corinne shook the small stray strands of hair that had fallen into her eyes out of the way and tossed the other part onto the floor too. Reese let his hands close, the knuckles red and sore though he doubted there'd be so much as a bruise to remind him of this even a few minutes from now.

Her blue eyes swam with tears, but her voice was fierce when she said, "You broke me like I just broke that ruler, and you do not get to come back into my life and break me again. Do you understand me, Reese?"

The door wasn't locked. They were not alone in the office. Anyone could come in at any moment and see them, and Reese didn't give one good goddamn. He went to his knees in front of her, shoulders bowed. Face pressed to the front of her skirt, so he could breathe in the scent of her.

"Yes," he told her. "Yes, Ma'am. I understand."

Chapter Twenty-Two

At the sound of that word, Corinne nearly went to her own knees. Fortunately, all she had to do was reach behind her for the support of the desk. Her ass found the edge. Her fingers curled into the hem of her skirt, sliding it up and over her thighs as Reese pressed forward using one finger to hook her panties to the side.

"No." She stopped him with a hand in his hair, pulling so hard it must've hurt worse than the rapping of his knuckles could have, even though she'd busted that ruler on them.

His lips were so close to her flesh that she could feel his breath, but obediently, Reese didn't touch her. When Corinne tightened her fingers even more, tipping his face, the dazed look in his eyes took her back to those long ago days when she'd owned him the way she had never owned another man since. She twisted her fingers, watching him wince and his mouth open, but he didn't mutter so much as a peep of protest.

"I have never had another boy since you. Do you know that?"

Reese closed his eyes. His hands slid along her thighs to rest against the backs of her knees, fingers curled. He shook his head as much as he could, imprisoned in her grip.

"Do you know how many times I've thought about that last time we were together, and what I could've done differently that might've made you want to stay?" Her voice shook, and she cleared her throat. "Do you know how often I wished you'd come to the diner that night when I asked you to? I waited for hours, Reese. You never showed. I never heard from you again. And I spent years blaming myself for driving you away because I demanded exactly…this…"

She tugged his hair again, then smoothed it to cup his cheek. He opened his eyes. She ran her thumb over his mouth until he opened for her, and then she tucked it inside so he could bite gently down.

"I have never asked another man to get on his knees for me," she whispered. "And I have missed you every day. I have longed for you every fucking second of my life. So don't you fucking dare, don't you dare think that you can..."

She couldn't finish, no words to say what she'd spent so many years thinking about. In the beginning, those first horrible hours while she'd waited for him to show, and then in the days after, she'd imagined herself calling him names. Cursing him. She'd imagined telling him to fuck off, to never darken her doorstep.

She drew in a breath. Swallowed hard. "You want me now?"

"I never stopped wanting you," Reese said in a harsh, strangled voice.

"Beg for it," Corinne whispered. "Fucking beg me for it."

Reese pressed his mouth to the inside of her bare thigh. "Please. Please, please, please, let me back inside you."

In answer, she slipped her panties to the side, giving him access. At that first slow swipe of his tongue, she put one leg over his shoulder. Her head fell back. She cried out, muffling herself by biting her tongue, aware that they were not alone in the office.

She was already coming when he pushed his fingers inside her, fucking along with the steady stroking of his tongue. Her orgasm rocketed through her, leaving her breathless and gasping and blinded with the pleasure.

Blinking, she looked down at him. His wet mouth. Passion-glazed eyes. She traced his lower lip with her forefinger.

A knock came at his closed, but not locked, office door. Sandy said, "Mr. Ebersole? I have a package here that was just delivered. Should I bring it in?"

As far as scandals went, Corinne guessed this would be one that would keep Sandy gossiping for years, but that wasn't why she pushed herself away from him and tugged her skirt down. It wasn't like she had to worry about losing her job for fucking the boss— Reese owned the company and the only person she had to answer to was him. But he would be humiliated if the secretary walked in to find him on his knees with a raging erection, his mouth still wet from Corinne's pussy. He would suffer for this, and that was something Corinne would not allow.

"Get up," she murmured. "Behind the desk. Now."

He was already moving as she did at the same time. By the time she got to the door, Corinne had slicked back the stray hairs off her cheeks and forehead and smoothed her clothes. She pulled the door open with a vague smile to find the secretary already reaching for the knob.

"Hi, Sandy. We were just finishing up a finance meeting. I can grab that package, if you want."

Sandy frowned, leaning to look past Corinne. Whatever she saw must not have been juicy enough to warrant more than a shrug though, because she held up the padded envelope. "Courier brought this from the real estate office."

Corinne half-turned, already taking the envelope. "I'll give it to him. We still have some business to go over."

"I was about to take my lunch, is that okay? Can I bring you anything?"

"I think I'm about to head out, myself," Corinne replied smoothly, looking finally to see Reese looking nonflustered and completely calm in his desk chair. He'd even managed to grab a few folders and a pen and looked as though he'd been hard at work.

Oh, he was hard all right, she thought and with that, the giggles threatened to overtake her. She bit her tongue hard enough to taste copper. Sandy gave her a glance, but Corinne covered up her impending hilarity with a cough.

"Yeah, me too," Reese said from behind her. "I'm suddenly dying to eat out. I can't think of anything I'd like better."

Sandy gave them both a curious but not suspicious look. "All right, well…if you're both going out too, I'll make sure to lock the office."

Corinne managed to keep herself together long enough to close the door behind the older woman, but then there was no holding back the flurry of half-hysterical laughter that surged up and out of her. Leaning against the door, she let it out, aware that more than a few of the chuckles were sharp-edged and almost sobs. She got herself under control quickly, though, and straightened.

"Bad boy," she told him. "Bad, bad boy."

Chapter Twenty-Three

Reese had ordered Chinese delivery, and with the door locked, he and Corinne were making a picnic on the floor of his office. He'd grabbed a shower, grateful for whoever'd had the forethought to put a full bathroom in the office. Now, hair still damp but back in his suit, he watched her spread out the cartons of fried rice and chicken lo mein on the tablecloth she'd snagged from the break room.

Corinne handed him a pair of chopsticks and a paper plate she'd already loaded with beef and broccoli from one of the plastic containers. "We have enough food here for ten people."

"Leftovers. I'm a bachelor, remember? This has to last me the whole week."

She rolled her eyes and settled back with her legs demurely tucked to the side, a plate of lo mein in her hands. "Still never learned to cook, huh?"

"Nope. Never had to." Reese took a bite of broccoli.

They ate in companionable silence for a few minutes before Corinne set aside her plate and gave him a serious look. "So."

Reese swallowed and wiped his mouth, then set his own plate down. "So?"

"We can't keep doing this…this hate-fucking."

Ouch.

"Is that what you think this is?"

"A little, yes," she told him.

"Do you hate me, Corinne?"

"A little," she whispered. "And it sure seemed like you hated me."

"Maybe I did. A little."

"Why did you come back here, Reese? The truth. Not some story you want to tell me, or tell yourself." Corinne leaned a little closer. "Why?"

"When I saw the report about how Stein and Sons was a good prospect for a buyout, I didn't even think twice. I knew I had to make an offer. It was a good excuse to see you again. That's it." The truth felt good.

"So...why were you such an unholy bastard about everything?" She still had that familiar head tilt, the one she'd always given him when she was trying to figure him out...or trying to figure out what to do to him.

He didn't have a good answer for that. "I've spent a lot of years forcing myself to forget or push aside the memories of how we were together. Until I saw you again..."

"And you *wanted* to see me again."

"Yes. More than that, I wanted *you* to see *me*." He cleared his throat, wishing it was as easy now as it had been back then to give up to her. "I wanted to show you that I'd been right to leave. If I'd stayed in Lancaster, I would never have become what I am today."

Corinne tilted her head to look him over. "You wanted to prove that I'd been wrong to ask you to stay."

"I wanted you to see how wrong you'd been not to want to come with me," he said.

"Because now you have money and power," Corinne replied quietly. "As though any of that ever mattered to me."

She'd always been able to read him. Hearing her say it shamed him, but he lifted his chin anyway, not wanting to show it. Her smile struck him right between the eyes.

She shrugged. "You wanted to show me up and prove a point by coming back here, and you also wanted to show me up and prove a point by making me run those ridiculous reports. Well, are you happy about it now? Do you think you got what you wanted? I am impressed, by the way, with everything you've accomplished. But I always knew you would make something of yourself. Even if you didn't think I did, I always knew."

As a younger man, he'd taken a lot of comfort from relying on her to guide him. His indiscretions had been minor. Her disciplines as much a game as anything they'd done. He didn't forget, though, how it had felt to trust her, to know that whatever she was asking of him, he would be able to provide. He'd learned not to need that guidance from someone else, but he'd never forgotten how it had felt to have it.

"This is stupid," Reese complains. Pen in his hand. Paper in front of him. Corinne has demanded he write lines.

"You're a procrastinator," she tells him calmly from her place at the kitchen sink where she's peeling potatoes for dinner, a job he was supposed to do but had left so long that she'd lost her patience with him. "If I ask you to do something, I need to know you'll do it. If you tell someone you're going to, you need to make sure you do. What good is your word if you don't keep it?"

He writes the first line, I will not leave my chores undone.

"Writing lines isn't going to make a difference, Corinne."

"No, edging your cock won't make a difference in this, because you like that," comes the retort. She turns, peeler in hand. "After the two hundredth line, when your hand is cramping and you're sure you can't do another one, maybe you'll remember the next time to keep your word."

"This is ridiculous!" He writes another line.

She laughs. "Yes, it is."

He does it anyway. When he has finished, she rubs his sore hand with warm oil and blows him, off and on, for an hour or so. That is a different sort of punishment and torture, but it is not discipline.

They both know the difference.

"Did you?" Corinne asked again. "Get what you wanted?"

He cleared his throat and looked at the desk, then back at her, amused to see that she was blushing a little. "Yes."

"It's been a very long time since I did anything like that. Actually, I've never done anything like *that*." She smoothed her skirt over her knees.

They stared at each other for a few minutes in silence, but it wasn't awkward. If anything, sitting quietly in her presence reminded him strongly of when they'd been together, when they'd needed no words. When simply being with each other was enough.

"The night you came to my house…"

She smiled. "Yeah?"

"Did you mean what you said?"

Corinne looked scared for a moment. Then slowly, she nodded. "Yes. I did. Everything. Did you?"

"Yes."

She looked down for a second, and when she looked up, the smile was back, this time with a glimmer of tears in her gaze. "Things are not the same as they were back then. I'm not the same person."

"I wouldn't expect you to be."

"You," she said firmly, "are not the same person."

"I hope not." Reese inched a bit closer, not reaching for her, though he wanted to.

Corinne cleared her throat. "You were very clear when we met in the restaurant that first day to talk about the offer. You are not my boy."

"I was being a dick—"

"No," she interrupted. "No. You were right. You are not my boy, and I don't want you to be."

His stomach twisted. Shit. All this, and he'd made an ass of himself for nothing. He could buy and sell a company, but he couldn't buy or sell her.

"I don't want a boy," Corinne continued. "I want a man. Someone strong. Capable. Mature. Willing to be a partner. I have a life and responsibilities and children now. They're my priority. And as much as I love fucking you, I have to put my kids first."

"I understand." He did reach for her hand this time, linking her fingers in his. "I wouldn't expect anything less."

"So if you just want to fuck around—"

Reese shook his head. "No, Corinne."

She cleared her throat. Then nodded once, carefully. Her fingers tightened around his. "We have to set some ground rules."

He leaned to offer his mouth to hers, waiting for her to take it. "I love ground rules."

"Mmmm." She brushed his lips with hers, not pulling away but not letting the kiss deepen, either. When he tugged her hand, she moved onto his lap, her skirt too tight to allow her to straddle him, so she sat sideways. "I think the first rule should be, no fooling around at work."

"That's a terrible rule."

When she took his lower lip between her teeth, nipping, Reese groaned, already getting hard again. His balls still ached from unreleased arousal.

She didn't let go. The sting increased, though she stopped just before it would've become actual pain. She knew him. After all this time, she still knew him.

Her tongue flicked over the sore spot. "Are you going to argue with me about everything?"

"Not about everything. No."

She laughed with a hitch in her voice and put her arms around him to tuck her face against the side of his neck. She spoke into his ear, soft feathering brushes of her lips on his skin making him shiver. "I'd like to do it right this time around."

He hesitated, then pushed her back enough so he could look at her face. Reese brushed a strand of hair off her face. "What was so wrong about how we were, before?"

"Obviously something, since we broke up." She shifted on his lap, easing the pressure on his growing erection.

He nuzzled her neck, loving the way it made her sigh and arch to give him better access. "You think we need something more formal? A...hell, a contract or something?"

She laughed again, this time pushing him away to get a good look at his face. "Oh, my. That sounds formal."

"People do it. They lay it all out, get it notarized, the works."

Her eyebrows rose. "Get out of here. That serious?"

"They do. It's usually a master/slave sort of thing, laying out the exact details and responsibilities..." He broke off at the sight of her expression. "What? No?"

"I thought that was something in books. Not for real life."

"One of the businesses I own is a travel company that caters to people in the lifestyle, planning vacations that incorporate kink." Reese shrugged. "There are lots of things in books that really happen."

"Pony stables?" Corinne whispered, looking both gleeful and horrified.

Reese snorted laughter, surprised she knew about stuff like that but realizing he shouldn't be. "Oh, yeah. For sure."

"Oh my God."

"Do you want that?"

Shit. There were a lot of things he'd be willing to do for her, but being a pony was absolutely going to stretch his comfort zone. Relieved when she burst into laughter, he took the chance to kiss her again.

"As much as I'd like to take you for a ride, no. I don't want you to be a pony. And I don't think we need a notarized contract. I mean, what are we talking about?" Her laughter eased, and she gave him a serious look. "I told you, if you just want to fuck—"

"No. That's not it. I'd like to see you."

"You do see me," she whispered and rocked a little against his cock.

Reese drew in a breath. "I want to see you, Corinne. Like dating. Like a relationship."

"Monogamous?"

"Yes." He paused. "Unless you want to see other people."

"Like I said, Reese, my kids are my priority. I don't really have time to go dating all over the place." Corinne smoothed her hand over his cheek to cup his chin.

His eyes went instantly heavy lidded at the embrace. "I like kids."

Her grip tightened until his eyes opened. "I haven't brought anyone around to meet my kids."

"I've met at least one already," he pointed out.

"That was different. You were my boss. Not my boyfriend."

Heat crept up inside him at the way she said boyfriend. They sat quietly for another few seconds as she let go of his chin to cup his cheek. She kissed him lightly. Tenderly.

"We can try it," she said against his mouth. "This. Us."

"No contract?"

"No contract," she said. "But I think I'll make you a list."

Reese grinned. "That's okay. I like lists."

Chapter Twenty-Four

There'd been a few hours of homework, then some TV, and now bedtime was looming. Peyton had already disappeared into her room, presumably to get on her laptop with friends in the last few minutes before she was supposed to go to sleep, but Tyler was procrastinating.

"C'mon, buddy. You were supposed to be finished with this before TV." Corinne scrubbed at her eyes, sleepy and more than a little irritated. "How long have you known you had to do this project?"

Tyler gave her a look that reminded her far too uncomfortably of the one his father used to give her when he was trying to keep the truth from her. "Well, I just remembered about it."

"Uh-huh. And you didn't work on it at all at your dad's?"

He gave her another guilty look. "Dad said it was okay, I'd have enough time to do it later. We were going to the movies."

Corinne frowned. "You're supposed to do your homework first, Tyler. Before anything else."

"Nobody else had any," he protested. "They'd have had to wait for me, and Dad said it wasn't fair that everyone should suffer!"

Corinne bit her tongue to keep herself from blurting out exactly how unfair it was that now she was going to be suffering because she had to oversee this busywork project that her kid really should've finished days ago but didn't because his father was too selfish to give up an afternoon of fun. She sighed and flipped through the packet of information. At least she didn't have to help him make a diorama. With a quick glance at the clock, she sighed.

"Okay, let's get working on this. I'm tired and want to take a bath."

"I can help him with it." This came from Caitlyn, who stood in the kitchen doorway with a plate of leftover pasta in her hand. "I'm super good at doing last minute projects."

Corinne laughed. "Auntie Caitlyn's the queen of procrastination."

Tyler frowned, looking back and forth between them. "Okay…"

"Relax, kid. We'll get your project underway. Let's go." Caitlyn settled at the table with her dinner.

The three of them worked for a bit, Tyler typing up notes based on things Caitlyn pulled from the textbook while Corinne checked off the list of items he needed to include. When Corinne's cell phone rang from where she'd been charging it on the counter, she glanced up but didn't answer it. She caught Tyler and Caitlyn sharing a glance though.

"What?" Corinne asked, frowning.

Tyler shrugged. "You should answer that, it might be your boyfriend."

Corinne's eyebrows rose. "Who says I have a boyfriend?"

By the way Tyler looked at his aunt, Corinne figured it out easily enough. Her sister shrugged, giving Corinne a look of exaggerated innocence. Corinne sighed.

"Me and Peyton don't care, Mom."

Corinne carefully kept her voice neutral. "So you've talked about it, huh?"

"Sure. I mean, you and Dad got divorced and he got a new wife. If you have a boyfriend who's nice to you that's okay." Tyler paused. "And to us too."

"I wouldn't be with someone who wasn't nice to you, kiddo."

Tyler gave Caitlyn another look. "Auntie says he's loaded. Do you think he'll buy me a new—"

"He's not going to buy you anything," Corinne interrupted sternly. "That's rude."

"Yeah, he's her boyfriend, not an ATM!" Caitlyn waggled her brows, making Tyler laugh.

Corinne gave them both a look that did nothing to stop the giggling. "I'm glad you're both amused."

"Sorry." Caitlyn sobered up, but barely.

It took another ten minutes or so, but finally the project was finished and Tyler packed off to bed with a reprimand not to let his work wait until the last minute again. Corinne came back to the kitchen to find her sister had cleared the dining room table and was wiping down the counters as the dishwasher hummed. She looked up when Corinne came in.

"He called again while you were with the kid."

Corinne took her phone off the charger. "Should I even bother to yell at you for telling them?"

"I didn't, actually." Her sister turned to lean against the edge of the sink. "They asked me, though, if you were seeing someone after you left me with them that Friday night and didn't get home until the wee hours of the morning. Peyton's the one who guessed it was Reese, by the way. I tried to play it off, but they're not so dumb."

Corinne pursed her lips. "No. I guess they're not. I should have told them, I guess."

"Are you going to bring him around? Is he really your boyfriend now? You haven't told me a damn thing, but you've been walking around all week like a cat that got into the artisanal yogurt."

"Very funny." Corinne rolled her eyes and swiped her phone's screen to see if Reese had left a voicemail. Two missed calls, one voice message. She held her phone to her chest for a moment, helpless against the giddy grin that crept over her face.

"Look at you." Caitlyn sounded surprised. "Wow. You're really into him. Even after all this time?"

"It's always like that in the beginning with someone."

Caitlyn gave her sister a look. "This isn't the beginning. You guys have had a thing forever."

"You can't count a thing that ended more than a decade ago as a thing, Caitlyn."

"Tell me you feel the same about him as you would any brand-new beau, and I'll believe you."

"I do, it's just the way you feel when you first start going out with someone. That's all."

"Liar," her sister said. "You're such a liar!"

It had only been three days since she and Reese had eaten Chinese food on the floor of his office. She'd promised him a list in place of a contract but hadn't yet finished it. They'd both been coasting on the giddy thrill of what had happened between them, she thought. The list, a discussion, putting words to what they'd agreed to be to each other…that was going to make it all too real.

"We're seeing each other," Corinne said.

"Exclusively?"

"Yes."

Caitlyn lowered her voice, looking conspiratorial. "And you're doing it with him."

"Oh my God."

"I knew it!" Caitlyn cried.

Corinne went to the fridge to pull out the bottle of seltzer water and poured herself a bubbly glass. She took her time sipping from it before she answered her sister. "It's all so weird, Caitlyn."

"Uh-oh." Caitlyn also went to the fridge, but pulled out a can of cola and popped the top. "Weird like how? Like whips and chains weird, or…"

"No chains. No whips." Corinne hesitated, then admitted, "Well, maybe chains? But probably not a whip. Maybe a flogger. Shit, I don't know. It's been so long since I did anything like this. I don't know what I want to do, or what we'll do. Shit. I can't believe this is happening. Reese Fucking Ebersole. After all this time. It's not real. Is it real?"

Caitlyn pulled a bag of pretzels from the cupboard and set it on the table, then waved her sister to sit. "You tell me."

"I don't know." Corinne fished a handful of pretzels from the bag and nibbled one.

"Nobody ever does, to be honest."

Corinne laughed. "Very profound."

"Keeping it real," her sister answered with a grin that faded after a second or so. "Look. It's time you get back out there. Some people never get a second chance with their one great love."

Corinne did not try to deny that description, though she wanted to. "He came back to me, Caitlyn. After all these years, he came back to me. That has to count for something, right?"

To her annoyance, she felt the rise of tears in her throat and had to clear it to hold them back. Her sister looked sympathetic. She didn't want sympathy. Shit, she didn't want this to be such a big deal.

But it was.

"Ride the wave, girl. Ride the wave." Caitlyn shook her head slowly. "What else can you do?"

"I could break it off with him now, before it gets out of control."

"You just got back together with him! What, are you crazy? Don't you dare." Caitlyn caught her sister's look and scowled. "Look, you bitch, some of us haven't had any sex in so long our vaginas have become a dry and dusty wasteland."

"So what, it's been like, a month?" Corinne had meant to tease, but at the sight of her sister's face, she stopped. "You're kidding, right?"

"I was taking a hiatus from the D. And the next thing I know, I can barely get a 'hey lady' from the guys hanging out in front of the mini mart." Caitlyn wrinkled her nose. "Even my dating profiles are all dead, unless you count the guy who told me last week that he wanted to test my gag reflex."

"Oh. Gross."

"Yeah, I told him that his message made me puke, so there was that." Caitlyn laughed, then looked serious again. "You're not going to break up with him, are you? C'mon."

"No. But I promised him a list of rules, and I really need to get on that."

Caitlyn's eyes widened. "So kinky."

"You asked!"

"Well, sure. I guess I'm just curious, that's all. I mean…you and Douglas never…did you? He wasn't…?"

"No," Corinne said a little sourly. "Definitely, he was not."

"Did you know that when you got married?"

"I was in love with him when we got married. I thought it wouldn't matter."

Caitlyn was silent for a moment, before she crunched a pretzel loudly. "It did, huh?"

"Well. Yeah. Sex matters. But we didn't get divorced because Douglas didn't like kinky sex." Corinne paused, thinking. "We got divorced because I wanted a partnership, and he wasn't being a partner. Not in the way I wanted him to be."

Caitlyn had heard enough stories about her sister's husband that it couldn't have been much of a surprise. She nodded, though. "But what you wanted was a guy who'd do what you told him to do. Right?"

"I…yes. I guess so." Corinne's brow furrowed. "When you say it that way, it makes me sound terrible."

"No. I don't think so. There's a lot to be said for being up front with yourself about what makes you happy," Caitlyn said. "If more people were honest about stuff in the beginning, they'd probably stay together longer. And I say this as someone who's never had a relationship last longer than oh, about six months."

Corinne was quiet for a moment or so, contemplating this advice. "Is it crazy for me to think that Reese knows me better than anyone ever has? Even after all this time? I mean, we've both changed, I think. I hope. And a lot of time has passed. But I still feel like he knows exactly how to push every button I have. The good ones and the bad ones."

"I told you, he's your *one*." Caitlyn grinned.

Corinne shook her head, not to negate what her sister was saying, but more in a thoughtful way. "I don't know about that. I'm not sure I believe in a one. But he's something. He was from the first time we were together, and all these years, I never stopped thinking about him. He says he never stopped thinking about me. Maybe this time we can make it work, right? Not fuck it all up. Anyway, it's way too soon to tell."

"You know, I'm all right staying here with the kids if you want to go on over there and give him what-for," Caitlyn said casually. "Get your list on, whatever."

Corinne laughed, sort of, but not quite embarrassed. "I haven't written it yet."

"Make him take dictation. Get it? Dick-tation!"

"I get it. God. You're like, twelve."

Caitlyn fluttered her lashes. "What can I say, it's a gift? But seriously, call him back, if he wants you to go over there, you can go."

"It's not a question of if he wants me to go over there," Corinne said archly. "It's a question of if I tell him I'm coming over."

"Ooh, hotsy totsy. How could I forget, you're the empress!"

Corinne laughed. Reese had sometimes called her his queen. "Something like that. Okay, you sure you don't mind?"

"Believe me, I have Interflix and a gallon of peanut butter chocolate ice cream, and nothing else going on. Go on. Just be back before the kids get up for school in the morning so I don't have to wake up early." Caitlyn grinned and made a shooing motion with her hands. "Go on. Go. You know you want to!"

"You're the best sister, you know that?"

Caitlyn preened. "Yeah. I know."

Chapter Twenty-Five

Reese had never felt as content as he did in this moment, his head cradled in Corinne's lap. They were supposed to be watching a movie, but it had been playing the entire time, and they hadn't paid much attention to it. Now, with her fingers running through his hair, he thought he might sleep—except that he didn't want to miss a second of this.

She had promised him a list but had not yet given him one. Back during their first time around, he would've pestered her about it, but time had tempered him. Or maybe he was unsure about what, exactly, to expect from Corinne's list. Uncertain if he was ready for it, no matter what he'd said.

"Tell me about the vacation company," she said now.

Reese shrugged. "It's a specialty thing. It started off catering to couples, honeymooners, that sort of thing. Over time the clientele became more focused. When I bought it, it was having trouble because the couple who ran it operated on good will, not written contracts, and they were getting screwed out of a lot of stuff by the venues that made promises and then didn't deliver."

"You can't promise something and not deliver," Corinne said.

Reese didn't think she was talking about the vacation company. His fingers curled with a twinge, a sense memory. "No. You shouldn't. What good is your word if you can't be counted on to keep it?"

Silence.

He didn't want to bring up the past, or the reasons why they'd broken up. Truth be told, Reese couldn't have said exactly why it had ended so abruptly and so badly. Losing his parents had been hard, especially because he'd never made things right between him and his dad before he died. Corinne had encouraged him to, and she'd been right. He'd refused to listen. He remembered being angry. Blaming

her. Later, he'd come to admit to himself that he'd done his share of
ruining what they'd had, if only because he'd learned there was never
only one person at fault. He wished he'd have figured that out
sooner.

"You never went on one of those trips?" she asked.

"Of course I did. I bought the business. I had to see for myself
how it worked. Just like I need to be in the office here," he said.
"You accused me of being hands-off, but really, I'm more a hands-on
kind of guy."

"Yeah, your hands are on," Corinne said. "I get it."

Reese grinned at her sarcastic tone, then said, "Yes, I went on a
few of the trips to see what they were like."

She stroked her fingers through his hair again. "Alone?"

"Once alone. Twice with someone."

She nodded, looking thoughtful. "What was it like?"

He wasn't sure what to say to that. He'd taken three of the
specialty trips, one to each of the locations his company sponsored.
Two different women. Amber had been the last one, and he was
certain that the trip had led directly to their breakup. Not that he
cared, much.

"It was better when I was alone," he said.

"Really?" She sounded surprised, not jealous. "Why?"

"More relaxing. The times I went with someone, it was a lot of
work," Reese said. "It wasn't like this, with them. I wasn't like this."

Corinne studied him with a small smile. "What were you like?"

"In charge."

She laughed. "Ah."

Reese turned his face against her thigh, closing his eyes. "It was
a lot of work, that's all."

"You dominated them?"

"Yes."

"Hmm." Corinne's stroking fingers paused for a moment, then
started again. Soothing. Rhythmic. Reese pushed into the touch like a
cat. "Tell me about it, puppy."

"You won't want to hear."

"I wouldn't have asked if I didn't want to know," she said.

Reese sighed. "The first woman was a casual lover who'd
expressed interest. She was more into the Daddy dynamic, which
didn't do anything for me at all. We didn't see each other again after

that trip, nothing nasty about it. We just didn't bother with each other."

"And the second?"

"Her name was Amber. We dated for about eight months."

"Why did you break up?"

Reese sighed. "She found someone with a bigger bank account."

"No small feat, I take it." Corinne laughed. "But before that, you took her on the kinky sex vacation."

"She wheedled her way into coming with me. She liked to be put on display. Paraded around. She was very proud of her body. She liked to be called a slut."

Corinne puffed out a breath he could feel on his face. "Oh, my."

"I didn't think she was a slut," Reese said. "What she wanted to do with her body was her own business."

"What else?" He could hear the approval in her voice, but he didn't open his eyes.

He nudged against her stroking hand until she started up again. "When she got...unruly...I disciplined her."

"How?"

"I made her write lines," Reese said after a moment, holding back a laugh. "She didn't like it."

"Did *you* like it?"

He didn't open his eyes. "I didn't hate it— Ouch!"

She'd dug her nails into his scalp. "Don't smart mouth me."

Corinne didn't sound angry, only firm and a little amused, but the tone of her voice...fuck, it made his cock twitch. It always had. He looked up at her.

"I felt disconnected from it," Reese said.

Her brow furrowed. Then she nodded. "Yes. I understand."

He smiled and closed his eyes again. "The whole point of the company is for kinky people to be able to visit these places that have everything set up for them to get their kink on. It was very much a scene thing. Lots of ritual and stuff. Very gothic. Naked people eating from dog bowls, that sort of thing. Amber got off on it. I didn't."

"Wow. That sounds intense."

He looked at her. "I could take you. If you want."

"Just because I call you 'puppy' sometimes doesn't mean I want you to eat from a dog bowl off the floor, honey."

"I could take you somewhere else. Anywhere you wanted to go."

She gave him another of those thoughtful looks. "You really got used to having money, huh?"

"It's better than not having money."

She laughed. "Yeah. I guess so."

"I couldn't take care of you back then," Reese said. "I know it was a problem."

Again, that thoughtful, contemplative look. "We had a bunch of problems, back then."

"We had a lot of good things too, Corinne."

"Yes. We did." She smiled, then said, "I said I would bring you a list of rules."

He nodded, thinking he should sit up, but not moving. Her fingers stroked through his hair, her nails scratching lightly on his scalp. "Yes."

"It's a short list," she told him.

Reese closed his eyes, smiling. "Okay."

The feather-light touch of her fingertips over his face traced his eyebrows. The bridge of his nose. Each lip, though when he opened his mouth to try to nip at her fingers she laughed and put her palm against his mouth.

"Bad boy," she whispered, and he looked up at her. Her eyes gleamed. She traced his lips again, and this time he resisted biting against the tickle. When she tucked her forefinger inside his mouth, he sucked gently on the tip; she withdrew it to paint slickness over his bottom lip. "The list has one rule on it."

"Only one?" He tried not to sound disappointed, but did anyway.

She laughed. "Yes. Only the one."

He did sit this time, shifting on the couch to face her. "Okay. I'm ready."

Corinne cleared her throat, looking a little nervous before she smoothed her expression with an obvious effort. She shook the hair off her forehead. Squared her shoulders. She looked him right in the eyes.

"Don't let me down."

He paused before answering, surprised at the simplicity of the single rule. "That's it?"

"That should be enough, shouldn't it?"

"I just thought…" He stopped himself.

"I know what you probably thought," Corinne said. "I think I know what you probably wanted."

He smiled. "Yeah? What did I want on the list?"

"You wanted rules about how you should address me. Yes?"

"Yes, Ma'am," he said with a grin.

"Here's the thing about rules, Reese. If you make a list of rules for the sole purpose of defining what has to happen when you break them, doesn't that sort of dilute the impact of the rules to begin with?"

He frowned. "Not sure what you mean."

Corinne took him by the front of the shirt and pulled him closer, her gaze tracing all the places her fingertips had touched only moments before. "It means that I don't want this to be about jumping through hoops. It's hard enough to find someone you like, much less someone whose kinks align. And ours align, don't they?"

Her fingers tightened in his shirt, digging into his chest beneath. Her mouth brushed his, but when he tried to kiss her, she pulled away. Reese's laugh had an edge to it.

"Yes."

"It means that I want a relationship based on mutual desires. Also respect and responsibility. It means that I'm going to take this seriously, and I expect you to do the same." The tip of her tongue flicked his chin.

"Yes. Of course."

"It means that I want us to take our time and relearn each other," Corinne continued. This time, instead of her tongue stroking him, her teeth nipped at his skin. She nudged his head back to get next to his throat.

Fuck, his cock was hard enough to break brick, just from the subtle pressure of her fingers on his chest and the brief, tempting sting of her teeth. "Yes, Ma'am."

She laughed, sweet and throaty, against his skin. "I love when you call me that. I always did."

"I know. See? I know a lot about you already. I know you like this," he added, sliding a hand between them to cup her breast and let his thumb pass over her nipple, already erect and taut through the thin material of her shirt and bra.

Her hissing gasp sent a slow, rolling bolt of desire through him. He wanted to bury his face between her breasts and pull up her shirt to get at her flesh beneath, but he kept his thumb just barely stroking over her nipple. He closed his eyes, concentrating on the sound of her breathing.

When she tangled her fingers in his hair and pulled his head back, he didn't move his hand. Corinne licked her lips. "This is not going to be all about sex."

"No, Ma'am."

"I expect you to actually take me out. On dates."

He grinned, letting his thumb stroke, stroke, stroke. Her nipple felt about as hard as his dick; he hoped she was starting to ache the way he was. "Absolutely. Anywhere you want to go."

"I...oh."

He pinched lightly then, sending a shudder through her that had her giving him a stern look. "Yes, Ma'am? You were saying?"

She put her hand over his, then removed it firmly. "It's late. I don't know about you, Mr. Bazillionaire Boss, but I have to work in the morning."

"Call in sick."

"Up." She pushed him until he moved away, then she stood. "I'm going home."

"But—" At the warning look she shot him, Reese gave a muffled groan. "Fine."

She laughed and bent to kiss his mouth, letting it linger until he grabbed for her hips. Then she slapped his hands lightly. "Nope. I'm going. And you're going to wait until I've left, and then you're going to take that pretty cock of yours, and you're going to stroke it until you're just about to come. But you're not going to."

"No?" He couldn't help grinning, even as the thought of it sent a wave of heat sizzling through him. His cock nudged the front of his jeans, beginning to throb.

"No."

"How many...how many times, Ma'am?"

She tapped her forefinger on her lips. "Fifteen. One for every year since we broke up the first time."

Shit.

"You want me to edge fifteen times?"

"Yes, puppy," she breathed, leaning to speak directly into his ear. "I want you to edge fifteen times for me. I want that cock hard and leaking and craving me."

"I already am…"

She laughed and nipped his earlobe, then danced away from him when he again foolishly tried to grab her. "No, no, no! It's late. Do as you're told."

He fell back onto the couch with a loud groan of protest, a hand on the bulge in his pants. "Yes, Ma'am."

"I'll see you tomorrow."

He cracked an eye open at her. "Really? Fifteen?"

"Now it's twenty," she told him, her expression going from playful to stern and her tone matching. "Keep arguing with me, I'll have your balls so blue you won't be able to walk for a week. Twenty times, and I want a photo each time you stop. They better be waiting for me when I wake up."

Reese got off the couch to go to her. "Anything you want."

"Uh-huh." She tipped her face to his for a kiss. Her hands snaked around to grab his ass, pulling him against her. "Sleep tight."

"I'd sleep better if you were with me," he said, risking the addition of another set of edges. As far as punishments went, it was worth taking the chance at changing her mind.

Corinne shook her head. "I can't. I have to get the kids up in the morning, and I do have work to do tomorrow. Unless you plan on running me ragged with a bunch of bullshit reports."

He winced. "No."

"You sure?" She gave him a steady look. "You're not going to turn arrogant on me again? Maybe you got more of a taste for it than you'll admit."

"Maybe I was just an ass," Reese said.

She kissed him again. "Yeah. Maybe that. Goodnight, puppy. I'll see you in the morning."

He walked her to her car, making sure she'd pulled all the way down the driveway before he went back in the house. His dick hadn't softened much—and in moments it was brick-hard again as he stroked, getting closer and closer to the edge.

He stopped, thinking of her. Fumbled with his phone. Took a picture. Texted it.

Good boy, came the reply, and he almost came right there.

Nineteen edges to go, he thought. It was going to be a long, long night.

Chapter Twenty-Six

"Here. I figured you'd need this." Corinne offered the mug of hot coffee to a sleepy-eyed Reese as she entered his office. She slid it across the desk, but kept out of kissing distance. As sexy as fucking in the office was, she was not going to succumb to the temptation. She'd woken to a series of increasingly hotter pics this morning, each photo sending another sizzle of arousal through her that still lingered, though she wasn't going to show it. "How was your night?"

"Long. Hard."

She laughed. "Uh-huh."

Reese leaned back in his chair. "C'mere, let me show you how long and hard."

"I already saw it." She sipped from her own mug, savoring the sweetness.

He drank some of his with a sigh of pleasure. "Thanks. I did need this."

"Of course. I know. I'm going to get back to my office, but if you want to grab lunch?"

Reese frowned. "Tony's on his way, babe, I'm sorry. I need to catch up with him on some things. And I have a meeting with the realtor who's going to take over the listing of my parents' house."

Corinne paused. "You're selling it?"

"Yeah. I mean, it's not in the best shape; it's going to need some work before someone's going to take it off my hands. I might just dump it though. I'm not sure I want to bother with a lot of work on it."

"Right." She kept her voice light, not wanting to make a big deal out of things. Of course he didn't want to live in the old farmhouse. A man with his kind of money and houses all over the place would find the old farmhouse beneath him.

"I can change my plans," Reese said.

She shook her head. "No, you don't have to. You do what you need to do."

"Dinner tonight?"

"Can't. I have stuff with the kids." She hesitated. "You could come over to my place for dinner, if you want."

Reese looked surprised. "Yeah? You want me to?"

"My sister kind of already outed me. Us. So...yeah. I think it would be good for you to meet the kids without it being a huge deal. I'm making meatloaf and baked potatoes. Nothing special."

"My favorite," Reese said.

She laughed. "We'll eat about six thirty, after trumpet lessons."

"I'll be there."

She wanted to kiss him, then, but didn't. "I'll let you get back to work."

"Corinne..." His voice stopped her at the door, and when she turned, he was there, one hand moving past her shoulder to keep it closed.

Instant heat.

"Yes?"

He took her hand and pressed it to his crotch, his cock hard beneath. "I want to come for you."

"No," she said in a low voice, rasping and rough. "Not yet. I want you to suffer a little for me, first."

She didn't pull her hand away, though he was moving it up and down on the hard bulge. She held her coffee out to the side, so it wouldn't spill. When he tried to kiss her, she turned her face.

"Later," she told him.

Reese chuckled and stepped back, adjusting himself with a wince. "I forgot."

"Forgot what?"

"What it was really like," he said, no longer laughing. "To obey."

She was going to drop her mug and throw him down right there, climb him like a tree and ride his face, no matter how unprofessional or inappropriate or... Corinne gave herself a mental shake. It had been a long time since her buttons had been pushed with such expertise.

"I didn't forget this, ever," she said. "I dreamed about it for years."

Reese swallowed hard. "Let me change my lunch plans. Let's go somewhere…"

"No," she told him with a small, determined shake of her head. "What did I tell you already?"

"This is about dating. Getting to know each other again."

"Yes. Which means we don't fuck in the office."

He smiled. "That's why I said we should go somewhere."

"You're making this very hard for me, Reese," she told him, and wagged a finger before he could reply with an innuendo. "Do *not* even say it. Get back to work."

He ran a hand through his hair, rumpling it, and nodded with a glance back at his desk. "Yeah. I have a bunch of things in motion. Tony's bringing updates on some new distribution resources. It means we'll be getting the product into some of the bigger markets. Not just Philly, also out toward Pittsburgh."

"Yeah? That's fantastic. You're really good, Reese."

He cocked his head to give her a look. "Did you think I couldn't turn this around?"

She had, in fact, wondered if his reasons for buying Stein and Sons might've clouded his actual ability to save the company from totally swirling down the drain. "Not because I didn't think you were good at what you do. But let's face it. Artisanal yogurts and ice cream…you'd have been better off just selling off all the pieces."

"I didn't want to do that. I made the commitment, so I want to make this company work." He backed up a few steps and pivoted to head for his desk, saying over his shoulder, "Not just to impress you, either. I don't usually hang on to companies I don't think I can fix."

She watched him settle into his chair. "I believe you."

He looked up. Smiled. How was it, she thought as she let herself out of his office and headed for her own, that in all this time, she had never stopped loving him?

She must have, she scolded herself as she forced herself to face her computer. Whatever love they'd had back then had been young, fluid, immature. It hadn't been meant to last. She was fooling herself to think that what she was feeling now was more than rekindled lust—it *might* become more than that. But it was not yet love.

Chapter Twenty-Seven

Tony had already snagged the back corner booth by the time Reese made it to the diner. The meeting with the realtor had run a little longer than he'd expected. The woman had been full of opinions about what he needed to do in order to make the house even close to salable, and while money certainly wasn't a problem, he did wonder how much effort would be worth the payoff. As he slid into the booth, Tony craned his neck to look past him.

Reese looked around too, already guessing what his assistant wanted to see. "She's not here today?"

"Damn it," Tony said. "I don't think so."

"She heard you were coming in and called in sick." Reese grinned at Tony's scowl.

Tony shrugged, looking at the menu and not at Reese. "You text a woman a few dirty pictures and then suddenly she ignores you."

"Dude. You did not." Reese held back laughter, but barely.

"Hey, she sent hers first," Tony said, indignant.

"Did you tell her you'd be here today?"

"No." Tony frowned. "I wanted to surprise her."

"How long has this been going on?" Reese scanned the menu, already knowing he was going to order breakfast, but not sure if he wanted a veggie omelet with tots or his standard eggs over medium.

Tony's sigh trailed into a groan. "A week. But I was going to try to take her out while I'm here. I booked a room at the Arts Hotel, by the way. You're covering the cost."

Reese raised his eyebrows.

"Hey, it's a business expense," Tony said with a grin. "I figured you didn't really want me cramping your style by staying in your parents' house, anyway."

"You don't want to stay there. The hot water is for shit and the heating isn't much better." Reese twisted in the seat to check for the waitress. When she came over, he asked, "Hi. Is Gretchen working today?"

"No, she's off. What can I get you?"

"Will she be in tomorrow?" Reese asked.

Looking faintly annoyed, the waitress shrugged, then looked a little wary. "I'm not sure…are you a friend of hers?"

"Don't worry about it," Tony put in quickly. "I'll just text her."

While they waited for their food, Reese pulled out his phone to check for a message from Corinne, but there was nothing. Disappointed, he put the phone on the table, ready in case she answered. Tony gave the phone a significant look.

"You waiting for something important?"

Reese gave his assistant a bland smile but didn't answer. Tony snorted laughter and shook his head. He pulled his own phone from his pocket and held it up, then set it on the table.

"Me too," he said.

An hour later, they'd finished their lunch and discussed all the new information Tony had gathered about the new possible markets. They'd gone over Reese's calendar and planned his travel—if there was a single thing that made Tony worth every penny Reese paid him, it was the man's ability to organize Reese's schedule. Just as Tony was ordering a slice of lemon meringue pie, so he could eat his feelings, as he said, Reese's phone buzzed with a text from Corinne.

Picture of your lunch.

It took him two seconds to snap a photo of the plate, empty but for a few tots he couldn't bring himself to finish. He sent it back to her without an accompanying message. He looked up to see Tony looking at him with a small, quirking smile. "What?"

"You Instaflixing your lunches now, or what? You're not into that sort of thing."

Reese shrugged. "How do you know what I'm into?"

"Umm, well, I've been setting up your email accounts for you for the past three years, so I'm pretty sure I have a handle on what sort of social media presence you've maintained. In other words, zilch."

"I know way too much about how those sites operate. I bought and sold more than one, remember? I'm a private guy." Reese's phone buzzed again.

Good boy.

Shit, now he had to shift in the diner booth to keep his cock from rising, and she'd know that too. When he looked up to see Tony staring, looking stunned, Reese had to fight to keep himself from covering his phone screen with his hand. His fingers twitched.

Tony's smile spread slowly as he leaned back in the booth. "Wow."

"What?" Reese said, annoyed. Not embarrassed, not exactly, because Tony had seen more than his share of Reese's life.

"How long has this been going on?" Tony said in a deadpan and perfect imitation of Reese.

"Almost twenty years."

Tony paused with a fork of pie halfway to his mouth. "Wha?" Reese grinned.

Another text buzzed in. *Show me your face.*

Shit, now she wanted a selfie? Without a word, Reese handed his phone to Tony, who looked at the message and laughed, then held up the phone to snap a picture for him. Reese took the phone back.

"You look mad," Tony said.

"She won't care about how I look. It's about giving her what she asked for." Reese sent the photo to her and put the phone back down.

"It's like that, huh?"

"Yes," Reese said. "It's like that."

Tony sat back in the booth and licked the tines of his fork. "She makes you feel like you'd do anything for her."

"Yep."

"I hear that." Tony shook his head and looked at his own phone with an exaggerated sigh. "Should I text her again?"

"How much do you want to see her?"

"A lot," Tony said. "But I don't want to be a creep about it."

The two of them sat in silent contemplation of this for a moment or so. Tony finished his pie. Then he ate the rest of Reese's tots.

Finally, unable to stand watching the misery, Reese pushed Tony's phone toward him. "Text her, man. You want to. Not a picture of your junk, though."

"That was once," Tony protested, already picking up the phone to type a message. "And I told you, she did it first!"

He put the phone back on the table. They both stared at it.

When it buzzed with a reply, Tony scooped it up with a grin as Reese pulled out a few bills and tossed them on the table.

"Have fun," he said as he left. "Try not to break the Arts Hotel."

Chapter Twenty-Eight

It had been hectic after school, though when was it anything less? Not for the first time since her sister had shown up to crash in the guest room, Corinne found herself more than grateful for Caitlyn's extra set of hands and wondered how on earth she'd been managing by herself for the past two years since the divorce. Her sister had even followed Corinne's hastily scribbled instructions on how to put together the meatloaf and baked potatoes, since Tyler's trumpet lesson was running late.

They walked in the door to the smell of good food and soft laughter and conversation. Corinne caught the higher pitch of Peyton's voice, and a lower, deeper rumble she immediately recognized. Reese was early. Or she was late. Either way, she bustled into the kitchen with her arms full of all the accoutrements of motherhood—trying to tell herself it didn't matter if he saw her this way.

She'd invited him here, after all. To meet her kids, to see her life, as brilliantly mundane as it was on a daily basis. She'd wanted to show him who she was now, in this life, even if the memory of who she'd been seemed ever so much sexier. *Chin up, shoulders square*, she thought. *You own him—*

She stopped herself abruptly.

She might've owned Reese Ebersole once upon a time, but she did not now. She remembered how it had been, though. At the sight of him leaning against the counter with a glass of red wine in his hand, one he was not drinking because he was holding it out to her as she entered the kitchen…at the sight of this man who'd left such a space, unfillable by anyone else, all Corinne could think about was owning him again.

"Hey," she said as he crossed to her. She offered her cheek for a kiss, aware that her kids were there with them, even if they didn't seem to be paying much attention. She took the glass of wine and sipped. "Mmm. When did you get here?"

"About ten minutes ago. Peyton was telling me about her school project."

Corinne hid her surprise. Of the two kids, Peyton was far more reticent than Tyler, who was already slinging off his coat and chattering at Caitlyn about the television program the two of them were currently binge watching. "She was?"

Peyton looked up from her ever-present cell phone. "Yeah, Reese said he could get me some contacts for job shadowing. I need to do three different careers."

"I can take her to Philly with me one day, get her shadowing in the promotions department for this small kosher grocery store chain I own. If that's okay with you," he added, meeting Corinne's gaze.

"Isn't seventh grade a little too early for job shadowing?" she asked Peyton, who rolled her eyes.

"Mom, I'm in advanced careers class, remember?

"Ah. Right. In that case, that sounds great. Hey, dinner smells awesome. Thanks, Caitlyn." Corinne let herself relax against Reese for a moment as her sister pulled the pan of meatloaf from the oven with a flourish.

Everything about this felt comfortable. Easy and natural, she thought as the kids finished setting the table with a minimum of arguing and Reese poured the adults all another glass of wine and the five of them settled around Corinne's kitchen table to eat. She'd never seen Reese interacting with kids, and in their time together they'd both been so focused on themselves the subject of marriage and kids had never come up. He was good with them, though. Friendly without being overbearing or trying too hard. He made them laugh. Caitlyn too.

He fit in this family.

When he caught her gaze across the table, both of them smiled.

Chapter Twenty-Nine

Dinner finished and cleared, the kids had been supervised with evening chores and homework and then bed. Corinne had refused a third glass of wine with a laugh and taken Reese into the den to watch a movie while her sister courteously disappeared upstairs. Now Corinne sat with her feet on Reese's lap while she scrolled through the Interflix list. His fingers curled around her instep, kneading away aches and pains she hadn't noticed until he was making them better.

"This," she said quietly and let the remote settle into her lap. "This is so nice."

He turned his head to look at her. "Very domestic."

"It's where most people end up," she told him.

Reese smiled a little, working his fingers up a bit higher on her calf, massaging tight muscles. "I never really thought I would, to be honest."

"No?"

He shook his head. "No. I worked too hard. Didn't ever put in the time with anyone, really."

"You didn't ever even come close to getting married?" Corinne shifted so he could get to her other calf.

"No." He paused. "Are you sorry you did?"

It was her turn to shake her head. "I have two amazing kids. So, no. I don't regret it. I'm sorry about the way things turned out, if only because at the end it was ugly for a bit, and it never feels easy to hurt someone. But I'm not sorry I got married."

He chewed the inside of his cheek for a moment. "What happened?"

"Oh." She laughed. "We fell out of love, I guess. And then he fell in love with someone else."

"He cheated on you?"

"I never asked him, but yeah. I think so." Corinne shrugged. "It doesn't matter anymore. He's happy with his new wife and the kids are okay, and I...well. Here I am with you."

Reese let his hand slide a little higher to caress her knee. "Do you ever think you'll want to do it again?"

"Get married?" Surprised, she blinked. "I don't know. Do...you?"

His answer was a smile. She poked her toes into his side, hard enough to make him wriggle away. He captured her foot and lifted it to his mouth to kiss.

It was way too early to even think about such a thing. She moved to kiss him, though, then rested her head on his shoulder. His hand came up to pet her hair, slowly. She breathed in the good, clean scent of him.

"This is so nice," she whispered.

His kiss pressed against her hair. "Yeah."

They sat that way for a few minutes in silence. Reese's breathing slowed. Beneath her palm, his heartbeat did too. He was falling asleep.

Also too early for him to be staying over. She rocked him gently until his eyes fluttered. "Wake up. You need to go."

He frowned, pulling her close to kiss her mouth. "Do I?"

"Yes. But the kids are with their dad this weekend. You could take me out on the date you promised. And I can stay over at your place." She nipped his bottom lip, making him groan, but pulled away before he could kiss her again. "Now, though, you need to go."

He yawned. "You sure? I could make it worth your while."

She poked his shoulder lightly. "You're so much more argumentative than I remember."

"Sorry." His grin said he was utterly unapologetic.

She put a fingertip beneath his chin, tipping it up and watching his eyes half-close. "Just be aware. I'm keeping a list, and it's not of rules."

"Uh-oh." He nipped at her finger, but she pulled it away. "I think I remember that list. What's on it?"

"A list of things you're going to need to be disciplined for," she said, meaning to tease, but as soon as the words came out of her mouth, she knew she meant it.

Reese's voice got husky. "Yes, Ma'am. I look forward to it."

"Kiss me again." He did, slowly, sliding his fingers into the hair at the base of her skull and tugging gently. She broke the kiss sooner than she wanted to. It was going to be really hard to say goodnight.

She made herself, though. She hadn't set any hard or fast rules about dating postdivorce, but it didn't feel right to have him sleeping there with the kids in the house, no matter how well they'd all gotten along. Not so soon. And if he slept here, she knew, they'd have sex, and having sex with her kids and sister in the house also felt inappropriate, especially the kind she wanted to have. The sort with a lot of loud noises.

"The weekend," she promised him with heat already curling in her belly at the thought of it. "We'll have the whole time together."

Chapter Thirty

Reese had texted her last night to pack a weekend bag, and now, as four thirty rolled around in the office, he showed up at her office door with his own bag in tow. "Ready?"

"It's not even five o'clock," she told him.

He laughed. "Who's the boss here, me or you?"

"I reserve the right not to answer that right now." She typed a few more things into her open document and saved it, then glanced at him. "You're serious, you're ready to go now?"

"Yeah, I let Sandy leave already. If we get on the road now, we might avoid the worst traffic on the Schuylkill."

"Is that even possible? That road is awful. I take it we're going to Philadelphia?" Corinne shut her computer down and came around the desk.

She looked fucking amazing in a navy blue skirt that showed off her sweet, tight ass and those legs...those legs. Reese gave himself a mental shake. "Yeah. If that's okay with you?"

"The kids get off the bus at Douglas's house on his weekends, and Caitlyn told me she had plans to visit some friends in Pittsburgh, so she's already gone. I'm free to go wherever you might take me."

"Perfect."

He'd planned what he hoped was going to be the perfect weekend to...well, not to impress her, exactly. Not to show off. To treat her as the queen she was. That was all. The way he'd always wanted to, but had never been able.

"You didn't tell me what to pack, so I threw in a bunch of things. If I need something special, we can run back to my house—"

"Whatever you need, we can buy."

She laughed, rolling her eyes a little bit, but looking pleased. "I see."

"Anyway, I hope maybe you're mostly going to be naked..."

Corinne clicked her tongue against her teeth. "Tsk, tsk."

"Is your list getting longer?"

"Oh, yes. Much, much longer."

He grinned, then grabbed her bag to sling over his shoulder. "Oof. Wow. What's in here?"

"You know, the usual things a girl needs for a weekend away with her boy. Chips, dips, chains, whips." She stopped at the look on his face and laughed. "I'm teasing you. Shoes. It's mostly shoes."

He hefted the bag. "It's two days, Corinne."

"I told you I overpacked!" She swatted him, and he snagged her wrist to dance her closer for a kiss, which she denied him by turning her head. "If you start that, we will never get on the road."

"Sandy's gone," he reminded her with a pointed look toward her desk.

Corinne shook her head and pushed him away, turning him at the same time toward the door. She swatted him on the ass. "And I told you, no fucking in the office. Let's go, c'mon. If we get stuck in traffic, I'm going to add that to the list and you will not be happy with what happens."

"Promises, promises."

In the parking lot, she stopped with a look of surprise at the sleek black Town Car and the uniformed driver waiting. "Reese?"

"I hate driving in traffic," he explained as the driver took the bags and settled them into the trunk. At her assessing look while they took their seats in the back, Reese paused. "What's up?"

Corinne glanced at the driver, now behind the wheel. "I just didn't think about us being chauffeured."

"Does it matter?" Reese buckled his belt.

In reply, she leaned back into her seat with a shake of her head. "No. Not really. Just feels fancy."

"Nothing's too fancy for you."

She gave him a familiar look. "Uh-huh."

"Is that a bad thing?" He took her hand, linking their fingers.

"It's just strange to me, that's all." She let her thumb rub the back of his hand.

They did hit traffic, of course, but even in the standstill moments it wasn't awful. The driver was capable enough to keep them moving the best he could. Reese's conversation with Corinne was entertaining. She held Reese's hand, tracing small circles on his palm with the tip of her finger and sending repetitive shivers of anticipation all through him.

In front of his building, Reese helped her out of the car as the doorman came out to take the bags. He tipped the driver, and, excited about showing off his apartment, he put a hand on the small of her back to lead her inside. She sidestepped him though, turning.

"Thank you…" She looked at the driver's name tag. "Terrance. For driving us."

"My pleasure, ma'am."

In the elevator, she looked Reese over, and though he hadn't said a word about how the driver had addressed her, she knew him well enough to guess. "Other people are going to call me ma'am, Reese. I'm a woman of a certain age, I don't qualify for the title 'miss' anymore."

"I know." Frowning, he pulled her into his arms. "I just don't like it."

She tipped her face to his. "You didn't say a word to him, that's all."

"What was I supposed to say?" he asked, surprised.

"He drove us for over an hour. You tipped him, but didn't bother to even look at him. The same with the doorman. You let him take the bags away but didn't even acknowledge him. I don't know. It bothered me."

The doors opened onto the penthouse floor, a small lobby with the broad double doors to his apartment on one side. His was the only one on this floor. The doorman would deliver the bags to the service entrance off the kitchen. Reese had intended to wow Corinne with this first look at his home, but her words stopped him from making the grand entrance he'd planned.

"Why did it bother you?"

"I guess I'm just not used to having people *serve* me," she said with a slight curl of her lip.

Reese had no idea what she was talking about. "You should be. You should be treated like a queen wherever you go. I'm trying to do that for you, Corinne."

Her smile looked a little forced. "I see that."

"C'mon inside. We can grab a drink, freshen up before dinner…" He spoke as he led her to the door, opening it and stepping aside so she could go through, first. "I picked this apartment for the view. Had it totally gutted and redone to open up the space so you can see the river from just about every room."

"It's gorgeous, Reese. Wow." She cast a glance and a grin at him over her shoulder. "Who knew New Jersey could look so good?"

He came up behind her in front of the living room's vast wall of glass overlooking the Delaware River. "New Jersey always looks better when it's on the other side of a river."

Laughing, she leaned into his embrace and sighed when he kissed her neck. "Mmm. That's good. But you promised me a drink, didn't you?"

"Kissing first," he murmured. "Please."

"How could I say no to you?" She twisted to face him, letting him back her up to the end of the sofa facing the windows. She gave him access to her throat, sighing again when he slid his lips over the soft skin.

His hands on her hips to make sure she didn't fall, Reese nuzzled at her collarbones for a moment before standing and pulling her upright. "Drinks. The powder room is through there, but you can use the master bathroom if you want. It's down that hallway."

"I'll do that." She pushed up on her tiptoes to kiss him again.

At the bar, he poured them both glasses of her favorite red wine and carried them into the bedroom. It had also been laid out to showcase the view, with glass on three sides and the bed facing the windows. No curtains other than a few billowy white gauzy ones the decorator had chosen. This high up and far away from any other buildings, there weren't any neighbors to peek in, and he liked the natural light. He could hear water running in the bathroom sink, so he set the wineglasses on the small table set between two comfortable chairs.

"Hey," Corinne said from behind him, and he turned. "This room...this entire apartment. It's amazing. I mean, I guess I didn't expect anything less. But wow, Reese. It's gorgeous."

"Not much like the old farmhouse. Or that shitty apartment on Queen Street," he added.

"I loved that apartment. It had character. It was cozy." Corinne took one of the glasses and sipped it as she went around the bed to look out the windows. "This *is* beautiful though."

He joined her, looking out over the water. "Are you hungry? I made reservations for dinner."

"You've thought of everything. I'd like to change first, if we're going to someplace fancy." She looked down at her work clothes. "My bag…?"

"I'm sure it's been delivered to the kitchen. I'll bring it."

One of the things he'd always admired about Corinne was how little time it took her to get ready. She'd changed her clothes, done something different with her hair and makeup, in under twenty minutes. She came out of the bathroom looking so good he had to take a step back with a low wolf whistle.

"Damn," Reese said.

She dimpled, twirling on stiletto heels to show off the sleek red dress that hugged her every curve. She stopped, hugging herself. "I can't tell you the last time I dressed up and went out to someplace nice without kids, without it being work related."

"You deserve to be taken out, Corinne."

She crossed to him, the high heels putting her nearly at eye level. "Thank you, puppy. You make me feel special."

"You are special." He brushed a lock of curling dark hair off her shoulder.

She hugged him. "Thank you."

Chapter Thirty-One

Reese had taken her a Creole place in Center City Philadelphia, a tiny restaurant tucked back along a cobblestoned street very close to the Betsy Ross House. They'd indulged in Chicken Bonne Femme, cocktails, steaming rolls glistening with butter. A bourbon bread pudding to die for. She was going to need a week to recover from this one meal.

Better than all of that was the way he'd doted on her entire time. Old school chivalry was far from dead, at least tonight. He held open doors, pulled out her chair. He ordered for them both, though he made sure to first ask her what she wanted this time.

"Something funny?" he asked when he caught her shaking her head.

"You. When you came back to Lancaster, you were such a pain. I never would've guessed we'd end up here."

"I had a chip on my shoulder," Reese admitted. "I'm trying to make up for that. For everything, I guess, that I didn't do the first time around."

"Things were different then," she said, meaning that both of them had been young. Broke. Trying to make their lives work out the best they could. She didn't blame him then for not being able to treat her to a three hundred dollar dinner. The truth was, he didn't need to be able to do that now.

"I want them to be different, now."

And of course they were. After dinner, he took her to a club with a waiting line outside so long it stretched around the block, but the two of them went to the front and were waved inside without so much as a glance at their driver's licenses. They were shown to a VIP section cordoned off with red velvet rope, and a table set with a chilling bottle of champagne and two flutes.

"I called ahead while you were in the bathroom," Reese said.

"You want a drink? Or should we dance?"

"Oh my God…I haven't been dancing in forever!" Giddy at the thought of it, Corinne looked toward the dance floor and the gyrating crowd. She was definitely not wearing dancing shoes. But when had that ever mattered?

Reese grinned. "Me neither."

She eyed him, moving closer so she wouldn't have to shout over the thumping bass beat. "I remember when you'd go dancing every weekend. You'd come into the diner wearing that black eyeliner, your hair all spiked. Dressed all in black. Once you wore a fishnet shirt…"

"Gah, don't remind me!" Reese cried. "I was a dumb emo kid."

"You were beautiful," she countered. "You still are."

For a moment they stared at each other, smiling but saying nothing. Reese took both her hands. "C'mon. Let's dance."

And they did. Stupid shoes be damned, Corinne discovered she had not forgotten what it was like to shake her groove thang. Reese, she saw, had not lost any of his former talent, either. Together, they bumped and ground until they were covered in sweat.

He tasted like salt when he kissed her. His cock, semihard, pressed her belly when he pulled her close. She lost herself in the moment, drunk not on the dinner cocktails or the bottle of expensive bubbly, but on him.

"Take me home," she cried into his ear, her arms slung around his neck.

Reese pulled away to look into her face. "Yeah? You're not having fun?"

"I want to be alone with you," she told him.

She didn't have to say another word. While she used the restroom, Reese called for a car that was waiting for her by the time she came out. They were back to his place in less than half an hour, and she'd held herself back from crawling all over him in the back of the car only because she wanted to tease and keep him on edge.

They rode the elevator in silence, standing across from each other. Still without speaking, they went into his apartment. When the door shut behind him with a click of the lock, Corinne found her voice.

"I want to see you the way you used to look. In my bag in the bathroom, there's some black eyeliner. Go put it on. And take off your clothes, everything but your briefs. Then come out here to the living room."

"Yes, Ma'am."

Fuck, how she loved that, his instant obeisance. The reverence in his tone, tinged with that underlying hitch of arousal. She could never pretend to understand why such submission tripped her switch, but it did, and she was so fucking glad it worked for them both.

It wasn't that she hadn't missed it over the years, she contemplated as she watched him disappear down the hallway and she helped herself to a bottle of cold seltzer from his bar fridge. She'd never forgotten how it had been to be in control, that was for sure. She'd done some reading about kink, mostly fiction, but a few reference manuals that had catered to the Mistress fantasy. The few times she'd searched for porn on the computer, she'd gravitated toward the clips featuring male submission. She'd known about her buttons, but somewhere along the way after breaking up with Reese the first time, she'd just stopped expecting them to get pushed.

She'd settled, Corinne thought as she sipped cool, bubbling water. Settled for men who made promises but didn't follow through. Men who'd let her down. Men like her ex-husband, who had never quite understood what it meant to put someone else first. Not her, not their kids, not really. It didn't make them bad men. Just not the right men.

Was Reese the right man? After all this time? She set her glass on the bar at the sound of footsteps coming down the hall. At the sight of him, her breath caught, jagged in her throat like she'd swallowed a burr.

He wore nothing but a pair of clinging, dark gray boxer briefs that perfectly cupped his ass and emphasized the thick muscles of his thighs. His cock pushed at the front of the soft fabric, not quite tenting it, but well on the way.

He'd slicked his dark hair into soft spikes and yes, oh fuck, he'd outlined his eyes with black that made them seem that much bluer. When he saw her looking, he stopped, one foot flat and the other, toes pressing the tile, so he could turn. Slowly, one side and the next. Posing for her.

His fingers curled slightly at his sides, but he kept his chin up as she came closer to look him over. She made a show of it, the inspection, running her hands over his body without lingering. Stepping back to let her gaze take in every inch of him. Now his cock strained at the fabric, and her mouth and throat went dry at the glimpse of flesh trying to peek over the waistband.

"Tell me what you like about this," she whispered.

Reese didn't hesitate. "I like feeling as though you like looking at me. That my body gets you excited. I like doing what you told me to do, turning you on. I like being…"

"What, puppy?" Curious, she ran a fingertip down the ridges of his belly but skated away before she touched his cock.

His voice rasped when he answered, "I like being a thing to you. I mean, I know I'm a person. But I like being this thing that brings you pleasure. It makes me want to do whatever you say."

"You like me objectifying you?"

"Yes."

"You like me adoring you," she added, still in a throaty whisper that he could have no trouble hearing.

"Yes, Ma'am. I fucking love it."

She took a few steps back from him on unsteady legs. Her dress unzipped in the back, and she let it puddle to the floor as she stepped out of it. Clad only in the brand-new panties and bra she'd bought especially for the weekend, she had a second to wish she'd added something sexier, a garter belt or something, but at the sound of Reese's appreciative moan, she stopped worrying.

When he moved toward her, she held up a hand. "I didn't tell you to move."

Another groan, this one less pleased, slipped out of him. "Yes, Ma'am."

She laughed and walked toward the windows, beginning to relax and enjoy this even more. The power, the control, made better by Reese's obvious arousal. What might've seemed contrived with someone else felt natural to her—to command. Demand. To expect obedience and receive it, unhesitatingly.

God, it felt so good.

She knew there were lots of games people played. Rules. She hadn't needed to live in the kink community to understand that much. Hell, she'd read that famous trilogy, who hadn't? Still, formality had never quite been their thing.

There were some new things she'd been thinking about though.

Without turning to face him, she could still see the hint of his reflection in the glass. He hadn't moved. She let her fingers press the window, feeling the chill. Her nipples tightened, though not from cold.

"My list," she told him. "It's gotten very long."

Chapter Thirty-Two

Standing in his briefs with a boner that could have broken bricks, Reese should've felt ridiculous. Especially with the makeup lining his eyes—shit, yeah he remembered doing that back in his club kid days, but he was well past that, now. Putting it on had come back to him though. The way to keep the lines smooth but smudgy. His father had always scowled at the sight of him heading out to the clubs, and a huge part of Reese's reasons for wearing it had been defiance.

His queen had asked it of him, though, so all he felt was pride that he'd pleased her.

Reese had grown pretty used to pride over the years. Arrogance, too, according to more than one of his ex-lovers and most of his business colleagues. What they'd seen in him, though, was different than this…this calm. This sense of peace, of waiting and being ready to please. It was not, exactly, that she was making him a thing and not a person, but that with her, doing this, Reese felt beyond himself. Bigger in a way he never did doing anything else, not making a deal, not pulling a company out of the ground.

Corinne settled herself on the armchair, her ass on the edge of the cushions. She smoothed her hands up and down her thighs and cocked her head to look at him with a small smile. "Take your briefs off and come over here."

He shucked out of the briefs immediately, instinctively wanting to grab his cock as it bobbed, tapping his belly. In front of her, looking down, he hoped she meant to take him in her mouth, but Corinne had other plans. She gestured.

"Over my lap."

Reese paused. "Huh?"

"My list. I told you what would happen, there'd be consequences. This is it. Over my knee."

"I'm too big."

She gave him another of those wicked smiles that burned him from the inside out. "Oh, I don't think so."

He remembered the crack of the ruler on his knuckles. This was something else that should've made him feel ridiculous, a schoolboy punishment. At the glance of her gaze at this straining dick, though, he knew there was no way he could pretend to her that he wasn't completely at her mercy.

"Oh, see?" she murmured, eyeing his cock. "Look how pretty."

She spoke to him differently when she was like this. Her voice changed. It triggered him to respond even more, letting his hand drift up his shaft so his fingers stroked through the glistening droplet of precome leaking from his cockhead.

Fitting himself onto her lap, though, that was more of a challenge. Awkward, to say the least, with his head hanging down, hands on the floor to support himself, his dick snugged somehow in the space between her knees and his own knees not close enough to the floor to touch. He was too heavy for her, he thought even as the warmth of her hand caressed his bare ass.

"Do I get to know what was on the list?" he asked.

"Oh, yes," she said as her hand caressed him. "Being argumentative. Speaking poorly of my apartment on Queen Street. You were generous to the driver, but you need to learn to treat the people who provide services to you like people, not servants. Being late—"

"I was early to get you leaving the office."

"Not that first time, when you came to my house. I told you very specifically, forty-seven minutes. You were late," she said sternly.

"That shouldn't count. That was before we came to an agreement."

"Argumentative," Corinne said.

"Argumentative is on there twice?" He closed his eyes, enjoying the warmth of her hand moving over his rear.

"It will be on there every time you argue with me," she said in that voice that got his cock twitching.

"I want to be better for you," he told her. "I've never said that to anyone else."

"I'm honored." Her hand teased the undersides of his butt

cheeks, tickling. "So. How many spanks do you think you should get?"

"Ten?"

She swatted him lightly, not nearly hard enough to sting. "You get twelve. To start. I want you to count them, and say 'thank you, Ma'am' after each one."

He laughed because she did, and twisted to look up at her. "You really...okay. Yes, Ma'am."

Still laughing, Corinne ran her hand over his ass again, like she was testing him out. "Hush. Yes. You get the spanks."

The first crack of her palm on his skin was more tentative than he expected, though it hurt worse than he'd thought it would. Felt better, too, a small sting followed by a spreading heat. He'd always liked a little pain, and she knew it, but the underlying elements of this had nothing to do with that. It was about giving up, giving in, doing what she asked of him; it was about the anticipation of the next smack.

After the fifth, he found himself pushing up to meet her hand as she cracked him. Rolling his hips to get his cock any kind of pressure, any friction at all in that sweet, slightly too open space between her thighs, if only she'd just squeeze him a little, it would feel so fucking good...

"Six, thank you, Ma'am," he said.

The next came. The sting was worse, the spreading heat centering in his balls and the base of his dick as much as in the meat of his ass cheeks. With his head hanging down, the blood was rushing, but that only made all of this that much more surreal.

By the eleventh, he wasn't sure he could last for one more, and not because it hurt. It would take a lot more than eleven or twelve spanks to really be painful. No, it was because his cock was betraying him, dripping clear, slick fluid all over her thighs and all it would take was a few stealthy thrusts to start easing him toward orgasm. It was all he could think about, really. Thrusting, grinding against the smoothness of her skin. It was strenuous, even, to bark out the words she'd demanded of him, and he knew the breaking of his voice would get to her.

"One more," she breathed. Her hand soothed over his hot flesh. "Your ass is so red, puppy. Such a pretty shade of red. I bet your cock is almost the same shade now. What do you think? How about another twelve? Maybe twenty. Fifty would get you in better shape, wouldn't it?"

"I don't know…"

Another crack came down against him. "You don't know, what?"

"Ma'am, twelve, thank you, Ma'am!"

"That was for not addressing me properly. You still get another. Do you understand?"

He groaned, laughing the tiniest bit. "Yes, Ma'am."

Again, her hand soothed over his stinging ass. Her fingertips traced the crack, moving down so slowly he was going to go insane. At the first gentle probe of her fingertip against his ass, all he could do was push upward, offering himself.

"Nobody else has had you here?"

"No. Only you, Ma'am."

He ached for her to touch him there. Fucking desperate for it. His hips pumped, but there wasn't enough friction on his cock to get him off and she wasn't pushing inside him, and all he could think about was that fuck, he was over her knee, she was spanking him, and he loved it, he loved her, he was going to explode if she didn't let him come…

"But you've thought about it, haven't you?"

"Yes. I dreamed about you." He pushed up a little bit to relieve some of the pressure on his hands. His wrists were aching, and that wasn't in the good way. "Please, Ma'am…"

"Please, what?"

"Please…give me the last one."

She laughed, hushed and rasping and sounding so fucking pleased with herself that he wanted to twist in her lap and grab her so he could kiss away that self-satisfaction, even as he knew he would never, ever do it. "You wouldn't rather I open this tight little hole?"

"Oh, fuck," Reese breathed. "That too. Please."

The final smack came down harder than the others, making him jump. He muttered out a thirteen and a thank you, Ma'am, as she'd requested, and waited for a moment, half-hoping she'd give him another dozen for his lack of appropriate enthusiasm. Definitely hoping she'd finger his asshole.

"Get up," Corinne said. "In front of me. Let me see that cock."

He stood, feet a little tingly but not quite fallen asleep. His prick didn't bob or move this time, so hard it lay fiercely upright, snugged up against his belly. He shifted his weight, feet shoulder width. She hadn't told him to, but his wrists crossed naturally at the small of his back.

"What did you like about what just happened?" she asked him.

He had to struggle to concentrate. Focus. "I liked the pain. I liked that you were doing it to make me think about being a better man, not just because I annoyed you. I liked feeling…"

"What?"

"Connected to you. Warm. I can't explain it. What did you like about it?" he asked her.

Corinne smiled. "I liked that you liked it, of course. That you were getting off on it. The sounds you made. Mostly I liked that you didn't have to let me, but you did. I liked that it was kind of silly. I didn't think I'd like it as much as I did. Come here."

He did at once. When she took the tip of his cock into her mouth, Reese couldn't stop himself from putting his hands on her head to gather her hair at the base of her neck. Corinne didn't protest, instead letting his prick sink deeper inside her heat. At the gentle sucking, he thought for sure he was going to explode, but she eased off in time to keep him from coming.

With her hand gripping him at the base, she looked up at him. "I should keep you on the edge all night."

He groaned. "Please don't."

"Mmmm." She took him in her mouth again, letting her tongue flick the underside of his head as her hand cupped his balls.

But she did, teasing him mercilessly for another twenty minutes with her lips and tongue. When he fucked into her mouth she slapped his ass, bringing back the sting. No matter how close he was, Corinne knew just when to pull back, blowing breath after breath across the tip of his throbbing, aching cock.

"Please, Ma'am…I need to come."

She hadn't moved from her seat on the edge of the chair. Gripping his cock firmly at the base, she looked up at him. "You *want* to come. That's not the same thing."

Reese would've argued with her if he'd been able to form the words. He absolutely needed to ejaculate—the need as fierce and insistent as anything he'd ever known. All he could manage was a soft mutter though.

Her hand slid along the shaft, not enough pressure to get him off, just enough to tantalize him. "Are you going to contradict me? Do I need to start another list?"

"No, Ma'am...oh, fuck. Please..."

"I love it when you beg me. I always loved it." She squeezed him again at the base, cutting off the urge to spurt, but barely.

He wanted to come. He *needed* to please her. So breathing in, breathing out, Reese clenched internal muscles and thought of baseball and did whatever he could not to let himself release.

"Legs apart."

He complied. Corinne slid her fingers inside her mouth and let them slide along his balls, then the seam of his perineum. At the pressure of her touch on his asshole, Reese gave a soft cry.

Corinne sighed. "Do you want to know how many times I touched myself over the years, making myself come, remembering you?"

"A lot, I hope. Ma'am."

She pressed harder, the feeling delicious and urgent, making him want to grind himself down on her or fuck into the empty air, anything that would relieve the building climax centered in his balls. She slid the tip of her finger inside the tight ring of muscle at the same time she covered his cockhead with her mouth. Reese shuddered, gasping.

"I loved how doing this would make you writhe and whimper and moan and beg for me. I loved it," she said against his shaft, the movement of her lips sending tickling sensation rippling through him. "I loved filling you with the toys."

"I loved it too..."

She went a little deeper, stretching him. Her tongue flicked the divot beneath his cockhead. "Do you have any?"

"No, Ma'am, no. I wish I...fuck...oh, fuck."

"Nothing? No ass plugs? You remembered how good it felt to be filled, but in all this time you never did it even by yourself?"

"Just my fingers, Ma'am..."

Her breath shuddered along his cock. "Oh...oh my God, really?"

"Yes."

"I want to watch you do that." Slowly, she withdrew and pushed at his thighs until he took an automatic step back on legs so weak he was sure he was going to fall.

Reese tried to compose himself. "What?"

"I want to watch you do what you did when you were alone. Thinking about us, about me fucking you. Show me." Corinne flicked an imperious hand at him, though her blazing gaze and tilted smile gave away her arousal.

Seeing how turned on she was sent a slow, seeping strand of precome leaking out of him, so much it actually dripped from his cock. She moaned when she saw it. Reese clamped a hand on the base of his dick to try and keep himself from jetting all over her. It was close, so close, but he managed.

"You want me to umm…jack off for you?"

"Yes," she breathed. "Please."

"Can I sit, Ma'am, I'm afraid I'll pass out otherwise."

"We can't have that. Do it however you need to, puppy. However you would've done it if I wasn't here. When is the last time you jacked off?"

"The day before that first meeting we had." Reese backed up to find the armchair behind him and sat, the material scratchy on his bare ass.

"Did you finger your ass?"

Heat burned the tips of his ears. "Yes, Ma'am."

Her delighted laughter sent another slow, rolling wave of desire through him. "Oh…I fucking love that so much. The day before you met me in that restaurant and you were such a prick, you were jacking your cock and fingering your asshole, thinking about me?"

"Yes, Ma'am." He settled into the chair, legs spread, ass hanging over the edge of the cushion. "Right here."

"Show me."

He gathered the slick precome from his cock and coated his fingers with it. One hand on his cock, stroking up and down just beneath the cockhead without palming it. The other, middle finger slicked with his arousal, pressed into the heat of his asshole. It went in easily enough to the first knuckle. His cock convulsed, balls tightening. More precome slipped out, and when he finally let his grip slide up and over the head of his prick, there was no more holding back. No teasing, no hesitating, nothing but the frantic, frenzied ride toward orgasm.

He wasn't even hitting his prostate in this position—just the sensation of his slippery finger stretching the tender, sensitive ring of his sphincter was enough right now to send ejaculate boiling up and out of his balls. It exploded from him with a force hard enough to send his eyes rolling back in his head. Spurt after spurt of hot fluid jetted from him, spattering his belly, his chest…his own fucking face, his mouth, and the taste of it, that musky, ocean flavor, pushed another wave of ecstasy through him.

Panting, muscles aching, Reese fell back against the chair with his hands at his sides. He didn't want to move. Couldn't.

Maybe he'd fucking died, he thought with his eyes closed, trying to catch his breath.

He lost track of the time he spent that way, but it must've been a few minutes because a soft touch on his knee opened his eyes. Corinne knelt in front of him, a warm wet cloth in one hand that she used to stroke along his skin. Cleaning him up. Taking care of him. When she'd finished, she got up to lean over him.

She kissed his mouth gently. "Thank you, puppy, that was gorgeous."

"I want to do for you," Reese said, though he couldn't manage to make himself get up.

"Don't worry," Corinne answered. "You will."

Chapter Thirty-Three

Corinne had not allowed Reese to give her an orgasm last night, not after watching him provide that glorious display. He'd been clearly exhausted after, and even though she'd been so turned on her thighs had been coated with slickness from her hungry, craving pussy, she'd instead forced them both to take a hot shower and go to sleep. She'd known he'd make it up to her, and besides, she hadn't told him that she'd come all on her own while watching him fuck his fist.

He'd started with serving her breakfast in bed, which had been a decadent treat. Then he'd gone down on her until she'd come twice, and after that he'd fucked her to another orgasm. Well worth the late start on sightseeing.

They'd spent the rest of the morning being tourists. Corinne had never explored Philadelphia, and Reese, despite living there, had never bothered either. They saw the Liberty Bell, the Betsy Ross House, Independence Hall. They'd grabbed lunch at the Reading Terminal Market. Barbecue brisket sandwiches, thick cut fries, and large chocolate shakes.

Now they were making the rounds of shops and bars on South Street. Holding hands. Stopping to look in store windows. Behaving like idiots, Corinne thought fondly as she made Reese pose for a selfie in front of a particularly funky splash of street art.

Across the street, a giant sign for CondomLand caught her eye. Next to it, though, was another shop. Smaller sign, but a better window display.

"Wow…is that what I think it is?" She pointed at the black leather bondage suit on the mannequin and shot Reese a gleeful grin.

Reese snorted softly. "Yeah. I'm sure. Please don't tell me you want me to wear one of those."

"Is that your hard limit?" She stood on her toes to kiss him.

"It might be."

She tugged his hand. "Let's go in anyway."

He sighed but complied, following her across the street and into the shop, which did not fail to delight her as much from the inside as it had from out. Long shelves lit with neon featured a plethora of sex toys in packaging ranging from discreet and classy to outlandish and porny. Something for every taste. Different racks held costumes and clothing, while an upstairs loft promised more treasures. While she hadn't planned this, Corinne already had a purchase in mind when she started toward the back wall with Reese in tow.

The first time around, there'd been no fancy sex shops for her to peruse. There'd been a few adult video stores in town, but they'd been seedy and gross. She'd done her ordering from an online catalog, hoping that the products she had to order sight—and fit— unseen would work.

"What are you looking for?" Reese asked.

"Something for you."

"Oh, man." He laughed, sounding embarrassed.

She looked at him, taking in the jeans, the button-down with the sleeves rolled to his elbows, the athletic shoes. The baseball cap. He looked so different than the all-black-wearing club kid he'd been, and different, too, from the high-powered business mogul he'd turned into. The frat-boy look made him seem younger.

"Don't worry, puppy," she promised. "You'll like it."

"I'm gonna go upstairs and look around."

"Okay," she answered absently, already consumed in her discovery of everything laid out on the shelves and wall hooks in front of her. "Text me if you need me."

"Help you find anything?" This helpful question came from a pretty young man wearing a black T-shirt that said HERS on the front in swirly white letters.

That, along with the thin leather collar at his throat, gave Corinne a small pause. She'd had only briefest foray into the world of real-life kink. Reese had the one-up on her in that department. The things they'd done in the past had grown out of fantasy and simply pursuing whatever it was she thought they'd both like, but somehow now, with all this information available to her, it seemed more important to educate herself.

Or something.

"I'm looking for some things for...umm...my boy." She cleared her throat, watching the clerk's face for any hint of surprise or distaste or anything that would make her want to turn around and flee the store.

He only nodded, looking thoughtful. "Yes, miss. What sorts of things are you interested in? We have really great new chastity devices that came in, people have had some great things to say about them."

"Umm...chastity...?"

He smiled. "Yeah, so, they're cages you lock up his cock in, so he can't get hard or come without your permission."

"Oh, wow." Corinne pressed her lips together, thinking about that. As much as she loved teasing and denying him, she wasn't sure locking up Reese's cock was exactly what she was going for. Not yet, anyway, though the idea had...potential. "I'm actually looking more for a harness and strap-on."

"Oh, sure. We have a really great selection over here, let me show you." He gestured, but allowed her to go first, staying a deferential distance behind her. "So, you've had a setup in the past and you're looking to replace?"

She nodded. "Yeah, but it was a long, long time ago. Like, over ten years."

"I was only twelve back then, so I can't tell you I know anything about what they were like, but I'm going to bet they've improved," the clerk said with a grin. "Let's get you fitted out. Do you want to start with the harness first, or the cock? What size are you going for? If your boy can take a lot of girth, we can start here."

Corinne, eyes wide, looked up at the racks of hanging dildos, some as long as her arm and twice as thick. "Something a little less intimidating to start, I think."

"Sure. Would you like a natural looking penis, with balls? We have some that can squirt, like ejaculation. I don't care for those, myself, they're hard to clean." He pointed. "Or do you want something that's not anatomically correct?"

"I guess the question is, do I want to look like I have a real penis or not?" She moved closer to the selection, considering. The one she'd had back then had been rigid, smooth, ill-fitting.

"Yes. It's really up to you, miss." The young man lifted a box off the wall. "Something like this is nice for beginners, or if your boy hasn't had anything for a while. It's curved here, for prostate stimulation. Three colors. Made of high quality materials, easily cleanable. Comes with a storage pouch, and you can fit it to any one of these harnesses over here, using an O-ring system, so if you find a harness you really like, you can switch out the cocks."

"This is so different than before." She laughed, self-conscious, and shook her head. "I ordered from a website with autoplay music. There were only a few choices, and you had to really hunt for them. Like nobody else in the world ever wanted to use one."

"Trust me, miss, there are lots and lots of people who want to use these." He grinned again. "Thank God, right?"

"Yes. Right." She laughed with him, then turned her attention back to the wall. "Let's find something really perfect."

Chapter Thirty-Four

She had not told Reese everything she'd bought, though she had ordered him to pick out a nice ass plug for himself from the shop's vast variety. She'd also allowed him to choose a set of truly frightening lingerie for her, something with a lot of complicated straps she was sure that once she was in, she'd be unable to get out of. It would make him happy, though, so she would find a way to wear it for him, because none of this was ever solely about her. It had been a good day, a really good one, full of laughter and good food and some great glasses of wine and actual conversation.

"Did we ever talk this way?" she asked him, her head in his lap on the couch.

He'd lit a fire, and the orange flames cast shadows on the wall. He leaned to pour another inch or two of wine into her glass. "We didn't have a fireplace."

"Smart-ass. You know what I meant."

"I don't think so," Reese said. "I don't think I'd have been able to. I'd never been anywhere or seen anything but the farm, pretty much. You were the one who always kept an eye on the news and stuff."

She sipped the wine, then set the glass on the table and wriggled in his lap. She loved the way he shifted a little at the pressure of her against his crotch. She'd had him put the plug in as soon as they got home, and she knew it had to be making him at least a tiny bit crazy.

"You had opinions," she remembered.

He laughed and stroked her hair off her forehead. "Of course I did. But they weren't very informed, I don't think."

"No, you liked to talk about philosophy and stuff like that."

"I did?" He looked surprised. "No way. I don't remember that at all. Me?"

"Yep. You. You'd argue with me about the existence of God,

life on other planets, that sort of thing."

He frowned. "And you put up with that?"

She sat up. "I liked it, at the time. I don't think I'd mind it, now. I love that we can discuss current events and financial planning, don't get me wrong…"

"You make it sound so sexy when you put it that way," Reese interrupted drolly, with a roll of his eyes. "So I went from freaky goth kid to boring old numbers cruncher, is that what you're saying?"

Corinne laughed. "No! Not at all. I like that we can have real conversations."

He kissed her, then said into her ear, "Even if we're talking about the ramifications of current political policy while I have something inside my butt?"

"It speaks to your powers of concentration." She turned her head slightly. "How does it feel?"

"Good. It reminds me every time I move that I'm doing what you asked me to do."

Arousal flooded her, peaking her nipples. "Ah."

Reese moved a little, tugging at the front of his jeans. "I'm half-hard from the pressure."

"Mmm," she breathed.

Just like that, she wanted him iron-hard, throbbing, and begging for release. She wanted him on his knees for her. She wanted his ass in the air while he opened himself for her…she wanted every piece of Reese Ebersole.

"Stand up," she told him.

He did at once, his instant obedience a burst of fuel on the already smoldering fire of her desire.

"I want you naked, but in the bedroom. Go take a shower and get on the bed for me and wait. I want you facedown, ass up."

Reese blinked rapidly as a soft hiss of breath escaped him. "Umm…yes, Ma'am. Okay."

The wine had given her a lovely warm glow, but watching his reaction intoxicated her even more. She waited until he'd disappeared down the hall and then went to the kitchen to put together a platter of cheese, grapes, and crackers. Some chocolate truffles they'd picked up this afternoon went on a small glass plate she realized with a start had come from her old apartment—she'd never known he'd taken it with him when he moved out and would perhaps have been angry about it at the time if she had, but seeing it now only moved her to an emotion so tangled and twisted she couldn't have put a name to it.

Nostalgia, melancholy for what might've been if they hadn't both been so stubborn and stupid. Bittersweet longing. Affection.

Love, she thought. Yes. Okay, so this was love, or at least the beginnings of it. And that was okay.

All of this was going to be all right.

Putting the food, along with the wineglasses and bottle, on a tray, she carried it carefully down the hall. She'd dallied to be sure Reese had ample time in the shower and to be waiting for her. She had anticipated he would be.

She hadn't been expecting this.

He'd lit candles. A dozen or more, some small votives and some pillars, placed carefully on all the flat surfaces of the room. In the middle of them, on the bed with the comforter and sheets already pulled down, he waited for her, exactly as she'd told him to. Head turned away from her, his arms spread, knees wide, ass up. She could see the rounded ring of the plug she hadn't told him to remove.

He had done what she'd asked of him, and it was beautiful.

Setting the tray on the table next to a few of the candles, Corinne crossed to the bed. "Good boy."

He smiled, but said nothing. His fingers twitched, though. He breathed deep, his body moving. His cock was long, thick, and totally hard, the tip just barely brushing the crisp white sheets.

"I'm going to fuck you," she said.

He let out a small sigh, but said nothing.

From the bag she'd tucked inside the guest closet he'd shown her, otherwise empty except for the dress she'd hung there, she took out what she'd bought earlier. The clerk had made sure she knew precisely how to put it together, so she didn't have to fuss with securing the dildo to the harness. She'd also picked up a bottle of special lube.

She had everything she needed, but she was far from ready. How had she managed this, before? Had they both simply been so young and lust-crazed that everything had seemed easy? Facing Reese on the bed, Corinne tried to focus on how turned on she was at the sight of him presented for her, but she was letting herself get distracted at how she was going to look once she donned the strap-on.

It helped that he wasn't looking at her. She slipped her legs through the spaces in the harness, adjusting it at her waist so the artificial cock pressed just right against her clit. The curve of the dildo was meant to press his prostate, which it wouldn't do in the position he was in, but she would worry about that in a minute or so. For now, she got on her knees behind him, the bed dipping as she did.

Her hands smoothed over his ass cheeks. "Tell me how it feels to wait for me like this."

"Exposed. Excited." Reese's voice was a little slurred, though not, she thought, from too much wine. "I'm remembering how it was before, but thinking it will be different now."

She ran her hands down his thighs, then up again, stroking his skin. She tugged the ring of the plug gently. "And this?"

He groaned at the motion of the plug. "Good. It's good…"

"What's it feel like?"

"Pressure. Fullness. It was almost too much at first; it's been a long time. But the longer I wore it, the more I could feel it, pressing me inside. My cock is dripping, Ma'am."

She looked. "There's a nice little wet spot there on the bed."

He thrust forward a bit. "I want to…I want to fuck against it… If I bear down, it's even better. Or worse. I'm going crazy for you, Ma'am. Please fuck me."

"Not yet." She toyed with the plug again, not pulling it out, easing off when she felt the toy begin to move.

Reese groaned and shook a little bit. "Fuck, it feels so fucking good."

Corinne smiled. "I'm glad. I want you to feel good for me."

She'd never had a lover who hadn't tried to get into her ass, but Reese had been the only man who'd ever responded positively to her getting into his. What had happened naturally for them had become weird with other lovers, and after the first time she'd been soundly and embarrassingly rejected, she'd never really tried to play that way with anyone else. So many things, she thought as she tugged again on the toy, had been special to only him.

"I'm gonna come," he muttered.

"No, you're not." She tugged the toy again, then let it settle back inside him.

"Please, Ma'am, I want to taste your pussy, I want to make you come first, please, or else I'm going to, and you won't…"

"I will, don't worry."

He quieted. "I want to make sure you're happy."

"I know, puppy." She kissed his butt cheeks one at a time, laughing.

He laughed, too, moving. "Ffffuck…"

Carefully, she eased the toy out of him, pleased to see that in addition to the candles, he'd also thought ahead to putting down a towel. She set the toy on it as Reese moaned, hips thrusting again a couple times before he stilled himself. She let her hand move between his legs to stroke him, feeling the slickness there.

"On your back."

He moved, rolling onto his back as she positioned herself between his legs. He was already pulling his knees back. Staring down at him, Corinne ran her hands over his skin—knees, thighs, belly. She gave his cock another couple strokes but stopped when it throbbed in her fist.

"Slow," Reese said.

"Of course."

She coated her fingers and the strap on with the thick, unscented lube. She used her middle and forefinger to press his tight ring, finding it already open for her after the use of the plug. Her fingers slid inside him with little resistance, and she curled them upward in a come-here gesture that had him bucking and crying out in seconds.

She stopped, her other hand flat on his belly to soothe him. "Hush."

Reese opened his eyes to meet hers. "Corinne… I haven't…"

"I know. Shhh."

He swallowed hard, licking his lips. She let her hand rub his belly in small circles. Her fingers inside him pressed upward again in a slow rhythm. She watched him close his eyes and move with her. After a minute or so, she withdrew her fingers and pressed the tip of the dildo against him. Then, slowly, she breached him, filling him until she'd settled inside all the way.

Reese muttered again. His fingers bit into the bed as he rolled his hips, pressing himself onto her cock. The motion pushed the end against her already pulsing clit. Corinne began to move, watching him carefully for his reaction. Going slow. Sliding in, then out, her nails scratching lightly at the insides of his thighs.

"Yeah, yeah, that," he groaned. "Harder."

Her nails dug into him. "Harder, what?"

His eyes flow open. "Please, harder, Ma'am…"

"Like this?" Harder, faster, she thrust.

She'd never seen a look like that on any man's face. Never before on his. Reese was clearly lost in the sensation, and watching him, Corinne felt herself tumbling into a swirl of tightly coiling desire that built with every thrust.

"Fuck me, Ma'am…please fuck me…"

She did, every smack against him sending another bolt of pleasure through her clit. Both of them spoke, fuck-talk. Words of love too. His gaze snared hers, not letting go. They were connected, both of them surging hard toward climax. Reese slid his hands across the bed and along the outsides of his thighs so Corinne could lace her fingers through his. Pumping inside him with short, shallow thrusts, she winced as his grip tightened.

His cock had gone a deep, flushed red and bounced with every thrust. A puddle of clear sticky fluid had formed on his belly.

"Yes, baby," she crooned, her own orgasm swirling, her cunt clenching. She stroked him, helping him along. "Come for me."

He did, a thick, creamy cascade of ejaculate hitting his chest. The sight of it, this visceral, visible proof his pleasure, tipped Corinne into her own orgasm. Subtle, rippling waves of desire tickled through her, forcing a gasp. Then another, louder as a second, stronger and surprising wave of contractions hit her. She shuddered with it, no longer thrusting. Incapable of anything but letting the ecstasy pound through her, leaving her breathless.

Still inside him, Corinne came back to herself aware that Reese's grip on her fingers had loosened. Blinking, she licked her upper lip, tasting sweat. She smiled. So did he. She eased out of him and rolled onto her side next to him to stare up at the ceiling, smiling again when he reached between them to take her hand.

"Was it always that good?" she asked after a moment or so of quiet. "Damn, baby, I just don't remember it being that good."

"I don't know how anything as good as what just happened could've ended."

That sobered her. Still thinking, she looked at the ceiling. Their fingers squeezed, gently.

"I loved you so much, Reese."

She felt him twist a little to look at her, but she didn't look back.

"I loved you too."

There could've been more to say after that, and maybe she should've found the words, but silence was all she could manage at the moment. They'd already gone over so much of this old ground, some of it in anger. All she wanted to do right now was bask in the afterglow.

Without moving much, Corinne unstrapped the harness at her hips and wriggled out of it. "I'm going to take a shower. You want to come in with me?"

A soft, contented snore was her only answer. Laughing quietly so as not to wake him, she kissed his cheek. She brushed his hair, damp with sweat, off his forehead. He was going to be sticky when he woke up, but for now she'd let him sleep.

"I still do," she whispered, thinking his smile was because of his dreams, but his answer trailed after her as she headed for the bathroom.

"Me too."

Chapter Thirty-Five

Before

"Bad boy, you couldn't wait for me to get home?"

Reese turns from the stove, where he's been stirring the pot of sauce Corinne told him he was supposed to let simmer. "Just tasting it."

She looks tired. She had class in the morning, worked the night shift at the diner before that, and is scheduled to go back in tonight. She's due to start her new job in a month, after she graduates. That will let her quit the diner, too, but until the job actually starts, her schedule is going to be insane. He told her she should quit the waitressing job, but she'd given him a look that made him feel stupid.

He hasn't told her about the money he got from his parents. It would be more than enough to cover the rent for the next two months, if she quits. More than enough to cover a lot of the bills too. But Reese has barely gotten used to the idea that both his parents are gone, and that money…it's his ticket out of here, for good. He wants to tell her, but it has to be the right time.

Usually she comes home from class and goes right to sleep, but today she's a little later than usual because she'd stopped at the grocery store. Reese would've done it for her, but he still hasn't managed to buy himself a car. Corinne slings her bag over the back of a chair and offers her face for a kiss.

"How's it taste?" she asks.

"Not as good as you." He kisses her, hands going to her hips, and though she responds, it's not with as much enthusiasm as he'd like. When he tips her back a little to nuzzle at her throat, Corinne shrugs out of his grasp to move past him.

She grabs a can of cola from the fridge and pops the top. "Will dinner be ready soon? I'm starving."

"I'll put on the water. You want spaghetti or rotini, or…?"

Reese pauses at the sight of her slightly slumping shoulders. "What?"

"Did you make a salad or anything? Garlic bread?"

"I was going to wait for you to get home."

Corinne turns to face him. "So dinner's not ready. Nothing is ready?"

"It'll just take a few minutes. You can grab the stuff for the salad, I'll start the water boiling."

"Never mind." She gulps cola. Without looking at him, she grabs her bag and disappears down the hall. The bedroom door shuts.

Irritated, Reese follows. She's already gone into the bathroom, stripping out of her shirt to stand in her jeans and bra, brushing her teeth. Hair pulled into a ponytail. She's gorgeous.

But when he moves behind her to kiss the back of her neck, Corinne pulls away. "What?"

She gives him a look in the mirror and bends to spit toothpaste into the sink. "Tired. Hungry. I'm going to grab a nap before work. I'll eat there."

"But I made dinner."

"You've been home all day long," Corinne says without turning, her lip curled. "You *didn't* make dinner. The only thing ready is the sauce, and I put that on the stove this morning before I left for class."

"I was filling out résumés. I worked out. I was busy, and there wasn't any point in making the pasta if you weren't home yet."

She pushes past him and into the bedroom. He follows. The bed is covered in laundry he'd been folding, and when she turns to look at him, Reese feels her contempt like a punch to the gut.

"You know, when I agreed to let you live here, it was with the understanding that even if you couldn't pay rent, you were going to do all this other crap."

He has been doing all the other crap. Most of it, anyway. He's doing his best, at least, and most of the time, he's done a pretty damned good job of it. "I'm not a housewife."

"No shit." Corinne snorts soft laughter that doesn't sound at all like she's amused. "Whatever, Reese. I'm going to try and get some sleep."

He grabs up the laundry she's about to toss to the side. "Hey, that's clean."

"Then put it away!"

"You don't just throw it on the floor, Corinne!"

"I wasn't going to throw it on the floor," she snaps. "I was moving it over so I had room to get under the blanket. Maybe if you had put it away, I wouldn't have to."

"I can't believe you're being pissy with me about this," Reese says as he tosses the clothes into a basket. "What the hell?"

Without a word, Corinne slips into the covers and turns away from him, her dark hair a tangle on the pillows. Muttering, Reese puts the laundry basket on the chair. He doesn't want to fight with her, not about this or anything else.

Pulling his shirt off over his head, then shucking his jeans, he quietly gets into bed behind her. Pressing to her back, he slides a hand around between her legs. Making her come will make her feel better. Let her sleep. Orgasms are good, right?

"Stop," she says after a minute, and when he tries again, she sits up to twist around. "I'm not in the mood."

"Fine." He sits up too. "I just wanted to make you feel good."

"Then pay attention," Corinne mutters. "I'm not a blow-up doll, okay?"

"Sorry. I guess I'm just a bad boy," he says, trying to tease. To be light about it, bring the conversation back to neutral ground and not anger. "Maybe you need to take me in hand?"

"Wow."

"What?" he asks, totally pissed off himself, now, because as far as he can see, she's being unreasonable.

"Is that all this is to you? What are you trying to do, make me mad so I'll punish you, so you can get off?"

That's not it at all, but he's not about to say so. Not when she has that look on her face, which confuses him but also makes him even angrier. She points at the basket of laundry.

"Go fold that. Put it all away. Go make dinner."

He's already getting out of bed, but hesitates. "I'm not a servant, Corinne."

Her eyes flash and her voice is cold but lacks that undercurrent of sexual tension that usually would have his cock twitching. "I told you to do something. I expect it to be done."

"Yeah, well, you know what, you can fold it yourself." With that, he gets off the bed and leaves the room.

The water's boiling in the kitchen, but fuck that, he turns off the heat without adding the pasta. He wants to go for a run, work off all this anger, and he strips down to his briefs in the kitchen. At the sound of her behind him, he turns, hands on his hips. And yeah, he notices how her gaze takes in his body, how she looks at him, and no matter how pissed off he is, he takes a gleeful, smug satisfaction in the glitter of her gaze.

"What?" Reese holds out his arms. Confrontational. Tensing muscles, putting on a show to be sure she notices the ridges of his muscled belly—all this time at home without finding a job has left him a lot of hours to work out. He knows she loves it too, the way his body's changed.

"Let me guess, the floor needs to be scrubbed. You want me on my hands and knees, Corinne? Yeah. Look at you. You're dying to see me down there on the floor."

"Stop it."

He can't. He's horny and angry, and all he wanted was to have some time with her before she has to go to work, and fuck all of this, he's spent too many days just trying to make her happy and now she's being a bitch because he didn't make the goddamned dinner? Sneering, he sinks to his knees, arms still held out, palms turned upward.

"This is where you like me, right?"

It's where he wants her to like him. He's pushing her; he wants to see the gleam in her gaze and watch her swipe her tongue over her lips. He wants her to order him to push his face into her pussy and make her come.

Corinne shakes her head.

"No? Seems like you liked it last night."

"What I like," she tells him in a low, angry voice, "is when you do what you promised you'd do. When you keep up your end of the bargain. When it's not just all about you and your dick."

The floor hurts his knees, but he doesn't get up. Instead, he crawls toward her, making a show of it, until he's at her feet. He bends as though to kiss her toes, but looks up at her.

"The princess wants her little tootsies kissed, right?"

She flinches and takes a step away. "How about you kiss my ass?"

She's turning, but he's on his feet fast enough to move in front of her, blocking her way. He's not sure why or how this became so enormously catastrophic between them. He's not sure how to stop it. They've argued before. Minor things. But nothing like this.

This feels like it could end up being permanent.

"It's not just about getting off," he says.

Corinne won't look at him. She presses herself against the wall, her arms crossed over her breasts. Her jaw is set.

"Corinne."

She shrugs. Reese sighs and tries to pull her closer, but she's too stiff and unyielding. He lets her go.

"It's not," he says again.

"Sometimes, it feels that way. I'm tired, Reese. Tired of working late and getting up early so we can manage to pay the rent, and I know in a few months it's going to get better, but it's not now. Okay? And I know you have your reasons about not wanting to move into the house, but…it would've made life easier. That's all."

His fingers curl into fists at his sides. "My parents died, Corinne. They're dead. I'm a fucking orphan, and all you can think about is that house? Oh, sorry. And your *career*."

He's hit her someplace soft, he can see it on her face.

"I'm sorry. I know it's been hard," she says.

"You have no idea how I feel."

She frowns. "That's not fair, Reese. Maybe if you talked to me about it, I could understand."

"What's there to understand? My mom had a stroke, and my dad died six months later of a coronary. Everything's tied up in probate. The money I got from selling off the livestock is paying for the lawyer. I told you that."

It's a lie. His parents had both had very clear and concise wills, allowing the estate to pass to him with a minimum of fuss. He has a bank account in his name with nearly ten grand in it, and the land and buildings are worth five or six times more than that, if and when he decides to sell.

He hasn't told her, that's all.

He doesn't want to tell her.

Things will change, once money is involved, and though, yes, it will make their lives easier it will also make it all different. It's not that he likes relying on her for everything, or that she has to work so hard to keep them afloat while all he'd managed to do was keep house. It's more than that. The money is his ticket to the bigger and better things he's always dreamed of having but had been certain he'd never get. The money is freedom.

It's his escape.

Chapter Thirty-Six

"I wish we didn't have to get up." Corinne burrowed deeper into the blankets.

"Go back to sleep for another hour or so." Beside her, Reese stretched, then curled to spoon her against him. "It's early."

"I need to get back. The kids will be home from their dad's before six, and I have lots of stuff to take care of before then." She yawned and pressed her bare ass against him, smiling when she felt his cock stir against her. "Mmmm."

It felt impossible that she could want him again after last night. After the entire weekend. She should've been so sated and worn out that she wouldn't have wanted sex again for at least…oh, at least another ten minutes or so she thought as his dick hardened against her ass. And Reese definitely should've been struggling.

"What kind of stuff could be better than this?" His fingers moved between her legs.

With a groan, she stopped him and got up, hopping out of bed before he could stop her. She admired him posing for her though, an arm flung behind his head. The sheets pulled down to expose his belly. She made an appreciative noise.

"I could look at you forever, just like that."

He bumped his hips a little, moving the bulge of his erection beneath the sheets. "If you lived here with me, you could see it every morning."

She laughed at the absurdity of that, then saw he wasn't laughing. "Reese."

"What? It would make sense, wouldn't it?"

Frowning, Corinne searched for something to put on over her nakedness. She found his discarded T-shirt and tugged it over her head. The hem hit her barely midthigh, but it was better than feeling bare.

"To move here, to Philadelphia with you? That makes no sense at all. My job is in Lancaster."

Reese snorted softly. "I'm guessing I could change that for you."

The heat that had been kindled inside her when she woke in his arms was rapidly being replaced by creeping ice. "Are you going to fire me?"

He frowned. "No, of course not."

"My house is in Lancaster. My kids," she said tightly, "live in Lancaster."

"I didn't mean—" He sighed and caught sight of her face. "Corinne, don't look at me like that. Isn't this better, here? Didn't we have a great weekend?"

"Yes, we did." She began looking for her clothes.

"So what's the problem?"

She turned, a pair of panties and a bra in her hands. "I can't move here with you. My life and my family and my job are in Lancaster. But let me guess, Reese, because it's so obvious I should've seen it before. You have no interest in making a life there."

His expression told her she was not far from the truth. But when she turned to head for the bathroom, he was up and out of the bed to follow her. She turned on the shower, not looking at him. Not wanting to turn this into an argument, but knowing it was heading there, because it felt so much like the last time she had to stare hard at herself in the mirror to be sure she hadn't somehow traveled back in time.

"You didn't think I was going to...what...live in my parents' old house? C'mon. My life, my business, it's here."

"You told me yourself, you have houses all over. Why not one in the place where I live?" she asked and stepped into the shower's hot spray. "You don't need to live in the farmhouse. You could buy something. It's not like you can't afford to, right?"

"And if I don't want to live in Lancaster?"

She didn't bother washing her hair, merely rinsed herself with a thin sheen of soap and got out to grab a towel. "Did you ever have any intentions of living there?"

Again, he didn't have to answer her with words. Disgusted and angry, Corinne wrapped the towel around herself and went into the bedroom to put her clothes on. Reese followed.

"No. I didn't. I intended to see you again, Corinne. The offer to buy the company was just an excuse to do that. I told you that already. But then I did see you, and I wanted to keep seeing you. But—" he laughed without much humor, "—surely you can see that it's impossible for me to actually *live* there."

"Because you never wanted to live there, right? You wanted out. You wanted to get as far away from Lancaster as you could. Even though it meant leaving me." Tears sparking her eyes at the memories of that last, final fight, she shoved her legs into skinny jeans and yanked a tunic blouse over her head. Her hair came free from the elastic, and she twisted it on top of her head again, ignoring the snarls. "So tell me something, Reese. Why did you bother? Why did you come back around, if you didn't think you'd want to stay?"

She let him take her by the shoulders and look into her eyes. She didn't want this to be a fight; she didn't want old pains to rise up and come between them. She lifted her chin, meeting his gaze head-on.

"I didn't know, until I saw you, how much I wanted to be with you again, Corinne. I had no idea."

"But now?" she asked quietly. "Now you know, right?"

"Now I know." He kissed her, and she let him.

She let him pull her close too, her cheek pressed to the warmth of his bare chest. She closed her eyes. She breathed in the scent of him.

"I've only ever wanted to take care of you, Corinne. And now I can, beyond anything we ever talked about back then. I wouldn't be where I am today if I hadn't left, if I hadn't used the money my parents left me to finish school and buy my first turnaround company—"

She paused, uncertain if she'd heard him correctly. "What do you mean, the money your parents left you? I thought there was nothing, that it was owed in back taxes and stuff, that's what you said. A second mortgage."

Reese looked uncomfortable. He took a step back, running a hand through his hair. It was his turn to look for something to put on, and as she watched him get into a pair of jeans with nothing beneath, she had time to piece it all together.

"Oh my God," Corinne said. "You...lied. You lied to me."

"Corinne..."

She held up a hand. He went silent. She shook her head, remembering long, hard hours of work and school and taking on all the responsibility for the two of them, especially those last few months before her first good job began and she and Reese had been at each other's throats constantly.

"You used that money to leave me," she said, her voice a rasping husk. "Is that what you did?"

"I asked you to go with me."

"No." She shook her head. "You asked me to leave behind everything I'd been working for, but you didn't tell me that you had money that would help support us. You let me believe that you intended to head out to parts unknown with nothing more than a couple bucks in your pocket. I had a job, a good job, lined up for me. I'd been busting my ass for years to get my degree so I could have more than a job. I could have a career, something you didn't seem to understand. I'd been supporting you—"

"And now I could support you," he put in.

She shook her head again, trying to take this all in. "Why didn't you tell me, Reese? Why lie? Did you think I would try to take it from you, or what?"

"I didn't tell you, because I knew it would change everything," he said angrily. "And I never liked being dependent on you, you know that, but once I found out about the money, all I could think was that if you knew I didn't need you that way, that it was going to change how you felt about me."

"I don't think it would've changed my feelings for you then," she said after a moment or so, "but I think knowing it is definitely changing my feelings for you now."

"Shit. No, Corinne. No, okay? Look, it doesn't have to change anything—" He tried to take her by the shoulders again, but she shrugged out of his grasp.

"You need to call the car. I want to get home."

Silently, Reese nodded and left the room. Corinne spent the next few minutes gathering her things, packing up her bag. She hesitated before taking the items she'd just bought on South Street, then left them behind. She found him in the living room, still wearing only the jeans. No shirt, no shoes.

"Are you coming with me?" she asked.

"No. I have things to do here too. Where I live," he told her coldly.

She did not want things to end this way. Not after such a great weekend. Learning he'd lied to her about something so big, though…it wasn't sitting well with her. Not at all.

"The car's downstairs," Reese said. "You should go."

So, she went.

Chapter Thirty-Seven

Before

It's cold outside and not much warmer in the house. She can see her breath, and while she'd tugged off her mittens upon entering the kitchen, she hasn't taken off her coat. Reese wasn't in the apartment when she got home. His note said he was here.

"Reese?"

Corinne hears a muffled noise from upstairs, and she follows it up the narrow staircase and down a hall to a small room with slanting eaves and a dormer. Reese's old bedroom, she can see that at once by the posters on the walls. The single twin bed is made up with what looks like a homemade quilt and several pillows. Trophies line the dresser.

"I didn't know you played baseball." She runs a finger along the golden figurines, then turns to face him.

"In high school. Yeah. I wasn't very good. I just didn't quit."

Things have been strained between them since the fight about dinner two nights ago. She's tried to make it up to him, but the problem with being with someone who likes it when she's stern is that in the fragile aftermath of an argument, it feels like any kind of discipline, even teasing, relates right back to the fight.

Anyway, they've been tiptoeing around each other since that night, and when she got back to the apartment tonight to find him missing, she'd been sure the note was going to say he'd left her. That he'd only gone "home" to the old farmhouse should've been more a relief—but it wasn't. Not quite. This relationship has been souring for months, and Corinne isn't sure how to fix it. At this point, she's no longer sure if she wants to.

"Are you hungry? I brought takeout from the China King. It's downstairs. Your favorite, beef with broccoli." She smiles, trying to tempt him into smiling back.

He doesn't. "Thanks. I'm in the middle of something. I'll get some later."

"Anything I can help with?" She sits next to him on the hard wooden floor and reaches for the file box he's been sifting through, but when Reese pulls it away, subtly but definitely moving it out of her reach, Corinne lets her hand fall onto her lap. "What are you doing, exactly?"

"Cleaning out some stuff."

She looks around the room and tucks her knees up, linking her fingers to hold them close to her chest. "Looks like this whole house is going to need a good cleaning out. That's a big job, puppy, are you sure you don't want—"

"I'm fine. I can handle it."

"Okay." She sits in silence for a few minutes, watching him. Waiting.

She can't imagine what it has been like for him, to lose both his parents so close together, and so unexpectedly. Her own parents are sometimes annoying, as all parents can be, but she sees them as often as she can. Since they moved to Delaware, it's not as often as she, or they, would like. To have both of them be simply…gone…Corinne can't begin to think of how terrible and sad it must feel.

She's tried talking to him about it, but Reese has said very little, other than to occasionally tell her there are problems with the estate. Lawyers to pay. Mortgages to settle. Back taxes to take care of. She hasn't pressed him about any of it, though she does wonder if surely, somehow, some way, there is a way they could move into this house and stop paying rent. It might ease some of the financial burden that has started to cause such a strain in their relationship over the past few months. It might help lead them toward some kind of future.

Maybe, she thinks, watching him sort through piles of papers without looking her, maybe the trouble that seems to have crept between them has nothing to do with money.

Maybe Reese just doesn't want to be with her, anymore.

"You know, I'm here to listen to you. If you need to talk."

"I don't need to talk," he says, still without looking at her. His voice is clipped. Cold. Distant.

"Reese." When he still won't look, she says it again, harder. Firmer. A tone that brooks no disobedience.

He has not so much as given her a glance. "I know you get off on bossing me around and stuff, but just drop it right now, okay? I'm not in the mood."

This, a role reversal and a tossing of her own words back in her face, stuns her so much she gets to her feet without another word. She can't find any. A breath hisses out of her, but she presses her lips closed to cut it off.

"Just because I submit to you doesn't mean you get to tell me what to do all the time or how to live my life," Reese says. "You don't always know what's best for me."

Corinne blinks back tears. "I didn't realize you felt that way."

"Well. I do."

"I'm sorry." It's all she can manage to get out, but the words taste wrong. Everything about this is wrong.

Everything between them has gone wrong, and she can't do anything about it.

"Will you be home later?" she asks, chin lifted, words gritting out of her, because she refuses to let him see her cry.

"I'm staying here tonight."

"And tomorrow?"

"I don't know," Reese says with a shrug. She's never seen him be so cold; she didn't know he was capable of it, though she shouldn't be so surprised.

"When do you think you'll know?" She hates herself for asking, for pressuring, but she can't help it.

"Shit, Corinne. I have no idea, okay? I have stuff to do here."

She nods, once, sharply. "Fine."

Downstairs, she puts the takeout in the fridge. The sound of him in the doorway turns her in relief. He'll apologize, they'll talk about things…it's going to be okay.

"Come with me," Reese says.

Corinne crosses her arms. They've talked about this already. He wants to move out of Lancaster, where she's still going to school. Where she has a job and a place to live. Where she will be working in a few months when she finishes her classes and starts with Stein and Sons, who were good enough to hire her before she got her degree.

"Where will we go?"

"Anywhere we want. Just out of this cow-shit-smelling town."

"And what are you going to do," Corinne says, a chill in her voice colder than the temperature outside. "Tap dance on the streets for cash? What?"

"I can get work."

"You haven't so far," she says and knows she's being cruel.

Reese could take the few steps across the frigid kitchen to take her in his arms, but he doesn't. "If I could just get out of here—"

"What's so bad about here?"

"Everything!" Reese's shout echoes in the kitchen. "Everything here is shit."

She shakes her head. "Not everything. I'm here. We're here together."

"I want more than this, Corinne."

More than this. More than her. More than them.

She has nothing left to say.

He doesn't stop her from leaving. He doesn't call for two days. When finally she breaks down and calls him, leaving a message on the answering machine, she tells him to come to see her at the diner. It will be her last day there, she tells him. She's going to take the next few weeks before the new job starts to get everything else in order. She's going to be there for him, is the unspoken promise, though what she says aloud is that if he doesn't want this to work, if he doesn't show, then they're over. If he doesn't come to meet her at the diner, he should never bother to call her, ever again.

Chapter Thirty-Eight

Corinne's office door was closed.

Reese didn't knock, but instead went to his own office and closed his. There wasn't much for him to do here. The staff that had been in place to handle the production had been doing a great job, and the new staff he'd hired to be in charge of distribution to the new markets would be coming on before the end of the month. The two new specialists who'd take over the creation, testing, and implementation of brand-new specialty products were also due to come onboard in the next couple weeks. At this point, Stein and Sons was going to succeed or fail, and him being on-site in Lancaster was not going to make much of a difference. Not to the business, anyway. Reese thought it would make every difference in his relationship.

At the soft rap on his door, he looked up. "Come in."

He thought it might be Sandy, but Corinne came through looking as smoothly confident as she always did. She had a stack of papers in her hands. She set them on the desk.

"Résumés for the office manager position. I thought you'd like to see them. I've gone ahead and had Sandy schedule the top prospects for next week, but if you want to be around for them, or if you have other suggestions..." She waited, expectant.

"No, I'm sure you've done a great job. You'll be working with them, anyway. Not me."

Her expression was neutral, but that didn't fool him. "Right. Well, anyway, those are your copies. Feel free to shred them or whatever you'd like. I'm going to the break room. Can I get you anything?"

"You don't have to bring my coffee, Corinne."

She let a small smile slip through. "I know I don't have to."

"Corinne, will you sit?"

She did. Her hands folded in her lap. She met his gaze straight on, but somehow managed to make him feel as though she were looking past and through him, not at him.

Reese frowned. "We should talk."

"About?"

Damn it. "About Sunday."

"Oh, Sunday, you mean two days ago, Sunday? Two days ago since I heard from you, that Sunday?"

"Stop it," Reese said sharply.

She sighed. "This is not the place for this."

"You're right," he agreed. "But I'm not going to let this go. So get your things, I'm taking you out for lunch."

"It's ten thirty."

"I don't care, we need to talk about this, and I'm not going to wait." He stood.

She stood too. "Fine."

* * * * *

They didn't talk about what had happened in his apartment or in the office on the way over to the diner. Corinne had sung along with the radio though, the windows down and the wind whipping her hair into a glorious disarray. She was so beautiful it made everything inside him hurt.

He wanted this to work. He didn't know if he could make it. He'd spent his life rebuilding businesses that were failing; sometimes, that meant breaking them apart to get at the only parts that could be saved and letting all the rest go. Sometimes, it had meant totally getting rid of everything.

Relationships were not businesses, Reese thought as he watched the woman he loved spoon sugar into her coffee.

Corinne tucked a bite of toast into her mouth and sat back in the diner booth with a sigh. "God. I can't stuff a single more bite into my gullet, I will explode. At the very least, I'll bust the seams of this skirt."

"I'll finish yours." He was already pulling her plate toward him. He'd eaten next to nothing since she'd walked out the door of his apartment on Sunday. He was voracious now.

Watching him, Corinne let her foot nudge him again beneath the table. He chewed. Swallowed. His foot nudged hers back.

Reese wiped his mouth with a napkin and leaned forward to take both her hands in his. She didn't curl her fingers into his grip at first, but softened after a second or so. He smiled, but she didn't smile back.

"This might not be the place," she began and tried to tug her hands from his, but Reese kept his grip tight enough to dissuade her.

"It's where I met you for the first time," he said quietly. "And it's where you told me to meet you for the last time, but I didn't show. I think this is exactly the place to have this talk."

Corinne shook her head. "No. I don't want to cry here in public."

"I don't want you to cry at all," Reese said.

She studied him. Again, her grip in his eased before she turned her hands to fully link their fingers. Reese let his thumbs stroke over the backs of her hands, but said nothing. After a moment or so, Corinne withdrew her fingers from his grasp. This time, he let her.

"It's been a long time," she said finally. "Maybe we ought to let it go. We had our little thing, but it doesn't mean—"

"Little thing? Let it go?" he interrupted. "Shit, no, Corinne. That's not what I want."

She had been the first and last woman Reese had ever gone to his knees for, but he was not the same man he'd been when they had last been together. She was not the same woman. He ran a hand through his hair, winced at how stiff it felt.

"Why did you come back here?" she demanded with a wave of her hand. "Surely there were other companies you could've bought. Other women you could've fucked. You didn't have to…you didn't…"

Her voice caught, and she straightened. Her eyes glistened, but she'd managed to keep the tears from falling. She shook herself, then spoke in a low tone to keep anyone around them from overhearing.

"I love the way you submit to me. Do you understand that?"

Reese swallowed hard. "Yes."

"I like to believe…I need to believe, Reese, that you love it too."

"I do, Corinne."

"My question to you is, does it go beyond the bedroom?"

Reese coughed, taken aback. "I'm not sure I know what you're getting at."

"Do you want to submit to me only in the bedroom?"

Stupidly, he tried to make a joke. "Any room is fine with me."

She didn't laugh. "You do as I tell you to do when your cock is hard, but that's all. Right?"

"That's not really fair."

"But it's true." She didn't sound angry. She sounded...resigned. "If I ordered you to sell your apartment in Philadelphia, to move here, would you do it?"

"I... Shit, Corinne. I don't know. No," Reese said. "Is that what you want? To order me?"

"That's the whole point. I *don't* want to order you. I want you to choose a life with me. The way you didn't, the first time around." She turned her coffee mug around and around in her hands, but didn't drink.

Reese pinched the bridge of his nose. "You want me to move here."

"I want you to be happy," she said quietly.

"It's not that far, you know. We could—"

"When I hurt you," Corinne interrupted calmly, "it's always knowing that it's my job to make sure it's not too much. I have the responsibility of making sure we don't go too far. That you're going to be okay. When I command you, when you obey, it's always my job to make sure I don't ask of you what you cannot do. Do you remember?"

He did. "You might ask me to do what I think I can't do, or what I think I don't want to, but you won't ask me to do what I absolutely can't do. I remember."

She looked sad. "It doesn't only apply in the bedroom. We don't need a notarized contract. I don't ever need to put you in a collar, or on a leash. But in this relationship, whether you are naked and on your knees for me or not, it will still always be my job to make sure I don't ask of you what you cannot do."

"What makes you think I can't do this?" Reese asked.

Her answer was a long, calm stare he couldn't interpret. "I need to get back to the office."

She was quiet in the car ride. No singing. No windows cracked to let in the breeze. When they got there, she left him behind and went into her office, closing the door firmly enough to let him know he would not be welcome to come inside.

An hour later, her resignation letter arrived via email.

Chapter Thirty-Nine

Corinne had, of course, given the minimum two weeks' notice. Four would've been better, but there was no way she could've lasted in the office with Reese. She hadn't needed to worry. He didn't come in to the office at all.

There'd been no going away party, no cake, no engraved watch to commemorate her service to Stein and Sons. As far as she knew, none of the previous owners even knew that she'd quit. The last she'd heard, the group of them had been planning to go on a family cruise, spending the money Reese had paid them. None of the new staff had even started. She'd promoted Sandy from secretary to office manager before she left, and the two of them had gone out for a celebratory lunch, but it had been strained and a little awkward.

"I'm okay," she told Caitlyn over glasses of wine and a platter of cheese and crackers. "Really. He gave me a huge raise when he came on, remember? I have money put away. I have three interviews lined up. I'll get another job. You don't have to worry."

Her sister frowned. "I'm hardly worried about you getting a job. Okay, maybe a little, because if we're both out of work, that could be bad. But that's not really what I'm worried about, and you know it."

"I feel very much at peace." Corinne tucked a piece of cheese in her mouth, then spread another with some spicy mustard and ate that, too. "You can't make someone love you, or choose you, and I didn't want to even try to force him."

"You didn't even want to think about a long-distance relationship? Philadelphia isn't that far away." Caitlyn also ate a piece of cheese.

"It's far enough. Sure, could we have tried it out? I guess so. Doing every other weekend. Talking on the phone during the week. Seeing each other whenever we could. Anything that's worthwhile takes work. Being together would've taken extra work. Not impossible. But once again, here it is, days later and not a word from him. How long should I wait?"

"You can't give up," Caitlyn said.

Corinne shrugged. "Sure I can."

"You don't want to give up. You love him."

"And?" Corinne shook her head. "So what?"

"If you just told him," her sister began, but cut off at the sight of Corinne's expression.

"He knows. He's always known. Sometimes, it doesn't matter."

Caitlyn was silent for a moment. "You can't mean that."

"He broke my heart once. Should I let him break it again? Let him go break someone else's heart. I don't have anything left." Corinne's phone buzzed with an alert she wasn't expecting, and frowning, she swiped the screen to see a message from her credit union app. "What the... Oh. No."

Caitlyn craned her neck to see. "What? What's wrong?"

"Someone made a deposit into my account." She showed her sister the screen. The amount was enough to make Caitlyn choke on the cube of cheese she'd been eating. Corinne gave her sister a grim smile. "Yeah. Right?"

"From him?"

"Who else could it be from?" She shook her head, already thumbing in his number. "I have to tell him I'm not taking it."

"Are you crazy? With that kind of money you don't need to work for a long time! If you don't want it, give it to me!"

Corinne gave her sister a look. "Forget it. He thinks this is all about money? Fuck that."

"Don't do anything crazy," Caitlyn said. "From what you said, five hundred smackers is like something he sneezes into a tissue and throws away."

"Oh, that's so gross." Corinne grimaced. Reese wasn't picking up. She didn't leave a voicemail.

She didn't have to, though, because a minute later, her phone buzzed again, this time with a text.

At the diner.

Meet me?

Then, a few seconds later, before she had time to answer...

Please.

Chapter Forty

Tony had brought along his tablet instead of a pile of folders. Reese preferred the paperwork so he could flip through it, take notes. Papers were physical and tactile. They felt more permanent.

He scrolled through the various pages. There wasn't much to note. At this point, the businesses in his portfolio, including Stein and Sons, were all running smoothly without needing any input from him—that was the point of it all, really. Hire good people to take over, and he could sit back and reap the benefits without having to be the guy overseeing every little detail.

"Coffee?" That rockabilly pinup waitress was back with eyes only for Tony.

Tony grinned and held out his cup. Reese rolled his eyes at the obvious simpering between the two of them, but waited until she'd gone before he tapped the tablet screen. "So, are you two a thing, or what?"

"We are not a thing. We are now, officially, partners." Tony gestured at the diner. "I'm buying this place."

Reese's jaw dropped. "What the hell? Are you quitting?"

"Do I have to? I mean, especially now?" Tony frowned.

"No. Of course not. I mean, if you can own and run a diner and work for me, more power to you." Reese blinked, still surprised.

"Gretchen's going to run it. I'm the money man. She has the practical experience."

"Sounds like you're going to make a good team," Reese said.

Tony shrugged, looking kind of irritated instead of happy. "That's what I think, but that girl is hard, man. She is hard like…like concrete."

"To work with?"

"To *be* with," Tony said with a scowl.

Reese's brow furrowed, confused. "So…you are or are not a

thing? I mean a dating thing."

"I have no idea what we are. I'm a damned booty call." Tony crumpled up a paper napkin and writhed a little in the diner booth, letting his head fall back with a groan. "She makes me crazy. This deal is taking forever to go through. I'm in a hell of my own making, man, and the worst part is, I could get out of it, and I don't."

Reese laughed. Tony gave him the finger. Reese laughed harder, though he softened his hilarity out of respect for Tony's clearly despairing situation.

"Can we get back to me?" Reese asked. "You know, business at hand?"

Tony waved a languid hand. "Yeah, yeah. Everything's under control. I handled all of it, just like you wanted. Some final paperwork needs to come through, but all the i's are crossed and t's are dotted."

"Good. Thank you. Now, get lost."

Tony groaned, but got up to slide out of the booth. Tony had taken his tablet when he left, but Reese had a single folder on the table in front of him. All he had to do was wait for Corinne to show up.

He had another offer for her.

Chapter Forty-One

"I don't have long," Corinne said without preamble as she took a seat in the booth. "The kids both have homework and stuff."

"Thanks for coming."

Did he have to look so good? It wasn't fair. She wanted him to at least look hollow-cheeked, shadow-eyed. Like he hadn't been sleeping. Something, anything, that would've shown her he'd been missing her.

"I'm not taking that money," she said, again without any hesitation. No point in beating around the bush. "You can't buy or sell me like I'm a business."

Reese smiled. "It's your severance package. If you'd read the contract amendment I had you sign when I took over, you'd have seen that."

"I did read it, as a matter of fact, because I don't sign contracts without reading them first," she answered sharply. "It did not say anywhere in it that you were going to give me half a million dollars for quitting."

"It said, if I remember correctly, that the severance package would include full benefits for six months as well as a discretionary bonus." He was still smiling.

Jerk.

Corinne sat up straighter. "I don't want your payoff. The severance I'm owed will be fine. I don't need a bonus."

"I gave it to you, and I'm not taking it back," Reese said complacently.

"I said I don't want it!"

At last, that smug smile faded. "It's not for you. It's for your kids. So you don't have to worry about another job, or uprooting or abandoning them."

"I can take care of my kids just fine, thank you," she snapped, keeping her voice low so as not to attract attention. "I don't need you to take care of them. Or me!"

"I want to take care of you, Corinne. For the rest of your life, if you'll let me."

Not the words she'd been expecting. Startled, she sat back. "What?"

Reese leaned forward. "You told me to choose. I'm choosing."

"What, exactly, did you choose?" She swallowed tears, hoping against every shredded scrap of hope she'd been denying she was holding on to.

"You. Us. If you'll let me, the kids. Your sister," he added with a grin that faded after a second so he could look serious.

He took her hand, and she let him, because she wanted to believe. She wanted to trust him. She squeezed, gently.

"You said you wouldn't ask me to do what I absolutely can't, Corinne. Right now, I can't live in Lancaster full-time. But," he cut in hastily before she could speak, "I can live here a lot of the time."

"You want to move in with me?"

"Yes. Some day. When we're ready. When it makes sense. Until then, I have a place I'm going to rent while I build something. I'm going to sell the farmhouse. I'll spend whatever time I need in Philly, but I'll make a home base here too. And eventually, if everything works out, we can talk about making a place together for all of us."

"You've thought it out," she said. "Sounds like you've really analyzed it."

"It's what I do," Reese told her. "Figure out how to make the pieces work. I want them to work with you."

"Me too." She leaned across the table to kiss him, then sat back. "I'm still not keeping that money."

"I'm going to take care of you the way I always wanted to, whether you like it or not," he shot back.

Corinne studied him, this man who'd once been her boy. She sat up straighter and gave him a long, cool look. Then a smile.

"My list," she said in that tone guaranteed to make him shiver and make his cock hard, "just got one item longer."

About the Author

Megan Hart writes books. Some of them use a lot of bad words, but most of the other words are okay. She can't live without music, the internet, or the ocean, but she and soda have achieved an amicable uncoupling. She can't stand the feeling of corduroy or velvet, and modern art leaves her cold. She writes a little bit of everything from horror to romance, though she's best known for writing erotic fiction that sometimes makes you cry. Find out more about her at **www.meganhart.com**, or if you really want to get crazy, follow her on Twitter at **www.twitter.com/megan_hart** and Facebook at **www.Facebook.com/READINBED**.

CPSIA information can be obtained
at www.ICGtesting.com
Printed in the USA
BVHW031211010320
573729BV00001B/204